Glen Wilson's Bad Medicine

A Novel of Unacceptable Ideas

Volume 4 of the continuing adventures of
Glen Wilson…

Other books by Ken Coffman

Fiction

Steel Waters
Alligator Alley, by Ken Coffman and Mark Bothum
Twisted Shadow, by Ken Coffman with Mark Bothum
Hartz String Theory
Endangered Species

Nonfiction

Real World FPGA Design with Verilog

The Armchair Adventurer
www.ArmchairAdventurer.net

Books can be ordered from:

www.bytechservices.com
1500A East College Way #554
Mount Vernon, WA 98273

This book is a work of fiction. Names, characters, places and incidents are the products of the author's fevered imagination or are used fictitiously. Any resemblance to actual events, locales or persons (living or dead) is entirely coincidental.

ISBN 0-975-43143-9

Published by:

The Armchair Adventurer
1500A East College Way #554
Mount Vernon, WA 98273

Dedication

For Dock Brown. When I was still a young and naïve country boy (I can't claim to be young any more), still wet behind the ears and with hayseed in my hair, Dock exposed me to the wide world of great chocolate, fine wine and intellectual adventurism. For example, Dock introduced me to the work of Ayn Rand, which, for better or worse, still guides my work and my ambitions. For this and more, I thank my good friend.

For literary inspiration, I thank Charles Bukowski. His work seems like a theme song for the denizens of the Seattle streets.

I wish to thank my "editorial board" for criticism, encouragement, guidance and proofreading.

Judy Coffman
Stacey Benson
Mark Bothum
Ken Lomax
Gary Croft
Dale Edwards
Colleen Bowen
Maureen Blando
Tommy Bolser

Author notes on Glen Wilson's Bad Medicine

I view the continuing adventures of our anti-hero Glen Wilson as a sort of bizarre spirit quest. Is he ultimately a force for good or evil in the world? I know, but I'm not saying. Yet. Glen has strange ideas for cleaning up the streets of Seattle. Do I think they'd really work? Sure, I do. However, our expensive social programs are not intended to make the streets cleaner and safer. Money lines the pockets of self-serving bureaucrats and ineffectual do-gooder activists. The end-result encourages irresponsibility and laziness. We don't have the will to really solve the problems of homelessness. Sure, some folks have bad luck and need a temporary helping hand. For those folks, private donations, faith-based programs, open-handed generosity and other random acts of kindness are appropriate. On the other hand, as talk show host Michael Medved says, there is no constitutional right to sleep on the streets.

KLC – March 2006

Email me at kcoffman@sos.net if you have questions or comments. As always, online reviews, good or bad, are greatly appreciated. For additional information, see www.kencoffman.com

Typographical, punctuation and grammatical errors are very pernicious and annoying. I proofread and edit and catch a lot, but still some sneak through. Here's your chance to make some money. Be the first to report an error, and as long as the dollars in my pocket hold up, I will send you a buck. I reserve the right to withdraw this offer at any time.

Cover Art Note

The images represent aspects of an indigent's life, the reflections in the panes being mirrors of their world and their transparency in near invisibility experienced as a non-person in society.

- Franz Hajnal

Part One

The velvet glove of kindness…

Notable Quote (unedited)

Please excuse any errors you might find in this book, this is only my first version and book to be made so their [sic] is bound to be some mistakes that I missed.

Rifts World Book: North Dakota
By: Sean Satterlee

INTRODUCTION

Murphy

The old DC-9 bounced once on the runway before the pilot abruptly pulled up. From her window, Margaret Murphy caught a glimpse of the scurrying coyote that caused the touch and go maneuver. The aircraft wheeled over the flat North Dakota landscape and swept around for another approach. She made eye contact with the Air Marshall on this flight, they were getting better at camouflaging themselves, but Murphy could tell he was armed by the way he shifted in his seat. Always, cops know cops. Murphy had been retired from the Florida State Patrol for many years, but she still thought of herself as a police officer. The pilot set the plane on the runway very gently to make up for the missed approach. As the plane glided to a stop, Murphy pulled her bag out of the overhead compartment and patiently waited for her turn to exit. By the calendar, it was mid-Summer, but the brisk breeze had an uncharacteristic chilly edge to it. The Bismarck Municipal Airport didn't use jetways, so the passengers, harassed by the stiff northwesterly wind, scuttled across the tarmac to the new terminal.

She stopped to use the restroom and examined herself in the mirror to make sure nothing was awry. She had cut her hair into an easy-to-maintain bob; it was streaked with mother lodes of gray. She was not a heavy woman, but not thin either. Perhaps meaty was a fair enough description. Her stomach was flat and her breasts still drew unwelcome stares even though she dressed conservatively. She didn't look tough at first glance unless the observer was perceptive enough to notice the calluses on her palms and her balance on her feet. She was always alert and coiled like a spring. Back in Sarasota, her judo master made sure she stayed in shape with endless tedious hours of drill and conditioning. There was a hint of world-weary depression expressed in the wrinkles of her forehead and the slight downward turn at the corners of her chapped lips. Looking only slightly butch, she didn't consider herself a lesbian because she wasn't attracted to women in general, only to her beloved Elke who waited back in Florida.

Successful police work required patience and following every lead to its natural and logical conclusion. Her friend, Glen Wilson, had disappeared from the face of the earth. Her mind stumbled on the word 'friend'. Was that the right description of what Glen meant to her? Former boss and suspect (person of interest) in a bizarre crime spree many years back in Florida. Catalyst. Agent provocateur. Raconteur. Bullshit artist. Her thought of him was more like family, someone she didn't choose, but was linked with forever, no matter what. Yes, friend was as good a word as any. In the past three years, Murphy searched for Glen without hope that he was even still alive. The political powers he crossed were ruthless. It was illogical to assume they would leave him breathing. Still, Murphy had followed hints and whispers into Canada, Mexico, South America (Bolivia), and once all the way to Hong Kong. All across the United States from Indio, California to Bangor, Maine.

Murphy wetted a paper towel and patted her cheeks. *Time to stop dreaming and get to work.*

The clerk at the Avis counter was reading a TV Guide which she quickly set aside. The paperwork was efficiently dealt with and soon Murphy was starting her Trailblazer and programming her familiar PBS station on the XM Radio. From scrawled notes, she entered coordinates into the Microsoft GPS system and the navigation computer plotted a northerly course up Highways 83 and 41. She cruised the quaint streets of Bismarck until she found Gun City Sports. The owner was a small man with florid leathery skin, he looked like he was at least part Native American. He wore turquoise-adorned necklaces, bracelets and rings. Murphy produced a federal firearms license and walked out with a used Smith and Wesson Police Special and a box of shells. The clerk agreed to buy back the gun if she returned it unfired and in good condition.

Highway 83 stabbed straight into the heart of North Dakota. The map software, linked with GPS coordinates, pinpointed an area northeast of Turtle Lake. There was nothing identified on the map, but a printed satellite image showed an unnamed and fenced-in compound slightly obscured by low trees. As far as Murphy could figure, it was precisely dead center in the middle of nowhere. On the radio, the talk show host threw softball questions at the Democratic Vice President. Murphy's thoughts drifted. Just past Wilton, she turned onto Hwy 41 and drove through Turtle Lake. She'd been on the road for 90 minutes and thought about stopping to pee, but decided she could hold it. Not much further to go. The turnoff was not marked and she missed it on the first approach. Backtracking much more slowly, she waved impatient pickup trucks around as she zeroed in on the location. There was no mailbox or other marking, though the driveway was paved as it weaved through a grove of bushy trees. The driveway ended at a gate. A squat concrete block building, painted industrial gray, was visible through the foliage. She pressed the button on an intercom and waited. Finally a disembodied voice crackled through the speaker.

"Yes, who is it please?"

"Retired Police Captain Margaret Murphy."

"You will not be permitted to enter without a security clearance and entry papers."

"Shut up and open the damn gate," Murphy barked.

It took a few minutes, but eventually the gate silently slid aside and Murphy drove through and parked her SUV. A small plaque announced the name of the facility: Prairie Meadows Medical Research Facility. Murphy tried to pat the wrinkles out of her skirt and tucked in her blouse. She marched up the walkway. When she reached the door, the remote lock buzzed and she pulled the door open. The air was stale and smelled ancient metallic, like medicine. A pair of burly orderlies escorted her to an office.

A man, dressed in a crisp white jacket and necktie, shook Murphy's hand and gestured for her to be seated. A woman, wearing a pale green pantsuit and sitting straight and rigid in her chair like a mannequin, was seated to his right. Her eyes did not appear to blink behind reading glasses that were attached to a shiny silver chain looped around her neck.

"I'm Doctor Floyd. I'm surprised to see you, we haven't had a visitor since, well, since when?" He directed his question to his assistant.

"Several years," she stated, barely moving her thin lips.

"Yes, several years, at least," Dr. Floyd repeated.

"I'm here to discharge Glen Wilson," Murphy said in a professional tone.

The woman answered. "We don't have a patient here by that name…"

Murphy pointed her index finger. "Don't play with me. Get Wilson and bring him out. Now."

"We'll need to see a discharge order signed by a federal judge. Who are you anyway?"

"My name is Murphy and I'm influential in matters that pertain to your federal funding. For starters, why don't you show me Mr. Wilson's commitment forms?"

This question was addressed by Dr. Floyd. "We don't get paperwork like that for our— clients."

"Then we won't be needing any paperwork for a discharge then, will we? I strongly suggest you stop trying my very limited patience."

They stared at each other for a minor eternity. Dr. Floyd sighed and reached for his radio. His assistant lightly placed a hand on his arm to stop him, but he shook it off. The intimacy of this gesture was not lost on Murphy.

"Chad, please bring out patient Wilson please."

"Okay boss," the radio whispered.

After ten minutes, as counted out by a large clock on the wall, a scrawny old man was escorted into the office by a large Native American orderly. The man looked shrunken. He wore a beard and had long greasy-gray hair. Under wild eyebrows, his eyes glowed with fierce intensity. He spun a guest chair and plopped on it with his head resting on the back. Murphy glanced at his hand, it was mutilated. It was Glen.

"What did you do to him?" Murphy asked Dr. Floyd.

"Excuse me, but we don't force our clients to eat."

Glen stared intently at Dr. Floyd, but addressed his statement to Murphy.

"It's about damn time you got here."

"You weren't exactly easy to find. We didn't know for sure that you were alive."

"Well, now you know. What was it, the balloons?"

"Balloons?"

"They allowed Mylar balloons for birthday celebrations, I set a few free with messages before they figured it out. Like airborne messages-in-bottles."

"No, we didn't find any balloons. It was the VOR interference. We got a good GPS reading from a Delta Airlines pilot."

"Ah. Are they going to let us stroll out of here without any trouble?"

"Yes, I think so."

"Alright then, let's not dawdle," Glen said, standing and kicking his chair out of the way. He stuck out his hand to shake with Dr. Floyd. "I'd like to say it's been a pleasure, but it hasn't, not at all," he said.

Hesitantly, Dr. Floyd accepted Glen's mutilated hand and shook with him. Murphy inclined her head toward the Doctor in a curt goodbye gesture. After leaving the office, they walked down the corridor. There were lots of openly-staring onlookers, but no one said anything or made any move to impede their exit. Outside, Glen climbed into the passenger seat of the Trailblazer and fastened his seatbelt. He stared out the window quietly as they rolled back toward Bismarck.

"Find a quiet place and we'll have some quick sex. I haven't been with a woman for over three years, so I'll apologize in advance for coming quick and promise to take my time and include you in the pleasure later."

"I don't think so," Murphy replied.

"Have sympathy for a broken old man, I've been living in hell. At least let me see your tits while you jack me off, that's the least you can do. It can be your random act of kindness for the day."

"If you don't stop it, I'm going to take you back so you can rot there forever. Try me if you doubt I'm serious."

"Alright Murphy, be that way. You can't blame a horny old guy for trying."

"Yes I can."

Not speaking, they drove for some time with talk radio chatter in the background.

"Three years in a box. I have a lot of catching up to do. McCord is president, eh?"

"Yes."

After a while, Glen spoke again.

"I confess that I'm wildly glad to see you, Murphy."

"Hmphh," Murphy grunted neutrally in reply.

Johnny Silver

Behind his drumset, Johnny Silver felt slippery. He slipped into a ¾ groove with a little syncopation on alternate bars. Playing slightly fast, the bass player had trouble thumb-popping his fat bass strings, but the crowd was fully sync'd: bobbing, slamming and screaming. Remnants of a flash mob sang, their body megaphones blared from the wall-to-wall crush. The air was so humid that trickles of condensation trailed down the brick walls. Sweat ran down his back and pooled on his drum throne. Synapses were firing at random in his head like a hint of lightning in a far-away thunder storm. He'd sipped hot-loaded fruit juice in the back alley during the break. He wasn't sure what exactly was in the drink, but he recognized that parts of the buzz came from synthetic Sparkle and Strobe plus Dick because he could feel his cock firm up as he bounced and stomped his bass drum and high hat pedals.

Johnny made eye contact with a little goth girl a few times. She wore huge black boots and a loose black silk blouse. One of her substantial breasts popped out while she was dancing and Johnny liked the way she left it flopping for a while before casually easing it back under cover. She looked familiar, Johnny might have hooked up with her sometime before, it was hard to keep track when you were the drummer for a hot local Skank band. The house manager flashed the lights to signify last call and Johnny led the band into the coda with a landslide of bass beats and a crescendo on the cymbals.

He slithered through the crowd and found the goth girl. They shouted into each other's ears, but Johnny's were ringing and the crowd was loud and he couldn't understand her. However, the message in the way she looked at him and grasped his arms was clear. Her tubby dance partner pouted and drifted off. The bass player tugged at Johnny's hair, having a day job he was always in a hurry to get the equipment into the van, pocket his share of the door take and go home. Johnny thought that was stupid; without the burden of a wife and kid, he could relax and party with the band after the show. His drums were electronic so it didn't take long to unplug everything and fold the pads into their cases. Everything compacted into a few small flight cases that were easily tossed into the van, then he was done with his work for the night. His share of the door was over $125 and they had sold a few CDs and T-shirts. Business was great for a weeknight.

The band celebrated their success by passing around a bottle of energy vodka, a premix of Skoli and ephedrine that made the blood rush in his ears but kept him from nodding off. The night was young. Goth girl wrapped her arms around his waist and Johnny made his goodbyes. Hand-in-hand they strolled downhill toward the waterfront. Under the viaduct, she pulled him into the shadows and they enjoyed a long kiss. Her hands caressed his ass as he pressed against her. She pulled an aspirin tin from her little handbag and took out two blood-red tablets. *One for you and one for me*, she whispered as she placed them in her mouth. He pressed his mouth against hers and accepted a pellet. *Let it melt under your tongue*, she suggested. The taste was bitter and almost immediately his heart raced and skipped beats in long pleasant pauses. The throbbing in his head eased. He'd heard of Vampyre, a secret synthesis from a lab in Bangalore, but it was very expensive so he'd never tried it. It would keep you up all night, stretch time and fragment the mind into separate intertwining consciousnesses. Johnny had heard that Vampyre turned sex into a marathon of chained-orgasms, the drug was very popular among the idle rich in Hollywood and Washington, DC. Party for 36 hours, then sleep for a week.

Goth girl pulled him out of the shadows. A shambling homeless guy yelled at them but Johnny stared him down and the bum wandered off. They stumbled closer to the water and entered a condo complex. Goth girl had a key to the front door and they rode the elevator to the 17th floor. She quietly opened the door and held her fingers to her lips to keep him quiet. It was a crash pad, there were several huddled sleeping bags arrayed on the floor they stepped over to get to her room. One of the dark lumps was moving and Johnny looked into the unfocused eyes of a flush-faced girl who was being humped slowly by a dreadlocked black man. She appeared to be on the edge of coming; her mouth stretched into a gaping soundless "O" as her head swiveled on her loose neck. Goth girl pulled him into her room. A pretty girl dressed in a long flannel nightgown slept with a pillow clutched to her chest. Goth girl pulled her roommate to her feet and escorted her out, then quietly pushed the door closed. She and Johnny were alone. The room had a small balcony over Elliot Bay. Johnny pulled the drapes open and slid open glass doors. To the south, container ships were being unloaded under bright spotlights and the lights of the city were reflected in glittery fragments by the choppy water. The air was cold against his inflamed skin. Goth girl joined him and handed him a thimble of oily fluid. He tossed it back in his throat and flipped the thimble into the night. Goth girl giggled. Johnny took off his shirt and held it out over the railing, then let it go. He pulled barrettes out of her short hair and pitched them over the side. He slipped out of his sneakers, into the night they went. She unzipped her big boots and handed them to him one-by-one. He lined them up on the railing and then pushed them over slowly with a fingertip. They hit the street a few moments later with satisfying thumps. Soon they were nude. Johnny took her hand formally and they pressed together in a slow dance. Her skin was warm and the sight of her body flooded his brain from four or five sets of eyes. All portals into his mind were open and saturated with images, odors and sound. Colors pressed into his skin. He pushed his girl back against the railing and prodded at her gently with his throbbing cock. With delicious slowness he eased into her.

He felt a heavy pressure in his chest and painful explosions in his head, heart and groin. He couldn't be coming so soon… A wrenching surfaced under his breastbone, like when he'd torn a ligament in his knee during a high school basketball game. He realized that his heart had stopped and he focused on the burning heaviness he felt in his chest. It took a long time before he got scared. He willed his heart to pump. The girl, misinterpreting his hesitation, tugged his buttocks and he penetrated her to the hilt. They stood quivering together until Johnny's knees gave out and he collapsed onto the concrete surface of the balcony with a sickening deadweight thud.

The apartment was surprisingly well equipped for medical emergencies and while someone called 911, ammonia vials were broken under his nose and CPR was started. They argued about shooting him with adrenaline but decided let the medics make that call. Seattle EMS was speedy and well-organized. They took control of the scene 11 minutes after the call was logged. This did no good for Johnny Silver; he was declared dead at 3:43 AM in the Harborview Medical Center emergency room.

Mary Swanson

The grounds of the Emerald Hills retirement home community were immaculately maintained by a crew of Japanese landscapers. Mary Swanson sat in the shade and split her attention between the crew raking leaves and the attendants carrying breakfast trays to the room-bound residents. Mary was infinitely grateful that she was still somewhat mobile and could enjoy her meals in the cafeteria. She was free to walk out the door and out onto the street, but there was nowhere for her to go. Besides, she didn't need to walk, the expensive rent at Emerald Hills covered a Cadillac Escalade that would take her anywhere around town she might want to visit. Examining her hands, she could not believe how old they looked. In her youth, she was proud of long painted nails and slim fingers that caressed piano keys and her deceased husband's private parts, but now her knobby knuckles throbbed with arthritis, sometimes more and sometimes less, they were never completely pain-free.

Mr. McMorris, the facility manager, only ten minutes late, came strolling in from the employee parking lot. There was a nearly imperceptible hitch in his step when he saw Mary waiting, but he bravely kept coming.

"Good morning to you, Mrs. Swanson."

"Good morning back at you, Mr. McMorris. I filled out a form, but I wanted to let you know in person there is a pawn missing from the East Recreation Room chess set. I looked on the Internet and I don't think you will be able to find a replacement piece, so I'm afraid that a whole new chess set will be required. I did some comparison shopping and I would say that a Windsor set from Bon-Macy's would be a good choice. It's on sale until the 27th, so I would suggest that your secretary make a credit card purchase right away."

"It might be prudent for the interns to monitor Mr. Bart's stools for a couple of days and see if it makes an appearance," Mr. McMorris replied. Earlier in the year, Mr. Bart had ingested china figurines which were eventually recovered. "In the meantime, perhaps we can find a temporary substitute, perhaps a salt shaker or the like might be pressed into service?"

"No, I don't think a delay is warranted at all. If we do recover the missing piece, then that set would make a fine back-up, but we need to make sure a complete set is available to the afternoon Chess Club members."

Mr. McMorris sighed. "As always, Mrs. Swanson, you are right and I will make sure this is taken care of right away."

"Thank you Mr. McMorris," Mrs. Swanson replied. With this task completed, she walked into the grounds to talk to the landscapers about a hose that was snaking near a flower bed. Unless the gardeners used extreme caution when they dragged that hose, there would be pretty pansies in grave danger.

Gerusha Andersen

Fully engaged with the morning rush, Gerusha Andersen collected orders as fast as she could. This Starbucks store near the University of Washington was one of the most successful in Seattle, their sales consistently in the top 10 for the state. Gerusha could remember faces very well; she scribbled hieroglyphics on the paper cups even before the customer got to the front of the line at the cash register.

"Hello 'G', can I get six pumps of vanilla instead of 5 today? I feel like I deserve a little extra loving."

"No problem, Lili, Grande Breve with whipping cream, a pump of hazelnut and 6 pumps of vanilla, coming right up for you."

Gerusha's next customer was a tall thin man with a hooked nose, a tall forehead and puffy white hair that swept back from his face like brushed cotton. He always dressed in a dark suit like an undertaker or politician. His eyes were captivating; it seemed to Gerusha that he could see through her clothes, her skin, and into her core. Gerusha didn't care if he had X-ray vision, she worked out regularly and was accustomed to being stared at. Let them look, she wore belly-baring blouses and lacy under-clothes on purpose to show off her figure.

"Hey, Walter, the usual? Triple espresso with a shot of licorice syrup? I saved you a raison sticky bun, if you're in the mood."

"Thank you Gerusha, that was very kind. Yes, I will take it. Do you remember the first time I came in here? Do you remember the first thing I asked for?"

"You asked for a nicotine espresso with a shot of belladonna. I never heard of it, but I looked it up on the Internet. You can get drinks like that in Eastern Europe, Albania maybe. That makes sense, you have a little of that accent."

Walter laughed. "I was born in the Bronx, but I picked up a little of that accent from my grandfather, I assume. You're very bright and observant while packaged very nicely, if you'll allow an old man license to say so."

The lady behind Walter was impatient. "Hey, I'm going to be late for work, can't you kids chit-chat later?"

Walter turned and looked down his long nose at the lady. "Of course, Miss, you are completely correct, there is simply no time to waste." He turned back to Gerusha. "It's always a pleasure sharing a few words with you, dear," he said while dropping a five dollar bill in the tip jar.

"The pleasure is all mine," Gerusha replied with a hint of a wink.

"I'd like a Frappucino with a shot of cherry, half a pump of caramel and two shots of vanilla with room please," the lady said after Walter moved out of the way.

"Coming right up," Gerusha said brightly, "Would you care for no-fat, low-carb, sugar-free scone to go with that?"

Overhearing this exchange made Walter smile as he waited for his drink to be finished.

CHAPTER ONE

Glen

Murphy and Elke's apartment was on the second floor of the Coral Mist apartment complex. After parking, Murphy dragged her roller case while Glen carried his plastic Big-K bag filled with the toiletries that Murphy bought him on their way in from the airport. The air was hot, still and humid. Glen had sweated through his t-shirt. They climbed concrete stairs. As Murphy worked her key into the lock, Elke, wearing a thin wrap over a one-piece bathing suit, jerked the door open. She held a furry yellow cat in her arms. Murphy embraced and shared a kiss with both. Elke stood back and looked Glen over.

"They turned you into an old man."

Glen pushed by and flopped onto the futon that filled most of their small living room.

"Nice to see you too, Elke," Glen said grumpily.

"Sorry Glen, that slipped out. Welcome back to the world."

"Thanks." He looked around the room. A window-unit air conditioner rattled and clattered. The room looked like a cheap motel, which it was before being turned into apartment units by a New Jersey real estate investment trust company. "I expected something better," he commented sourly.

"We're saving our money for a townhouse out in Palmetto. We bought into a presale, it's on a canal and will be done in a year or so."

Another cat peeked through the doorway from the kitchenette. It was a thin gray tabby.

"Cats, huh?"

"Yes," Elke said proudly, "they are our babies. This is Mia," she said offering up the yellow cat, "and that's Becky by the kitchen and Blackie is the one sleeping on the clothes hamper."

As if hearing his name, Blackie lifted his head and sniffed the air. He was mostly white with a black face.

"I'll call that one Al," Glen said.

"Blackie?" Elke asked.

"He's making a reference to Al Jolson. That's racist and rude, Glen. Knock it off."

"I suppose the cats are okay as long as they stay away from me. Where do I sleep?"

"You're sitting on it, the futon folds down. This is only a one-bedroom unit."

"Bullshit. Hey, I could sleep with you both and make up for lost time. I don't care if you girls make out as long as I can watch. There's plenty of me to go around, I could service you both."

"Did he say 'service'?" Elke asked. "That's kind of cute."

"Yeah, in an old-fashioned obsolete disgusting pig male sort of way, I guess," Murphy said to Elke. To Glen, she said: "If you don't stop this nonsense, you'll be sleeping under the freeway with the other tramps."

"I was better off back in the nut house," Glen muttered.

"Excuse me, I didn't catch that," Murphy said ominously.

"I said, thank you for welcoming me into your lovely home, this will be fine."

"That's better," Murphy replied. "Elke dear, are there any of those Buffalo wings left? I'm famished."

"And I could use a beer, a dark one if you have it, a microbrew or import would be nice," Glen said, sitting upright on the futon.

Elke furrowed her forehead as she thought. "We don't have any beer, but I think there is a raspberry wine cooler. I'll get it for you."

Glen buried his head in his hands. "Cats, a lousy futon and no beer. Lord, strike me dead now and end this inhuman torture."

"Do you want the cooler on the rocks?" Elke asked cheerfully.

The Powers that Be

Willie Thomas, special assistant to the White House Press Secretary's liaison, walked through his office and nodded to his staff. He took a bundle of newspapers from his Office Manager and seated himself before his large desk. The desk was spotlessly clean and polished; the only items on its surface were a laptop PC and a gold Cross pen. Willie's hair was still damp from a shower after his session on a treadmill at the private section of the K Street Fitness First health club. An intern brought him a china cup on a saucer and poured him strong coffee from a stainless steel carafe. She quietly closed the office door when she exited. Willie unfurled the Wall Street Journal and scanned the headlines. He had skimmed the Washington Post and the New York Times when his Office Manager poked her head in and excused herself for interrupting.

"Yes, Madelyn?"

"Sorry to disturb, sir, but there is a Mister Stephens here to see you."

"Stephens?" Willie thought about this, but could not quite remember who this might be. "I don't know him, how did he get this far?"

"He has a badge, sir. DEA."

"Very well, give me two minutes, then show him in."

Madelyn nodded and pulled out. Willie folded the newspapers and put them into a desk drawer. He aligned the Cross pen until it was perfectly parallel to the edge of the PC and brushed lint off the desktop. He stood when Stephens, a very large black man with graying hair at his temples, strode confidently into the room. When they shook hands, Willie felt like he was grasping a fistful of bananas. Stephens looked slightly familiar, but Willie could not place him.

"Good morning, Mr. Stephens, please take a seat."

"You can call me Steve. You don't remember me, do you?"

"I have to confess that I can't quite place you. Would you care for coffee? It's Batangas barako from the Philippines and quite good if you like strong coffee." As if via telepathy, Madelyn whisked into the room and left a cup on a tray with cream and raw brown sugar. Willie poured Steve a cup and handed it over. Steve took a sip, nodded with appreciation, and then set it down.

"There is no real reason you would remember me, I'm usually stationed in Miami. I helped bring down Noriega and Sanchez, so my picture got in the newspapers a few times. I don't believe we've ever met face to face. I'm here to talk about something that is a bit of a hobby."

"Yes?"

"A man you've become acquainted with by the name of Glen Wilson."

Relieved that the topic was something 'safe', Willie relaxed and leaned back in his chair.

"Yes, Glen Wilson. I wondered if I'd ever hear that name again. The man who would be king. Like Icarus, he flew too close to the sun and crashed back to earth. If I recall, we have him stashed in Nebraska or some damn place."

"North Dakota."

"Sure, that sounds right. If I can be frank...?" Steve nodded. "He came very close to being part of the feed at an Iowa hog farm, if you follow me." Willie said. "I hope I'm not getting too graphic?"

Steve chuckled. "I'm not the overly-sensitive type."

"No, I expect not. I decided to keep him alive, but to this day, I'm not sure why. Loose ends can be very troublesome. I had the idle thought that he might be useful someday. Regardless, what about this Glen Wilson has prompted this pleasant visit?"

"He's out."

"How did that happen?"

"His friends tracked him down and they conjured up an invisible release order. He walked right out the front door."

"Interesting. And you're here…?"

"I thought you should know."

"You have history with Mr. Wilson?"

"Extensive."

"So you must have a suggestion?"

Steve sat back and rubbed his hand over his face. He sighed.

"I hadn't thought that far ahead."

"Do we have a line on him? Where he is right now?"

"He's currently located in Sarasota, Florida."

"Well now," Willie said as he stared at the wall and steepled his slender fingers. "I don't suppose you're looking for a job, Steve?"

"Nope. I happened to be here in DC and I thought you should know." Steve leaned forward. He seemed uncomfortable. "I know Glen and I have nothing against him personally. However, he has a way of coming out on top. His enemies fare poorly, often very poorly. I don't know how this happens."

"Are you concerned for my personal safety, Steve?"

Steve chuckled wryly. "No, not for you. I don't even know you." He put his elbows on the desk and cupped his chin. "I'll tell you what keeps me up at night and haunts my dreams," he said quietly.

"Go on."

"What if he decides to get even with us, all of us?"

"You and I?"

"He actually won his Congressional race in Alaska, right? And he became president of the United States."

"Sure, technically, for a few hours you could look at it that way."

"And it was all stolen away from him."

"You think he might blow something up?"

"No, nothing so direct. I may simply be losing my mind, but what if he's spent the last few years dreaming up some way to even the score with us. You, me, Americans, the government? The established powers?"

"I'll tell you what, Steve. We'll keep an eye on Mr. Wilson and if he gets, uh, too rambunctious, we'll take care of him. Okay? Maybe the hogs in Iowa will get extra protein in their feed?"

"As much as I hate to suggest this, it might be more prudent to do something more proactive. It troubles me that this genie is out of his bottle, figuratively speaking. I suggest you send a team to Florida, figure out his price and pay him off. Defuse him."

"I'll mull this over and seriously examine all the options. There is a bigger picture here to consider. I think the Republicans are going to do much better in the next election and I don't much like the prevailing sociopolitical winds. As I sit here, I have a vague notion in the back of my mind that Wilson may be useful to us. I need time to think through all the potential impacts and ramifications."

"I caution you not to be too clever about this."

"Honestly, Steve. This is one guy and from what I can see, not all that bright of one. He's not even a footnote in history. Let's maintain perspective." Willie stood and extended his hand to bring the meeting to a close. "I thank you so much for stopping by."

Steve looked troubled, but nodded. "Good day to you, sir," he said before turning and walking to the door.

Mary Swanson

Mary did not like to sleep during the day because she had enough trouble sleeping through the night, but sometimes she'd drowse off in her chair. Often she would dream about her late husband Bert, a police officer for 32 years on the Seattle force. Bert was a soft and gentle man. She propped him up during a police brutality investigation and, on the street, she made sure he was always ready to shoot first and ask questions later. The street vermin deserved no better. There were plenty of sad stories from cops who let their guard down or hesitated. Sadly, Bert died in his sleep less than six months after retiring.

Mary knew she had a reputation for being tough, but she stood by the results. Her sons not only survived, but brought honor to the family name doing Marine duty in Iraq. Even though she rarely (never) saw them, she knew they were good fathers to their children in Houston and Philadelphia. Bert drove a squad car in the Central District and Mary made sure he always carried a cheap throw-down pistol and shiv (a sharpened screwdriver or something similar) to press into a deceased thug's hand. It wasn't usually necessary, because most of the bangers had some sort of weapon at hand, but you always needed a backup plan to survive the inquisition the cops had to go through as part of their job. When Bert shot a teenager in the back (three times), it was Mary who thought to claim the kid was threatening another officer in front of him. They would have never survived this episode except for the cell phone and quick alignment of stories among the shift officers. The contrary witnesses that stepped forward were not credible, a stroke of luck. A jury will believe a cop's story even when contradicted by a convicted drug dealer, even if the dealer had apparently gone straight and was pastor at a small local black church.

On one occasion, Mary slipped a blade into jail to make sure a witness was put down. He fell victim to a jailhouse brawl while the security cameras were conveniently malfunctioning. This operation took courage and cashing in many favors, but somehow the plan worked. It was not something Mary was proud of, but sometimes extreme measures were required. She often missed Bert, but he'd discovered Viagra and wouldn't leave her alone, so in some ways his demise was a blessing. He'd left a pension, Social Security and a generous life insurance policy, so Mary was safely ensconced in this luxury retirement community, healthy and pampered, but often bored.

Waking from her reverie with a start, she realized that it was almost time for the Doctor Phil show. She led a quilt group that sat in front of the TV and worked on a 9-11 anniversary memorial for the New York Fire Dept. If she did not round up the ladies and make sure they attended to their assigned tasks, this quilt would never get done.

Truth is Stranger than Fiction, Item 1

Blueprints Promising Programs
Seattle Social Development Project (SSDP)

Program Overview:
This universal, multidimensional intervention decreases juveniles' problem behaviors by working with parents, teachers, and children. It incorporates both social control and social learning theories and intervenes early in children's development to increase prosocial bonds, strengthen attachment and commitment to schools, and decrease delinquency.

- Blueprints for Violence Protection from the University of Colorado at Boulder Center for the Study and Prevention of Violence

CHAPTER TWO

Glen

Glen stood looking over the balcony and let the sun bake his body while he sipped warm beer from a plastic bottle. He was wearing skimpy Speedo swimming shorts and his gray skin hung loosely on his frame in wrinkly folds. He looked like a half-dead prisoner of war, but he didn't give a shit how he appeared to the tourists strolling on the sidewalk below. Elke and Murphy exchanged sections of the newspaper as they enjoyed their morning coffee with croissants and occasionally glanced outside at Glen. He'd been sleeping on their futon for a week, hanging out, surfing the Internet, watching TV and listening to talk programs on the radio as he tried to catch up on the events of the world. He was listless and seemed broken. In the afternoons, he went on long walks down the beach, but otherwise he stayed in the apartment or out on the balcony.

The newspapers were set aside; Murphy and Elke sat with their fingers intertwined when Glen entered the dining area and sat down.

"Okay ladies, I want to make sure I understand the situation. My mom died and her house was razed and turned into a fast food joint."

"A Jack in the Box," Elke offered helpfully.

"My house burned to the ground and all my money and gold is gone. The bank accounts were confiscated. When you checked my safe deposit box at the bank, it was empty. I have nothing to show for everything I spent my life doing, I'm flat broke."

"We're sorry Glen, they tracked down and took everything. But don't worry, we have money saved up," Murphy said gently. "Plus, Walter and Bennie's business is doing well, they would give you a stake and get you going again."

"I'm a damn charity case. A pathetic loser. Tapped out."

"We'll help you."

"I don't want your money so there's only one thing left for me to do." Elke and Murphy exchanged worried glances. "Desperate times call for desperate measures," Glen continued.

"Glen, you're not thinking of… suicide, are you? That's no answer to anything."

"No dummy, this is something much worse. If things keep drifting along like this, I'm going to have to think about getting a motherfucking *J-O-B*."

Mayor Harry Silverberg

The Mayor of Seattle was a mess, he'd buttoned his shirt wrong and his hair was mussed. Gray stubble sprouted from his unshaved chin. The doctors had given his wife, Evelyn, Halcion and she was standing quietly by a window sipping hot tea. They kept offering Harry pills, but he pushed them all away. He insisted they show him his son's body; it was ghastly with needles stabbed in its veins and lurid burns on the chest from the defibrillator. The worst part was the smell, like fried pork, but Harry might have imagined that. The scene was nightmarish. Photographers kept trying to get his picture and he sent the State Patrol out to create an isolation zone. He held his wife's hand, but she was not focusing. He asked an aide to drive her home and irrationally, he decided to walk to his office. It was very early in the morning and his office was at least a mile from where Harborview Medical Center perched on First Hill, but Harry wanted to get away from everything. He found a corridor that led to an exit propped open so the nurses could sneak outside to smoke. He walked through the parking lot. No one paid any attention to him at all. He looked back at the main entrance, it was a bustle of activity and at least two flood lights illuminated local TV reporters as they bloviated their blather. He stood looking over the city from the red medevac helicopter landing pad, staring beyond the expensive twin stadiums into the busy container-ship harbor. A hobo camp in the trees stretched between the hospital and the freeway. The trash scattered around depressed him even more. He found a walkway and walked down toward Yesler. There was a rat running down the sidewalk and a guard dog rushed and scared him, only a well-chewed chain link fence separated him from the gnashing teeth. He crossed I-5 on Yesler.

The city was mostly asleep except for a few delivery trucks, including the early morning run of the Seattle Post Intelligencer. He supposed editors were cursing because the death of the Mayor's son missed their AM edition deadline. There were people sleeping in doorways and on park benches and a bum was prying, with a length of angle iron, at the door of one of Seattle's six-hundred-thousand dollar self-cleaning city toilets. He was approached twice with offers of smoke or junk. A low-riding Honda Accord cruised by with a repetitive hiphop thump emitting shock waves like an earthquake. His town was turning into a shit-heap. Literally, judging by the smell of an aromatic pile left in an alley. A transient asked him for spare change and Harry absently handed him the content of his trouser pocket.

"Hey, don't jive me man, I know you can afford to buy me a bowl of soup."

Harry lifted his eyes from the sidewalk. The transient wore a navy pea jacket, a greasy ponytail and had a bloody gapping hole in his front teeth. *From a fight? Some low-budget back-alley dentistry?* Harry realized he was being backed against the locked gate of a pawn shop.

"Beat it or I'll call the police," Harry said as he pulled his cell phone from the holster on his belt.

The transient knocked the phone out of his hand and stomped it.

"Cops don't come down here much. Give me your wallet and we'll call it even."

I'm being mugged, Harry realized. He pushed off the gate and slapped the transient's ear with a cupped hand. This was a disabling blow intended to burst an eardrum and no way for a mayor of a progressive and civilized city like Seattle to act. Harry was surprised at himself, but the Air Police training he absorbed in his Air Force stint apparently still lived inside him. Police Technical School at Lackland in Texas, then a year tour in Viet Nam. Justice delivered by old-fashioned hardwood night stick.

"I'll kill you, motherfucker," the transient said. However, he said this while back-pedaling. Harry took a quick step toward him and the homeless guy turned and ran away shouting curses over his shoulder. Harry could not understand what he was saying. Except for a woman trying to sell him a food stamp card for ten bucks, no one else bothered him on the remainder of his walk. It took a moment for the security guard to recognize the perspiring and disheveled Mayor when he entered the municipal office building, but soon Harry was in his office staring out his window over the city. Every time his thoughts touched on any memory of his son, it felt like black smoke poisoned his mind. He had a breakdown of sorts as his thinking became derailed. On his bookshelf, there was a ceremonial bottle of Tequila, a gift from Mazatlán, one of Seattle's sister cities. It tasted terrible, but after many little sips his mind settled down. His desk was covered with budgets and proposals for endless social programs. Expanding the number of beds in a homeless shelter. Giving away cell phones so transients could receive phone calls and, presumably, job offers. A rule preventing the police from asking if a detainee is a legal resident of the United States. Building more of the expensive toilets that the bums vandalized and defiled. Stopping the roundup of drug addicts in the city parks. *All this shit to deal with while my son's body grows cold on a slab at the morgue. Maybe it's time to try something different to make this a city where families want to live. To do something about the bums which harass the tourists, the drug addicts that scare the kids in the parks, the taggers that defile the walls and overpasses, the gay cruisers that have taken over the public restrooms and the bangers that terrorize the minority neighborhoods.*

Harry realized he was drunk when he tipped over the tequila bottle; it hit the floor and sprayed brown fluid across his carpet. He'd been doodling on a legal pad, his son's name, a sketch of a girl he'd loved in Saigon (his wife would be shocked at how clearly he remembered and could accurately draw her almond-shaped eyes, the birthmark on her neck and her perfect miniature breasts) and a man's name. Glen Wilson. *Glen was no friend of mine. Truth be told, I'd shed no tears if he got the payback he deserved. Still, he had a mysterious and inexplicable way of getting things done. His friends prospered and his enemies suffered. Recently, his name was mentioned in a business journal covering a hot local biotech company. Maybe this city needs a man more known for breaking heads than marching in the Gay-Lesbian-Transsexual-Transvestite Pride Parade.*

A wave of nausea erupted from the pit of his stomach and he barely got his garbage can between his legs before his gut emptied itself in an acidic outpouring of brimstone and bile. The feeling of responsibility for the death of his son was unbearable.

Did I kill my son by indulging him? He wanted to play drums in a rock band instead of going to college and I let him do it. Everything we did together, Disneyland, Yellowstone, all the baseball games, putting up with his beating the shit out of his drums at all hours day and night, dealing with the pregnant girlfriends and the misdemeanor charges for joyriding in cars and shoplifting. All this young life leading up to acute occlusive intracoronary thrombus. Why can't they just say his heart exploded like an engine run at red line too long? I didn't kill my son. This God damned fucking city killed my son.

Mary Swanson

After dinner, Mary walked down the corridor toward her room to sneak a cigarette. She hesitated outside Queenie Jefferson's door. There was a scent that Mary recognized instantly. Death lay behind that door. Queenie was Mary's main rival for leadership among the ladies of Corridor C. If Mary suggested the ladies work on sorting old clothes for the Goodwill, then Queenie would suggest writing letters to Congress about retirement benefits. If Mary suggested adopting Salvadoran school children, then Queenie would recommend baking cookies for a local church youth group fund raiser. A thorn in Mary's side and usurper of the legitimate monarchy of the Corridor C ladies' group. Now, if Mary's instinct was right, the path to power was clear and unobstructed. She allowed one brief moment of glee before composing herself and walking to the nurse's station to report the sad passage of her rival.

Truth is Stranger than Fiction, Item 2

When CPIs [Chronic Public Inebriates] are discharged in the morning from our City's shelters, missions and sobering services, their first priority is to obtain alcohol. It is the nature of their addiction. Seeking low-cost, high-alcohol content products, they will actually line up outside stores waiting for the 6:00 a.m. opening. Then they quickly initiate their daily cycle of inebriety.
[...]
I've kept a careful record of the deliberations, the study and the actions of our work group since 1996. That written record fills thirteen three to four inch wide 3-ring binders. Stacked one sheet on top of the other, it measures about 40¾ inches of documentation.

- Excerpts from testimony during a public hearing of the Office of the Washington State Liquor Control Board on the creation of an Alcohol Impact Area in the Pioneer Square area of Seattle by Patrick Vanzo, employee of the King County Department of Community and Human Services on November 19, 2002

CHAPTER THREE

Glen

Nigel Wombaski was a leathery old man with yellow teeth and a raspy voice earned by a lifetime of smoking and drinking. He wore a white short-sleeved shirt and wide yellow necktie. He stared over his reading glasses at Glen.

"This is a numbers game, Mr. Wilson. The more traffic we run through our doors, the more business we book. Your job as OPC[1] is to get QPs[2] to fill the chairs out there and our job is to make the sale." He gestured at the large room next door that was filled with run-down desks and folding chairs. Sales people were divided between desk dwellers and closers that roamed and took over when the client had been sufficiently softened up by the liners that gave the grand tours. "We're good at our job and we have high expectations that you'll do your part. You get asses in those seats and we'll get the signatures on the bottom line. Your resume says you have a lot of sales experience, but it's light in the details. What did you sell and for which companies? Your name seems familiar, but I guess it's a common name, am I right?"

"You're right," Glen replied.

"We pay every day in cash, you bring your sign-up sheet. For every client that shows up and gets logged into the computer, you get five bucks. The clients have to sign and if you fake names, we dock your pay. I've seen everything, so don't even bother to pad the sheets. We have clumpers[3] on the street, so stay in your assigned territory and don't do anything that will get us in trouble with the cops. I don't want to see you beat up in an alley, if you follow my thought. You gotta get both the

---

[1] OPC, Off-Premises Contact. A street canvasser that coerces people into attending timeshare sales presentations.

[2] QPs, Qualified Prospect. These are the targets for the timeshare sales, people who meet the profile for potential timeshare purchases, typically low to middle-income tourist couples. Typical criteria include ages 28-75 years old, both husband and wife must attend, no single men, but single women over 30 are okay, must possess a major credit card (not a debit card which has more customer-friendly rules for reversing a transaction), must have photo-id, must be employed and be citizens of the USA (or Canadians that already currently own a timeshare).

[3] Clumpers. Enforcers (thugs) that roam the streets and police informal territory agreements.

husband and wife or it don't count. These days, you'll get a lot of live-togethers, as long as they can show a check or utility bill that has their address and both names, they count. These days, we sell a lot of timeshare units to fags and dykes, that's good business, I don't give a shit, you sign them and we'll sell them. We have the best exit program blaggers[4] in the state. If the marks buy something, we SPIF[5] you another fiver. One of our canvassers made fifty-five thousand last year, there is no limit for a man with moxey. You'll find clients everywhere, in the grocery store, on the beach, lining up outside the toilets and sitting outside restaurants. They get a toaster oven and a free dinner at Chez Andre's. You show up during a slow time and Andre is good for a discount on a chili dog or something that will keep you going. Sun Village Resorts is a top-class operation and we have high standards for our sales associates." He looked Glen over and sighed. "We'll advance you 50 bucks on your pay to get a haircut and some sort of leisure suit from the Goodwill store. Mention my name and they'll cut you a 10 percent discount."

So, I had a job of sorts. I've always thought it highly important for the public to keep me in the high manner to which I've become accustomed; otherwise, you'll have to face me on the street peddling timeshares. Did this seem like a setback? To go from being President of the United States to hustling timeshares to drunken tourists? Well, duh! On the other hand, I believe the sales gig is an honorable profession. The world revolves around commerce and everybody is selling something, whether they are honest about it or not. The politician on TV? Selling. The engineer? Selling his labor and creativity. A professor at a prestigious university. Selling. There is no avoiding it. A preacher? Selling the word of God at retail. I still consider selling timeshares a worthy use of my time, even in sort of a backhand manner. People will spend 35 grand a year sending their kid to Harvard for an expensive business education; getting scammed by a timeshare salesman teaches the same tough lesson, but a lot cheaper. A bargain.

Let's face it, I'm an artist at this stuff. I don't keep the brochures in sight, they are stuffed inside a newspaper. I try to strike up a conversation. 'Where are y'all from?', 'Those are great shoes, where did

---

[4] Blaggers, literally liars. These people try to make any deal before the QPs are allowed to leave the premises. Weeks in alternate years? Cheaper travel club packages? It's a bonus if they anger non-buying QPs so much that they leave without collecting their "free" prizes.

[5] SPIF or SPIFS, Sales Person Incentive for Sale, a bonus typically awarded for up-selling or meeting a quota.

you find them?', "Have you seen a little brown puppy running around loose?'. Anything to get a dialog going and the next thing you know the QP is nodding his head and thinking a 45 minute low-pressure presentation won't be so bad in exchange for a deluxe toaster oven and a gourmet dinner with free drinks. Gotcha. This is an art, should I make my pitch to the man or the woman? Should I play them against each other? Who will make the buying decision?

This is a tough business, but the numbers work out. I sign up 50 couples and 25 of them show up. I've made $125 in cash that Uncle Sam will never get a whiff of. Mr. Day Job must make $200 in order to see this much cash after the state and local feds take their cut. Then, with his $125, he can pay sales tax, property tax, tariffs, access charges and other fees. Who is the thief? Of the 25 couples that appear for the presentation, two will sign the contract and I'll get another hard-earned ten bucks. Minus the $50 cash advance that somehow turned into $60. Whatever. If I stick with this game, there is no doubt in my mind that I'll work my way up the food chain, I would move into lining, clumping, table-selling, closing, managing a line crew, then finally running my own crew. I could clear a million a year playing the game as straight as it could be played, maybe a few million if I was willing to cut and run with the money and relocate every year. That's the way the world works and there is always a place for a man who can make a sale.

Mayor Harry Silverberg

The Seattle City Council was in session in the Council Chamber at Seattle City Hall. Seven of the nine members were present and seated around a large oak-trimmed conference table. Council President John Drake was reading a reading revision to a Council Bill and most of the members appeared to be listening except for Golden who was whispering into his cell phone and Lymph who was tapping on her PDA. The door slammed open; Mayor Silverberg walked in and seated himself at the table. President Drake stopped reading. "Let the record show that Mayor Silverberg has joined us," he said. The Council Clerk nodded and typed the information into her laptop computer. Silverberg was disheveled and breathing hard as if he'd climbed the stairs instead of taking the elevator, which was true.

"Carry on, don't let me disrupt the meeting," he said slowly, but still slurring his words.

The Council members exchanged worried glances.

"I lost my place," Drake said. "Let me begin again. Agenda Item Number One - Council Bill Number 114940, relating to regular property taxes; providing for the submission to the qualified electors of the City at a special election called on September 14, of a proposition authorizing the City to levy regular property taxes for up to seven years in excess of the 101% limitation and any other limitation on levies in Chapter 84.55 RCW for the purpose of providing City services, including providing Seattle School District public school students, Seattle youth, and their families with educational and developmental services; authorizing the creation of a new subfund; creating an oversight committee; and authorizing implementing agreements..."

"More money for social programs," Silverberg interjected with derision. "Tax and spend, fully fund the nanny state bureaucratic infrastructure. Feed the pigs at the government trough. I hate you goddamn useless motherfuckers."

Drake waved at the clerk to stop recording.

"I move we call adjournment and delete the Mayor's comments from the record."

This motion was seconded and affirmed in seconds.

The clerk stood and stated "Meeting adjourned."

"We talk and spend money, but we don't even try to solve any of the real problems with our city."

"Mister Mayor, you are not yourself. We understand. Go home, get some rest and come back when you're feeling better. We feel terrible for your loss."

"My son is on a slab in the morgue and you cocksuckers are flapping your lips about raising taxes. I hate you all, I really do."

The Council members slipped hurriedly out the doors and left only Drake and the Mayor.

"Harry, listen to me. You need to go home and take care of yourself and your family. We'll forget everything that happened here. Don't worry about it."

Silverberg slumped at the table.

"I've lost my son..."

"We understand and feel your tragic loss. Go home and take care of your wife. Take a few weeks off."

Silverberg seemed to get a grip on his emotions. He sat up straight and looked around the room as if he did not know where he was. "I'm so damned sick of all the bullshit. What is the limit of a contract I can issue under my signature without competitive bids and all the other bureaucratic horse crap?"

"I'd have to check with the attorney's office, but I think it has to be less than a million dollars. You're not yourself, it's understandable. Don't do anything rash."

Drake took his arm and eased him toward the door. Security was standing by and Drake waved them over. "Drive him home, he needs to stay away for a while." They escorted Silverberg down the hallway. There were a lot of people watching, but none would make eye contact.

"Poor bastard," Drake uttered under his breath.

Mary Swanson

Mr. McMorris elegantly kissed Mary's hand and led her to the visitor's chair in his office. He made sure she was settled and comfortable. He glanced at his calendar, it was her hair day. Her hair always looked the same to him, a fluffy cloud of gray arranged in pin curls on her head.

"I can see that the beauty parlor has performed its usual masterful work, your hair is lovely. Is there anything I can get you, Mrs. Swanson? A cup of tea or cold water, perhaps a snifter of brandy?"

"Oh, Mr. McMorris, you have a keen sense of the absurd. I'm perfectly fine, thank you."

McMorris settled into his leather chair and made church steeples with his fingers.

"Pray tell, Mrs. Swanson, to what do I owe the immense pleasure of your company on this lovely afternoon."

"It's a shade on the humid side, wouldn't you agree?"

"Now Mrs. Swanson, I know you are far too busy to take time from your schedule to discuss meteorology with me. How may I assist you?"

"If you'll permit me, Mr. McMorris, I have a list."

"Of course you do, madam."

"First of all, there is a lamp malfunctioning in the public restroom. It would be very welcome if you'd remind maintenance to clean up any oily smudges left behind when they replace these light bulbs, we don't want a repeat of the unsightly mess they left in Mrs. Tennenbaum's room last year when the fluorescent tubes were replaced."

"Duly noted."

"You will shortly be receiving a request from Mrs. Taylor to switch rooms with Mrs. Ovid. I would strongly suggest this request be denied as the current arrangement of rooms was carefully designed and has been working well. Once we approve one of these requests, then

Veronica will want to switch with Edith and so on until we have complete chaos in the corridor. We must nip this unpleasantness in the bud, so to speak."

"Very well."

"Last year, you agreed that consideration could be applied to repainting the cafeteria. I have taken the liberty of acquiring paint samples and I would like to strongly recommend Prairie Peach, which I believe will be quite attractive. Of course, the drapes will have to be replaced with complimentary colors."

"Of course," Mr. McMorris sighed. "Is there anything else on your list?"

"Yes, I noticed the passenger rear tire on the Escalade appears to be slightly low in pressure, I suggest we get a mechanic to look into the matter. Perhaps there is a slow leak that should be addressed before it becomes a hazard. Also, I noticed that the compass in the mirror needs adjustment, it appears to be set to the wrong latitude and therefore often displays an incorrect heading. Also, the nurses in the West Corridor seem to be receiving an inordinate number of personal phone calls, this ties up the lines in cases of emergency and we run the risk that incoming calls will be blocked. Someone will have to check the union rules, but my judgment tells me that the volume of calls is excessive. A word to the nursing supervisor should suffice, I'm sure."

"I will make sure this gets immediate attention, Mrs. Swanson. Is there anything else?"

She took a moment to review her notes to make sure everything had been mentioned.

"Not at this time, Mr. McMorris. See you tomorrow at this same time?"

McMorris finished making notes, then walked around his desk and took Mrs. Swanson's hand to help her rise from the chair.

"Of course, Mrs. Swanson. Until then, I hope you have a pleasant, if somewhat humid, afternoon."

CHAPTER FOUR

Mayor Harry Silverberg

Back in his office, Mayor Harry paced. He could march seven diagonal steps from bookcase to window before spinning and marching back again. Remembering his boot camp days, he could hear the Drill Sergeant's jodie song, which lent order to his fractured thinking.

Down by the river
HELL YES
I saw a man go down
HELL YES
It was Sergeant Springer
HELL YES
Should we let him drown?
HELL YES
Should we hit him with a stick?
HELL YES
Should we brain him with a brick?
HELL YES
Should we fuck him up?
HELL YES
Should we hold him down?
HELL YES

Harry picked up his phone and dialed his executive assistant leaving voice mail. While doing this, a little voice in the back of his mind whispered. *This is a mistake.*

"I served with a Buck Sergeant in Viet Nam, a guy named Glen Wilson. He had family here in Seattle, see if you can locate him for me. You may be able to track him down via some of the other guys I served with. Sergeant Frank Daly, Major Powell Thompson, Master Sergeant Steve Stephens. The Army will have records. Spread the word, find Wilson, get him on the phone and do it now."

Glen

Glen was hosting dinner at Barnacle Bill's Seafood restaurant. He generously told the ladies to order whatever they wanted, but reflexively frowned when Elke ordered a crab cake appetizer for $3.95. He was wearing his Goodwill leisure suit with a tie hanging loosely around his neck. The tables were so old that they were adorned with cigarette burns though smoking had been outlawed in Florida restaurants for at least 15 years. A ceiling fan rattled as it half-heartedly stirred the thick hot air. The ambience was nothing much, but Barnacle Bill's served a decent-sized portion of fried grouper on angel hair pasta that Glen liked. They sipped sweetened iced tea and watched the old folks stream in for the 4:00 dinner specials.

"So, you're one of those annoying time share guys…" Elke commented.

"Don't knock it, I made $180 yesterday. If I keep it up, I'll get promoted to street supervisor in a week or two and that's an extra ten bucks a day, easy money."

"Don't you need a permit to work the streets?" Murphy asked.

"Only if I get caught."

Murphy looked uncomfortable. "Are you making enough money that maybe you could rent your own place?"

"Hey, I kicked in fifty bucks for the rent last week, don't put the strong arm on me."

"What do you think the next step is?" Elke asked, clearly trying to change the subject while scraping dried crud out of her teaspoon with a thumbnail.

"I can work my way into a table job where the commissions are very good; particularly if I can get the rube to upgrade to a Presidential suite or add a travel club membership. I could easily make a grand a day."

"No, I mean after this time share stuff. You won your election in Alaska, there must be a long term plan, something big, bigger than big. It's sad to see the infamous Glen Wilson sleeping on a futon and hawking timeshares on the street. Besides, this is stupid. Benny and Walter are worth billions, they'd give you an executive job or finance any kind of business you'd care to start."

"I could say the same for you. You could call in a favor and buy a better place tomorrow, something even better than that condo on the canal you talk about. For me, I'm in my fifties now, perhaps the ride is over and this is as good as it gets. I matched myself up against the professionals in Washington, DC and got my ass kicked, put in my place in the universal pecking order and learned my valuable lesson in humility. Maybe I'm finally cured of my grand ambitions."

It took many seconds before they parsed what they were hearing. The girls made eye contact and started giggling. Elke raised her plastic cup to Murphy and made a toast.

"To Glen Wilson on a futon," she said.

"From Commander in Chief to time share canvasser. The irrepressible Glen Wilson."

"You girls are not even slightly funny," Glen grumbled. "Shut up and eat your grouper, it's getting cold."

Back at the apartment, the telephone was ringing stridently. Murphy hurriedly opened the door and dashed inside.

"Wilson? Sure, he's right here." She handed the phone to Glen who was already peeling off his shirt and tie. They listened to Glen's side of the conversation with curiosity.

"Wilson here. Yeah, sure I remember you, Silverberg. What's up?" Glen listened to a long speech while scratching his hairy stomach. Something caught his attention and his eyes became alert and alive with a glint they had not seen since their congressional run in Alaska. He gestured for a pen and motioned for Murphy to hurry up.

"I'm sorry, how much did you say?" The phone squawked and Glen scribbled notes onto the margin of his time share brochure. He covered the mouthpiece and hissed at Murphy. "What's your checking account number and bank routing number? Quickly!"

"What?"

"Goddam it Murphy, give me your checkbook and make it snappy."

Murphy wore a sour look as she fished in her handbag and pulled out her checkbook. "I have seven hundred dollars in that account, you'd better not make me go overdraft." Glen grabbed it out of her hand and read off the numbers into the phone.

"Alright, I will come when the deposit shows up. No, not until I see the money. No! Get the money transferred and I will come with a contract in hand. And you're paying all reasonable expenses. Right." Glen slammed the phone into its cradle and pumped his fist in the air. "Yes!," he said with a tight grin on his face.

"What's going on?" Elke asked.

Glen turned and allowed an impassive expression to cover his glee. He took a deep breath.

"I think I'm back in business," he said calmly. "They are going to wire money to your bank account. I have a job."

"What about the time share business?"

"Fuck the time share business," Glen said with a smirk.

Murphy and Elke

The lobby of the Florida First Federal Savings and Loan Bank was nearly empty. To kill time, Murphy and Elke were playing cribbage with a travel game. They sipped tepid coffee from Styrofoam cups and glanced at the clock. All Glen would tell them was that a bank transfer was supposed to be executed at exactly noon local and they were supposed to wait for confirmation. When they pressed him for the amount and for details of his new job, he grinned his characteristic toothy grin. They both found this very irritating, but he was not talking.

"Excuse me, Madames?"

Most of the bank workers were dressed in business casual attire, but this man was wearing an immaculate black suit. The lighting gleamed on his bald head. He shook their hands with soft and perfectly manicured hands. "If the Madames would care to join me in my office I have biscotti and a fresh carafe of Gevalia coffee."

After Murphy put away their cribbage game, he led them behind the counters and down a hallway to a small, but ornate, office where they were seated.

"I apologize for the delay, but for a transaction of this nature, we have procedures for validation that must be observed," he said as he poured coffee into miniature cups.

"First of all, I want to make sure you know that Florida First Federal is a full-service banking company and we serve many wealthy clients with mutual fund and other investment opportunities. We have a full array of methods for putting your funds to work for you."

"Give us the current balance, please," Murphy said.

An emotion of disapproval appeared briefly on the banker's face before his compliant expression re-established control. He handed Murphy a slip of paper and Murphy held it out so Elke could read it too.

$1,001,729.48

With a thumbnail, Murphy measured the digits and checked the decimal places.

"That's a million?" Elke asked.

The banker nodded: yes.

"Interesting," Murphy and Elke said together. They looked at each other and laughed at the synchronicity. "Must be some job," Murphy commented. "Okay, we have a friend named Glen and we need to open a checking account for him."

"Banking rules are very strict on these matters, we require the customer to appear in person—" Murphy gave him a stern look. "But in special cases, we can overlook the details. In what name shall we open this account, ma-am?"

Mary Swanson

The meeting of the Corridor C Ladies Quilting Club started. Mary Swanson was secretly pleased that her deceased vice president (Queenie Jefferson) would not be disrupting the flow of her agenda. Mary clapped her hands sharply.

"Ladies, please take your seats. Who are we missing? Oh yes, Mrs. Platt, please go round up Mrs. Yelt, perhaps she is napping and has lost track of the time, thank you very much dear. Let's have a moment of silence for Mrs. Jefferson. Now, if Mrs. Cooper will lead us in our group prayer, then we can get started."

After the prayer, Mrs. Cooper raised her hand.

"Yes, Mrs. Cooper."

"I move that we write a letter to management requesting a small patch of Daffodils be planted in Queenie's memory. She loved Daffodils when they blossomed every Spring."

"Yes, that is a splendid idea, Mrs. Cooper. Go ahead, draft up a letter, once I've reviewed it and made corrections, we can get it printed and signed by all the ladies. Is there anything else? Any action items from our last meeting to discuss?"

Mrs. Bomton stood and read: "Queenie suggested we put a red, white, and blue piping around the edges of our quilt."

"Well, we won't be concerning ourselves with that topic, will we?" Mary stated. "Let's go ahead and delete the suggestion from the record. Now ladies, lay out your squares and let's have a look at them while Mrs. Platt sets up the quilting rack."

They worked for several hours until the meeting broke up at the 4:00 dinner bell.

"Mrs. Yelt, could you stay for a few minutes, please?" Mary asked.

Mrs. Yelt, a diminutive Hungarian, looked nervous when she nodded her head. Once they were alone, Mary spoke to her intensely.

"Mrs. Yelt, you were late for our meeting."

"Yes ma-am, I fell asleep in front of the TV. I'm very sorry."

"This is not the first time."

"It will not happen again, I promise."

"I don't want to take drastic measures. Please have respect for the other ladies who take our quilting seriously and make the required effort to be prompt."

"I'm very sorry."

"Also, Mrs. Yelt, your stitches are not going uniformly through the backing, we don't want to create a quilt that falls apart on the lap of one of the sad New York Fire Department widows, do we?"

"No ma-am, we don't. I've been on new medication and my hands don't work like they used to. I will take extra time with my stitches."

"I suggest you spend time before our next meeting with Mrs. Taylor, her stitches are perfect and beautiful, you could learn a lot from her."

"Yes, ma-am, I will do exactly as you suggest, I'm sure that will take care of the problem."

"Because—"

"Please don't say it, Mrs. Swanson."

"I don't want to think of how the ladies would vote if your membership status was questioned. If you are chronically late and you do poor work, well, you remember what happened to Mrs. Kelley."

"She tried to start her own quilting club, I remember."

"And you remember how that worked out for her, don't you?"

"Yes, ma-am, I remember, I swear that I will pull myself together."

"Very well then, Mrs. Yelt, let's consider the matter to be put behind us for now."

With tears of shame in her eyes, Mrs. Yelt said "Yes, thank you very much, Mrs. Swanson," before scuttling up the corridor like a terrified kitten. Watching, Mary could not resist allowing a small cruel smile to grace her lips. She was going to have discipline in her Quilting Club, or else.

Truth is Stranger than Fiction, Item 3

[Teen Homeless Service] Providers were positive about the potential for making some changes requested by youth

- Accommodation for pets
- Unmarried young adult couples
- Later wake up times could generally be accommodated in overnight shelters with additional resources

From the Final Summary Report, YOUTH SHELTER UTILIZATION: Breaking Down Barriers and Building a System of Care
By the Street Youth Task Force, King County, Washington State, March 2002

CHAPTER FIVE

Glen, Bennie and Walter Reunited

The 757 slewed and the right wing dipped alarmingly until the plane slowed and gripped the runway. Glen glared at the pilot as he exited the aircraft.

"Been driving long?" he asked sarcastically.

Glen was dressed in his polyester suit and flipflops. Everything he owned was stuffed into a canvas zipper bag. The plane ticket was prepaid, but Glen assumed he'd have to spend his last fifty dollars on a taxi ride to City Hall. He was surprised to see a limousine driver, dressed in a formal black suit, waving a sign that said 'Glen Wilson'.

"I'm Wilson."

"Very good, sir. Are we waiting for checked baggage?"

Glen handed him the canvas bag. "No, this is it. Let's go."

The limousine weaved through Seattle while Glen sipped a Pepsi on ice and looked longingly at the array of bottles: Cabo Wabo Tequila, Skyy Vodka, Chivas Regal and Baileys Irish Cream. Glen had not been drinking since his internment (beer did not count), but he was not sure why. *Waiting for the right moment,* he mused wryly. He hoped he was not developing self-discipline in his maturity. In front of a modest four-story brick and chrome building in the shadow of the Fremont Bridge, the car pulled to a stop. It was drizzly and Glen grimaced as his uninsulated feet hit the cold pavement.

A stainless steel casting of the infinity sign hung over the front entry.

"This does not look like city hall…" Glen commented.

"It's not. This is Immortality, LLC."

"Hmmph," Glen grunted.

The front lobby was plush with potted plants and framed prints illuminated with bright LED lighting. The receptionist, dressed in colors that matched the décor, was a stunning cheer-leader type. There were several people idling in the lobby, Glen recognized them as hungry sales-people examining and measuring him to see if he was 'someone'. The way he was dressed, in a cheap rumpled suit and plastic sandals, he could have been a street bum or a genius Bay Area software engineer. The receptionist handed him a preprinted badge embossed with an old picture and his name. Glen clipped it to his collar and leaned over the counter. The receptionist wore a nametag that said 'Gerusha' pinned to a furry mauve cashmere sweater. She wore a wireless headset and her thumbnails were adorned with the infinity sign in silver paint.

"That's a curious name," Glen commented. "It means stranger or exile in Hebrew. I used to have a ferret I called Gerusha. So tell me, are you doing anything tonight that you can't cancel?"

"A couple of phone calls and I'm all yours," Gerusha whispered as she pushed her business card across the polished granite surface of the reception desk. "Call me on my cell phone."

Glen stood straight and looked around suspiciously. The sales-droids were trying to listen in but they were far enough away that Glen could safely ignore them. He leaned over the counter again.

"Kalal is Hebrew for making complete or perfect, if obscure Hebrew words are your thing," Glen said hopefully.

"Is it true that you discovered Bennie on the street in Orlando and gave him your business card?"

Glen was confused. Gerusha laughed at the expression on his face. She gestured toward a brass bust in the corner. Glen walked over to it. The inscription read 'Glen Wilson, Long Life to our Friends and Death to our Enemies'. He walked back on weak knees. The salespeople were inching closer.

"I don't think I like this. The little beard makes me look like Trotsky or something."

"If you need a friend in Seattle, you can call me anytime, Mister Wilson, day or night," Gerusha whispered.

Walter Crowley, dressed in a perfectly-tailored ivory suit, burst through glass-trimmed security doors. His white hair, longer than Glen remembered, was brushed back from his face and he wore delicate gold-rimmed glasses. He gathered Glen into a bear hug. Embarrassed, Glen extracted himself and offered his hand to shake.

"Glen, we're so delighted you came by," Walter said with a well-burnished baritone voice.

"I was on my way to see the Mayor. It's great to see you, Doc. You're looking well."

Walter used to operate a roving magic show under the moniker Doctor Zalooq.

"And you look like shit on a stick, if you don't mind me saying. We wanted you to come right away, but Murphy said we should leave you on your own for a while. Bennie and Emma are going to shit briquettes when they see you. I paged Bennie, but he's in one of his labs, he'll turn up sooner or later. Emma is coming in from the Eastside, she was shopping with Melinda Gates and their kids, she'll be here shortly. Let me show you around." They pushed through the glass doors and

Walter punched the button for the elevator. On the top floor, they walked through a cubicle farm. Everywhere, there were staring eyes. The cubicles were designed like automobile cockpits with large flat computer displays and reclining seats. Unconscious, Walter led Glen to a corner office which looked out over the canal. The Space Needle and the tall buildings of Seattle seemed close enough to touch. Walter gestured toward a small oval table and waved at papers in a binder.

"What's this?" Glen asked.

"The largest public offering in history. We're going to raise 10 billion dollars in exchange for 5% of the company. We have almost a billion in angel seed money from Gates, Ellison, Buffet, Allen, they're all in. Ellison tried to steal us over a year ago for 8 billion. I wanted to grab the money and run, but Bennie insisted we hold out. Of course, he was right, he's fucking golden, I'll tell you. It's all laid out in the documents, take a look for yourself."

Glen closed the binder and pushed it away. "What are your products?"

"We're into everything. Bennie designed a magnetic levitation system for mass transit. He prototyped an ion processor that mimics brain activity, an infinitely configurable thinking machine. Everyone is onboard with that, governments, corporate data centers, the entertainment industry, everybody. There are many other things, however, our big money is in biotech, we're selling longevity and health."

"What's the secret sauce?"

"I don't think anyone but Bennie really understands, it's a mix of stem cells, hormones and radiation that rejuvenates the body at the cellular level. It might be the single greatest human invention ever and it's made us rich, all of us."

"Excuse me?"

"Let me show you your office." Walter took his arm and led him down a private hallway to the opposite corner of the building. He gestured at the name engraved in the glass. 'Glen Wilson, Director of Sales'. The doors opened to expose the same breathtaking view as Walter's office. The room was carpeted and held a large desk, but no other furnishings.

"You do whatever you like with the room, it's all yours. Hire a decorator and go crazy."

"I don't understand."

"When we put the company together, Bennie penciled you in for 2.5%. He thinks he'd be selling stuffed lizards out of the back of a van in Orlando if you hadn't intervened. You are one rich motherfucker, didn't anyone tell you? Murphy and Elke have a piece too, the whole team was in from the beginning. If you want to work, the job is yours, but to tell you the truth, this shit sells itself, the market has gone crazy. Let's see if we can find Bennie, he's been dying to see you."

Walter strode out of the room and chatted with a lady a few offices down. She tapped keys on her computer and gave Walter the answer he was looking for.

"Come on Glen, Bennie is in Lab 4C, let's go see what he's up to."

They walked down an austere concrete stairway and past clean rooms where workers in head-to-toe blue suits worked around exotic equipment. "We do prototype chips here," Walter commented as they walked by. They stopped at a huge metal door that looked like the entry to a walk-in freezer. Walter heaved at the latch and the door eased open slowly. A tall and thin black kid, wearing overalls and safety glasses, turned with a grumpy look on his face. Benjamin Franklin Jackson had grown at least a foot since Glen had last seen him. Bennie's face exploded into a huge grin.

"Glen!"

"Hello Bennie." Bennie embraced Glen and squeezed the breath out of him with his wiry arms.

"Don't break my ribs," Glen complained.

Bennie broke his clinch and stood back to look him over.

"It took us a long time to find you."

"Too damn long, but that's old news. What are you doing?"

"Yeah, Bennie, you're supposed to be working on regression of the Stockholm data, but you're always down here. What are you working on?"

"Let me show you." Bennie ushered them toward the center of the room where a large propeller mechanism, constructed of dull gray metal, was suspended on a chrome frame and swivel. "This is quite interesting. Take a close look, do you see any wires? Take my word for it, there are none. The impeller is suspended on very good bearings, go ahead and give it a spin."

Glen pushed and the impeller, though very heavy, started rotating smoothly and quietly. Bennie stopped it. "Here's the interesting part." Watching a LED readout, he rotated the frame until the impeller was at an angle. It started moving and was soon spinning slowly and evenly. He picked up a heavy iron crowbar and handed it to Glen.

"Okay," Bennie said proudly, "see if you can stop it."

Glen jammed the crowbar into the frame and the impeller slammed to a stop.

"Shucks Glen, that's not what I meant," Bennie cried out. He pulled them behind a protection barrier and they watched through a battered Lexan shield. There was a shrill sound like the fabric of the universe shredding. The crowbar bent and warped as if rubberized. Pieces flew apart and arced through the air to embed themselves in the concrete reinforced walls with an ear shattering roar. Soon the impeller was spinning again at its quiet and steady rate. Bennie walked from behind the shield.

"Is everyone okay? I should have warned you, the frame and impeller are made with carbon nanotube string reinforcement, much stronger than iron."

"Alright, I'll bite," Glen said. "What makes it spin?"

"Yes, that is the question isn't it? The earth travels through space at 660,000 miles per hour. The impeller is impregnated with a rare earth and it seems to be either reacting to gravity waves or catching a little piece of an ether wind. My thought is that they are aspects of the same thing."

"I thought Einstein discredited the idea of 'ether' almost a hundred years ago."

"Fields create action at a distance. You'll call me a charlatan if I suggested nothing connecting the magnet and the iron filings of your grade school experiment. Look, when I tap this table top, you hear it because sound waves travel through the air and stimulate your eardrum, that's an action at a distance with the air as the intervening medium. I can't accept action at a distance without a medium to carry the force. The medium could be called ether."

"You're giving me a headache, just tell me the bottom line. What is happening with this propeller thing and what good is it?"

Bennie looked exasperated. "The bottom line is, if my analysis is correct, as long as I keep this ethermill rotated perpendicular to the ether wind, it will spin at a constant speed and emit a huge energy."

"So British Petroleum and Exxon will hate you. What's the downside?"

"Well, I'm using about a gram of the metal I call Etherium. Estimates are that there are only about 7,000 grams of this stuff available in the earth's crust."

"So, we need to get to the places where Etherium can be mined before the oil companies get to it," Glen said.

"Sure, I guess," Bennie said. "I hadn't thought of that."

The lab door flew open and they turned to look at the girl who entered. She was a small Eskimo about five-foot-four inches tall. Her highlighted hair was woven into French braids and she wore a silky pantsuit with high-topped sneakers. Her grin was like dawn, her white teeth gleamed from her round face and she wore rouge that accented her cheekbones. She was very nearly the most beautiful young girl that Glen had ever seen. She walked right up and kissed him on the cheek.

"Welcome back, Glen."

"Emma?"

She spun on her heels. "Yes, 'tis moi," she said brightly while inserting herself between Bennie and Glen. "If these yuppie-scum technogeeks haven't bored you to death, let's go grab food, we need to get a meal in you. There will be plenty of time to admire Bennie's high school lab experiments later." With that, she pulled them away.

As they gathered in the lobby, Glen walked over to talk to Gerusha. She was gabbing with one of the salesmen leaning over the counter. Her bright eyes flicked between Glen's companions. Absently, Glen accepted the salesman's proffered business card, slipped it in his coat pocket and motioned for him to move aside.

"Are these guys always hanging around here?"

"Business is bad in Seattle, I think we're the only company in town buying anything right now. These guys are okay."

"Be careful, you can be judged by the company you keep. Do you have a boyfriend or husband or something that would be a problem if I offered to take you to dinner tonight?" Glen whispered.

"I can free myself up. I'd be delighted to join you," Gerusha replied.

"And do me a favor?" He gestured toward the bust. "Do something about that thing, it's embarrassing."

"Maybe they'll let me take it home," Gerusha said.

"For Christ's sake," Glen complained before Emma tugged him away by pulling at his jacket.

Peter Harris

"How're you doing, Red?" Peter asked while ladling a serving of steaming vegetable soup into Red's plastic bowl. Overhead, glowing red letters spelled out: God's Infinite Love Mission.

"My new sign is doing good," Red said, grinning through brown gappy teeth.

"Let me see it."

Red looked around to make sure no one was watching too closely. He crafted his messages carefully and didn't want the other transients stealing from him. He unfolded the sign.

Job outsourced
Gas too much
No Job, no Gas
Don't be Dutch

God Bless

"You're right Red, that's a good one. Are you staying at the shelter tonight?"

"No, too many rules and too much preachin'. I can sleep in a trailer at the U-Haul place as long as I clear out before the customers come in. When it gets colder, I'll use the shelter. Or I can go down to LA, they got good soup in LA too, y'know?"

"The cops a problem?"

"Cops is always a problem man, but not bad. They are busy with the Mission Babies, the hobos by the freeway and the bangers under the viaduct. As long as I stays out of their way, they leaves me be."

He tucked his sign under his arm and picked up his soup bowl and ambled to a picnic bench.

"Take care out there, Red," Peter called after him.

Mayor Harry Silverberg

Harry stopped pacing, picked up his phone and dialed his assistant. "Where is that goddam Wilson? His plane landed hours ago, he should be here."

"Sorry Mayor, no one has heard from him. We'll show him in right away when we see him."

"That cocksucker bastard piece of shit is jerking me around like he always does. I'm going to cut off his dick and feed it to the Sea Lions over at the fucking Ballard Locks. He probably took the money and is spending it on whores and ganja in Barbados. Goddam it! Get off your thumbs and find his sorry ass."

"Yes, we will. Please sir, I speak for many in the office, we find your language offensive and oppressive…"

"Spineless twit!" the Mayor shouted as he slammed down the phone.

Gerusha Andersen

Martin sat in their dark apartment and sipped a cup of hot Chai tea. The apartment was on the sixth floor of a converted Belltown loft. His suitcases were packed and arranged by the door. Gerusha unlocked the door latches and walked in from outside.

"I thought you'd be gone by now," Gerusha said while dropping her purse and keys on a small entry table.

"After two years, I thought I'd earned more than a phone call. Talk to me, Gerusha."

She pulled clips out of her hair and shook her head to release her blond waves.

"This arrangement was a convenience for both of us. It was great in its time, but that's passed and we should move on."

"At least tell me who you're dumping me for? Is it one of those PhD bio-guys at Immortality? One of those zillionaire dipshits throwing their option money around?"

"Look Martin, if you want a goodbye BJ, then unzip and whip it out. But it'll be the last you'll get from me, then you'll take your shit and pound the pavement, you're out of here, it's over."

"It could have been good for us. Another couple of semesters and I can take the bar exam. If you want to get married, we could do it once I've passed the bar and my career gets going. I could have loved you, you cold-blooded stainless-steel bitch."

She kicked off her high heels and took a martial arts stance.

"Are you going or do I have to throw your ass out of here?"

"I'm going, Gerusha. I wish you luck in your quest. You'll make a fine trophy blond for one of those rich assholes you work with. Or they'll fuck you inside out and you'll find yourself back at Starbucks serving iced lattés and counting out pennies in the tip jar. You'll regret treating me this way."

Gerusha sighed. "Can the hyperbole and beat it, will you, Martin? I'm tired and I need to take a shower and shave before dinner."

"I hope you nick yourself and bleed to death," Martin said as he picked up his bags and walked out.

Rubbing her eyes, Gerusha gently pushed the door shut with her shoulder. *Thanks for the image, asshole,* she thought as she went to her bathroom and prepared herself for her big date.

She'd spent many hours in that lobby staring at the statue and wondering what kind of man this Glen Wilson could be. When she started the job, there was little else to do. The lobby was barren except for her little desk. The statue was one of the first furnishings. The rest of the building was nearly empty, but slowly furniture and equipment began arriving and the lobby got busier. Glen Wilson. *Did she imagine his aristocratic brow and the determined tilt of his chin? That his wide forehead must be home to great and noble thoughts?* Hours earlier, she could only imagine meeting the legendary man, now she was joining him and the rest of the executive team for dinner. Did she misread his hunger for her in his eyes? She would let him dominate her, use her, fill her. Even if he used a condom, she could use the contents later to impregnate herself and carry the great man's child. This thought was pushed away as too crude; she was always letting her imagination get carried away.

After complete thoroughness in her shaving, she plucked her eyebrows into an arch like a magazine model. She applied a blow dryer to her feathery hair, then douched and carefully painted her finger and toe nails. She arranged candles by her bed and made sure the lubricant was handy in case he tried to take her too quickly. Layering her clothes thoughtfully, she put on a red thong with matching bra, followed by a charcoal dress and high heels. She twirled in front of the mirror and decided she was finally and truly ready. Then she tried to figure out what to do for the remaining couple of hours. To avoid wrinkling the dress, she did not want to sit down, but eventually perched carefully on a bar stool and riffled through the pages of an Us magazine. The hours passed slowly. She swore the clock ran backwards at times, but eventually and glacially it was time to go, and so she went downstairs to meet her taxi.

Glen and the Team Have Dinner

The group streamed through the front entrance of the Union Place restaurant. They were shepherded to a semi-private dining area. Emma guided people to their seats and urged everyone to move until she got the mix she was looking for. Glen got a kiss on the cheek from a very pregnant woman that he did not recognize at first, but once she took Walter's arm, Glen realized she was Angela. She wore a garish wedding set on her finger and Walter's hand comfortably on her substantial ass.

She was pretty in the face but had gained a lot of weight. From the doorway, Gerusha waved until she got Glen's attention. He motioned for her to join them and the burly greeting staff parted to allow her through. She was scrubbed and stunning, wearing a black cocktail dress which was cut high on one side to expose her long legs and cut deep into her chest to mostly cover her nipples, though a brown hints of areola were visible when she moved. She had sprinkled a dusting of sparkle on her cheeks and cleavage, so she glittered like a walking disco ball. Emma scurried and pushed chairs around to clear a spot next to Glen. The dinner party was complete with, clockwise around the table, Glen, Gerusha, Bennie, Emma, Walter and Angela. A photographer waved a digital camera equipped with a huge lens and Emma motioned for him to enter. All shifted their chairs to face the camera and smiled except for Glen, who was distracted and peering down the front of Gerusha's dress when the flash froze the image. A waiter walked around filling wine glasses but Angela turned hers upside down. Emma and Bennie's glasses were removed from the table because they were too young. Glen covered his glass with his palm. Walter looked at Glen with curiosity, Glen leaned over and said "I don't think I drink or smoke any more." Walter looked surprised, only he and Gerusha were taking the wine. He shrugged and raised his glass in toast.

"To our Guru!"

Glen looked at Bennie, but found everyone looking back at him.

"I'm supposed to be the guru? That's horseshit," Glen muttered.

"Please say a few words," Angela urged.

"Speech!" the crowd chanted.

Glen, with a sour look on his face, picked up his ice water and stood. He looked around the table and gathered his thoughts.

"Obviously, I'm glad to be out in the world again and to those that helped me escape from my private hell in North Dakota, I thank you." He took a sip. "I'm not sure I properly expressed my appreciation for the work that went into our big win in Alaska, that was a sweet victory. We went against the political power structure and they beat us silly in round two. So, screw politics." This was echoed around the table. "And to absent friends, our team is not complete without Elke and Murphy. They told me that your company was doing well, but I had no idea you were doing this well. Why aren't they here?"

"Murphy wants to do one last tour with Toxic Shock and then she'll take over security for us. She hates the weather here, so she wants to keep her home base in Florida. We'll all be back together soon," Walter explained. "Let's go around the table and catch Glen up."

With Glen's help and leveraging her weight on the table, Angela managed to get her feet under her. She turned toward Glen and raised her ice water.

"Walter planted a bun in my oven, so we got a quicky shotgun marriage, bought a small house in a great neighborhood on the Eastside and we're going to have a boy named Seth. And soon, I hope, because I'm going crazy with the damn vitamins and clean living."

"Can I touch your belly?" Glen asked.

"I'd rather you didn't," Angela replied. "I hate that," she said as she settled back in her seat.

Walter stood. "After you were disappeared, I came to Seattle with Angela. I thought about starting up the road show again, but we were coming out of the tech depression and biotech money was starting to free up. I found it was just as easy to flimflam the vulture capital guys as the general public, so with ideas from Bennie, we put a business plan on the street and soon had angel money coming in. We were able to hire really smart people and work them hard in exchange for stock options, like Microsoft in the early 80's. Bennie conceived a method of rejuvenating cells and the initial tests in Brazil went well. If I can get him to stop screwing around in his playground labs, we'll roll out and start cranking up the money machine."

"I hate to be a spoiler, but what about the FDA?" Glen asked. "It can take a decade to get approval from those bureaucratic dickwads."

"We were paying attention to your lessons, Glen. We set up a clinic on the border between Brazil and Bolivia. For a price, they let us do whatever we want down there." Walter leaned over, grinned and said in a stage whisper: "We promised free treatment to President Delacruz and his family. At a million bucks a shot, we have people lined up for years. They fly down, spend a few weeks in the clinic, and then come back as new people. It raises interesting legal questions, they are genetically the same person, but they are not literally the same flesh."

"Pardon me for asking, but what exactly are you doing?"

Walter pursed his lips and scratched his head. "In a way, we're selling a second lifespan," he said furtively.

"What's the catch?" Glen asked.

"Umm, well, we'll talk about all the minor details later," Walter replied. "Cheers," he said raising his glass and then settling in his seat.

Emma stood up and placed her hand comfortably on Bennie's shoulder. She was small, but her gray eyes were steady as she scanned the table. "I'm supposed to be going to Seattle U, but things have been so hectic that I'm only taking one class this semester, Business Law, an easy 'A'. I have to get back to my studies because Bennie says he won't marry me until I'm a college graduate."

"Bennie never went to college…"

"Bill Gates got him an honorary from Harvard, the weasel." To Glen, she said: "I didn't get a chance to know you very well in Alaska and I hope to rectify that situation now. Welcome back to your life." She kissed the top of Bennie's head before she sat back down.

Bennie scribbled notes onto a tablet. He was dressed in farmer-style overalls where the many pockets were adorned with pens, screwdrivers and personal electronics. He looked around the table and then stood. He was easily six foot tall now and maybe 160 pounds. Wearing patchy sideburns and a sparse mustache, he looked about 13 years old.

"Steganography. Pattern recognition. Water marking. I wrote algorithms that work quickly to sift and analyze raw data and insert or extract encoded data. We have neural artificial intelligence machines that work well, this technology goes way beyond digital signal processing."

"Just stop it Bennie, shut up and figure out what you want for dinner," Emma complained.

"Yeah, Bennie, you're supposed to be working on the human study data instead of screwing around with your diversions," Walter added.

"No, I was getting to my point, you guys are going to like this."

Walter rolled his eyes. "Sure."

"Listen," Bennie continued, "I've been scanning the world's archives of photographs from Getty Images and Corbis—"

"And wasting half the world's bandwidth!"

"—and I've found codes. For example, impressions in clay from Peru are encoded, they are not random. Also, I found stones from Iran that have binary-coded dimples. Language, intelligence."

"So, what old messages have you found? New chapters of the Bible or something?"

"This stuff is much older than that, something like 25,000 years, way older than the Bible."

"What does it say?"

"I don't know yet, we don't even have context for deciphering the codes yet. But, I have proved that these things are not random, there is intelligence passed through the ages. This is big!"

"Yes, Bennie, we get it. When you figure out the message, we'll all be very happy for you. But please keep in mind we have our IPO coming up and you need to focus on our core business, okay?"

Bennie looked disappointed. After he sat down and refocused on his tablet, Emma rubbed his neck and shrugged to the people around the table in apology.

Gerusha looked around.

"You don't have to speak," Emma said kindly.

"No, its okay," Gerusha replied as she stood. She took a deep breath and a fortifying sip of her wine. "My name is Gerusha and I was born in Redding, California. I have an two-year degree in Business Admin from California State U, Chico. I moved up here to Seattle…"

"Bullshit," Walter complained.

"No biography," Emma whispered gently.

"Alright." Gerusha took a deep breath. "Months ago I was a barista at the Starbucks on Roosevelt when Walter offered me a job in the lobby. I'm a receptionist, but I have larger ambitions, much larger. I want to thank Glen for inviting me to join you tonight. It is a great honor. That's all."

Glen made a command decision. He grabbed the wine bottle and took a deep drink.

"I guess I'm drinking again," he announced. Everyone watched him expectantly, but that's all he said until the restaurant servers walked around the table distributing menus a minute later. Glen set his aside and stood. "Okay, I'll say a few more words. This team is spectacular, each and every one of you. However, I don't want to sound like a hippie, but I think you're in danger of selling your souls. Don't get me wrong, I love money and I crave the power and freedom that money buys. But, making money for its own sake, well that's a waste of the talent I see here." He drained the wine bottle and handed it to a server. "More," he whispered.

"Glen, you're our soul," Bennie said. "Will you lead us again?"

"Bullshit. If anyone, I think Murphy is our soul. However, I do have something I've been thinking about for the last couple of years. I haven't worked the whole thing out, but it's big, really big."

"So tell us already."

Glen sat down. "No, not yet. Besides, I have a job here in Seattle and everything will have to wait until I finish this contract, then we'll go from there."

"At least give us a hint."

"Nope."

"Prick," Walter hissed. Gerusha looked shocked that Walter could be so rude. She took the wine bottle from the wine steward and filled Glen's glass herself. Palm up, Glen motioned for her to fill it to the brim. Already, his cheeks were rosy and he had a wild gleam in his eyes as his body reacted to the alcohol.

"Gotta tinkle," Angela announced.

She stood and walked toward the restrooms. After a moment, Glen followed. She walked past the bathrooms, through the kitchen and out the back door into the alley where an overflowing dumpster radiated stench. Angela leaned against the building and pulled out a Virginia Slim cigarette as Glen pushed through the doors and joined her.

"The doctor lets me have one a day, but this is my second."

"Give me one, I guess I'm smoking again too." Angela lighted his cigarette with a thin gold lighter. "How are you doing?" he asked.

Angela sighed. "Sometimes I think I'm going to scream and jump out of my skin, but usually it's okay. I may surprise myself and be a good mother. Walter has been a prince, but sometimes I think," she said, gesturing toward her tummy, "he sees us as a lab experiment. He scares me sometimes." Changing the subject, she asked: "What's the deal with you and the receptionist?"

"I've haven't been with a woman in over three years."

"Oh, I figured that was something you'd get out of your system in Florida."

"I was busy, it never came together for me that way. Do you think Walter ever found about our affair?"

Angela was exasperated. "One fuck is not an affair and for both our sakes, we'd better hope he never finds out. It's not something I'd expect him to be mature about. There's no telling what he might come up with for revenge for a betrayal like that."

"Of all of us, Walter's the one I thought might fly apart at the seams first. But we'll burn that bridge when we get to it."

He took a deep drag on the cigarette and started gagging. Suddenly, the wine and big dinner came spewing out in a torrent. He barely turned his head to avoid spraying Angela.

"Christ Glen, that's attractive."

He coughed and spat. His mouth was filled with bile and acid. He took another drag on the cigarette and threw it into the mess.

"Got any breath mints?"

"No," Angela said, holding the door open for him so they could go back inside.

"I think I feel better now," he said as he walked by her.

"Gross," she replied, waving her hand to dissipate the smell of his breath. He escorted her to the restroom, then entered the men's room. He pissed then stood at the sink and splashed his face, rinsed out his mouth and spat. The restroom attendant handed him a warm towel.

"Got any breath mints?"

"How about mouthwash, sir?"

"Perfect."

Glen exited the restroom at the same time as Angela. Walter looked at them intently as they came back to the table. Glen held Angela's chair as she maneuvered her belly against the table then seated himself and took a drink of ice water. His pushed his order of prawns and angel hair pasta into the middle of the table. He appeared to be deep in thought, then reached over and speared a prawn. The waiter offered to take his plate, but Glen waved him away.

"I guess I'm hungry after all," he said. "Bring me a Bad Medicine, that's vodka and Alka Selzer, and make it a double."

"Excuse me, sir?"

"You heard me, dissolve a couple of Alka Selzers in a cup of cold water. Add a double shot of vodka, nothing expensive, whatever the house brand is. A cherry on top would be nice. Bad Medicine. When I finish that one, bring me another just like it, okay?"

"Yes sir."

"Also."

"Yes sir?"

"Is smoking allowed in here?"

"Yes, sir, if we close the doors and turn this into a private party. I must warn you sir, there is a surcharge."

Glen addressed the table. "Who's picking up the bill?"

"Corporate business expense," Walter said.

"Great, bring me cigars, good ones, got it?"

"Yes, sir."

"Hey Glen, tell Gerusha about being president," Bennie said.

"President of what?" Gerusha whispered to Bennie.

"Of the United States," he replied.

"It lasted about four or five hours until they figured out that I was actually going to lead. I wrote a couple of executive orders, they are probably out on the web somewhere, I guess. That was all it took, then the beltway bandits took me out of it."

"Excuse me? President of the United States? That's mad," said Gerusha.

"It's a long and twisted story and I'm too tired to go into it. Can't we talk about something else?"

There was an embarrassed silence around the table until Gerusha gathered her courage and asked: "What happened to your fingers."

Angela groaned. "Don't bring that up, he comes up with a different bullshit story every time. I'm sick of it. A nazi got one and a drug kingpin got the other, or was it an accident with a lawnmower or a mishap while changing a tire on your rental car. How about a joke instead?"

"Sure," Glen replied.

"Alright, you know those pictures of the bride and groom in the newspaper? Do you know why many of the brides have this huge grin on their faces?"

"No, why?"

"Because she knows she's performed her last BJ."

This relaxed things around the table as they dug into their food. Glen drank two of his special drinks, then switched to vodka and tonic water. Emma discreetly convinced the waiter to weaken his drinks, but Glen, unaccustomed to the alcohol, got steadily drunker anyway. Gerusha's dress hiked up her thighs. Under the table, Glen's hand found her leg and explored freely up and down its silky length. She was tanned and did not wear nylons, her skin was soft and warm under his palm. She kicked off her high heels and rubbed a foot on his. She ordered a Rockstar energy drink on the rocks and studied her tablemates. These people were legendary, wealthy beyond all her dreams and she was overflowing with joy at being with them tonight, but ambition and envy ate at her. She wanted to be part of the rich and powerful, but she didn't have the skills or intellect. Glen was her ticket, but who and what was he?

Is there any chance I will be expected to pay any part of the dinner bill? No, the company is paying. The entrées were thirty bucks or so, times six people. That's over two hundred dollars with tip. The wine looks expensive, Columbia Winery, but several years old. Twenty bucks a bottle? Fifty? Drinks were probably five bucks apiece, how many? Glen had at least seven and those cigars? What would the Union Place charge for a Dominican cigar? Ten bucks? Twenty? Turning the room into a private dining room incurred a surcharge. Another hundred dollars? Perhaps more? These guys were rich, they could afford it, but with $2,700 take home a month, this dinner could cost two weeks pay when it's all added up. I always have to worry about how much things cost, wouldn't it be heaven to not worry about such things? I see these people walk in and out of the lobby and I fend off unwanted phone calls from charities, stock brokers, timeshare salesmen, and people offering up can't-lose business opportunities and real estate ventures. But who are they? Many people in Seattle would give their left nut (or ovary) for five minutes with these people, yet here I am listening to them talk about money and stem cells and software algorithms. Why can't I relax and enjoy it? Because, tomorrow I may be back at the reception desk or *worse. What if I upset someone and get fired? I could be back at the coffee shop trying to remember how much foam the customer wants on his cappuccino or whether she wants room in the cup for cream and sugar.*

And what's with this Glen Wilson? It's obvious that the people at this table love and respect him, especially Bennie, the genius nigger-kid, no don't even think that word, it might pop out sometime, the genius black kid from Orlando. Truth-be-told, Glen seems like a loser, a clown. That suit? It smells like a thrift shop castoff. And he's old, he's probably impotent, I've never fucked a guy so old. Will he be so drunk that he can't even get an erection? Would it be so embarrassing that he would never want to see me again? Where can I find Levitra at this hour of the night? I know the apartment is clean, but did I remember to change the sheets on my bed?

Get a grip, girl. You're going to blow this opportunity if you get too tense or needy. Desperation does not sell. Confidence. Poise. You're pretty and your grooming is nearly perfect. Will he notice the small crook of my nose and that my bottom teeth are buckled a little? He's an old man, he should be thrilled to have a young girl friend. Am I kidding myself? Am I just a convenient piece of ass to him? Could I ever possibly be his girlfriend? I have to play this smart, I can't make it too easy. Men like a challenge. The thrill of the chase. Get the ring first, there is wisdom in that old saw. Why buy the cow when you can get the milk for free? But these days things are different. Everybody hooks up, it doesn't mean anything. Maybe he's old-fashioned. How old is he? Fifty? Maybe even sixty? He looks scrawny and unwell, he needs sun.

I need to turn off my brain. If necessary, I'll go back to the Starbucks, who cares? The tips were good and a lot of that that was cash I didn't pay income taxes on. I could do it. Martin would take me back if I sweet-talk him. These people are just people. Screw them if they don't like me, I don't need them. I wish I could buy a pair of shoes at Nordstrom's without giving up dinners for a week.

The dishes had been long since cleared away. Emma and Angela nibbled small bites from a community slice of cheesecake. Gerusha tried to distract Bennie from his scribbling by talking to him about SuperSonics basketball, but Bennie unconsciously ignored her. Emma made eye-contact and shrugged.

"Don't take it personally, there's nothing that can be done when he's like this," she whispered.

Glen, looking embarrassed and tipsy, stood on rubbery legs and held out his glass. In response, all the people at their table raised their glasses too.

"I'm obsessed by the knowledge that, 12,500 years ago, this very spot was covered by a sheet of ice one mile thick! And, it wasn't caused by fucking SUVs or Freon from goddam air conditioners." Glen drank from his glass and slammed it down on the table. He swayed on his feet and then collapsed. Emma and Gerusha were quick to try to support him. Gerusha got under him and he regained his feet, though unsteadily.

"I have medical training, I'll take him to my place and make sure he's alright," Gerusha whispered to Emma. After consideration and glancing back to make eye contact with Bennie and Walter, Emma nodded and allowed Glen to be led away. The party was quieter but carried on bravely after they were gone.

Staggering down Union Street near Third Avenue, a man, dressed in many layers of old clothes, emerged from an alley.

"Hey, you guys got a quarter so I can get a cigarette?"

Gerusha steered them around him. He moved until he blocked their way again.

"Hey, I'm talking to you. You got money, gimme some, you can afford it."

Glen stepped up until he was nose-to-nose. Gerusha tried to drag him away, but he pulled his arm out of her grip.

"Tell me friend, do you like it here in Seattle?"

"Yeah, I guess so. It don't get too cold, not like Minnesota where I came in from. The meals are pretty good and the cops don't bother us much. So, you going to give me your wallet and purse, or what?"

While they were talking, Gerusha worked a pepper spray dispenser out of her purse. She brandished it and the bum backed away.

"Hey, you don't have to be like that," he said over his shoulder as he scurried away. "Stuck up bitch," he shouted before disappearing around a corner.

Glen leaned against a brick wall to catch his breath.

"Is there a lot of street trash in Seattle?" he asked.

"More and more every year," Gerusha commented.

He looked her up and down as if he'd never seen her before. The street lighting cast shadows over her face. "Where are we going?"

"You can crash at my place."

Glen looked up and down the street as if seeking a familiar landmark.

"You have any aspirin there?"

"Advil."

Glen thought for a moment. "Okay, that will work," he said. "Let's do it."

Truth is Stranger than Fiction, Item 4

City of Seattle Budget, total revenue, from www.cityofseattle.net
In thousands.

	2002 Actual	2003 Adopted	2003 Revised	2004 Endorsed	2004 Adopted
Revenue Source					
Total Taxes	$542,071	$555,538	$547,890	$571,091	$558,391
Licenses/Permits	$10,213	$12,990	$12,021	$13,062	$11,325
Parking	$10,674	$12,613	$11,745	$13,713	$13,829
Court Fines	$14,178	$19,776	$15,845	$20,083	$16,016
Interest Income	$3,053	$3,592	$1,851	$4,002	$1,899
Entities	$16,674	$7,551	$9,046	$7,820	$8,969
Reimbursements	$41,134	$38,709	$38,580	$39,521	$37,756
All Else	$1,725	$911	$798	$937	$892
Total: Revenue & Other Financing Sources	639,722	$651,678	$637,775	$670,228	$649,076

King County Budget, from www.metrokc.gov

Revenue Source					
Property Taxes	$225,751	$232,027	$232,103	$239,002	$238,965
Debt Service	($13,493)	($14,621)	($13,721)	($13,334)	($13,334)
Sales Tax	$62,261	$61,154	$60,549	$62,062	$62,062
Interest Earnings	$12,518	$9,140	$9,554	$10,416	$10,416
Other Revenues	$199,666	$198,261	$208,605	$195,240	$206,186
Total	$495,593	$494,633	$505,349	$509,021	$512,931

"... and I balanced a 3 billion dollar budget in King County..."
— From a campaign advertisement by Rod MeKenna, running for Attorney General in Washington State, in 2004.

CHAPTER SIX

Gerusha Andersen

The alarm clock, set to a pop music station, slowly increased in volume. Gerusha opened one eye, then the other. She was sorely tempted to press the snooze button, she had set the alarm early enough to get to work a half-hour early to prove an obscure point that made sense the night before. Something about being dedicated to the job even though she was up late and part of the elite dinner group. She got up and peeked at Glen who snored raggedly on her pull-out couch. His hair was mussed and he looked several years older in the harsh morning light. She considered slipping into his bed and giving him a hand job, but decided to stick with her 'hard-to-get' plan. She showered and dressed in more casual than usual clothes, accented with a colorful Polynesian scarf. She slipped out of the apartment and caught a Sound Transit bus. She opened the front door with her keycard and arrived at the reception desk right at 7:30. After checking her quick makeup job in a compact mirror, she saw an instant-message icon flashing urgently on her computer. Paula, Walter's admin, was paging her.

"Don't torture me, what happened last night?"

"Did Walter come in yet?"

"Everyone is here. Bennie is in one of his labs. Walter looks like he's dragging ass a bit, but he's working the phones to the East Coast already. He's already gone through three cups of coffee. Did you have dinner with everyone? I'm dying to hear about it."

"Yes, we had an expensive dinner. I didn't see the bill, but I'm sure it was a thousand dollars or more."

"Did you get any stock tips? Should we short Icos or buy more Loudeye?"

"It wasn't like that. Bennie spent the evening scribbling in a tablet and Glen got drunk."

"Who all was there?"

"It was a small group. Walter and Bennie, of course. Glen, Walter's wife Angela and Bennie's girlfriend Emma. That was it. They talked a lot about two women named Murphy and Elke. If I understood, they are lesbians and helped with the Alaska campaign. I'm sure we'll see them hanging around at some point, I think offices on the sixth floor are reserved for them. Murphy does something for that guy Raz with the band Toxic Shock. Raz is gorgeous, I saw TSS in concert at White River playing with Linkin Park."

"And Glen, tell me, damn you."

"He spent the night at my place."

"You slut! Was he any good, is he big? Was he considerate? Did you have to take him up your ass?"

"It wasn't anything like that. He passed out on the couch."

"Liar."

"It's a fact."

"I don't believe you. What was he like? Is he a drunk?"

"He seems like those sleazy creeps that sell broken down pickups to the Mexicans on Aurora Avenue. But, I think there may be more to the guy than that. This is crazy, but the way they were talking, Glen was the President of the United States for a little while."

"How old is the guy? I remember all the presidents. Between Nixon and Carter, you mean?"

"No, after Allen North and the VP were killed in that weird train accident."

"I don't remember reading anything about a President Wilson in the newspapers. He won the congressional seat in Alaska, but was recalled for something, something about voter fraud, I don't remember the details."

"These people we work for are all a little strange."

"Yes. How about Glen, do you have a date for tonight? Does he have someplace else to stay? Will he stay with you tonight, do you think?"

"I have no idea. I left him a key. We'll see, I guess."

"You are so lucky. This could be your big break."

"Maybe."

"If he wants another girl in bed, I'll come right over. If things don't work out between you, give him my number and tell him I'm real good in the sack, okay? Tell him I'm not clingy. I'll meet him anywhere and do anything. Make sure you say that, anything and anywhere."

"You're a cold-blooded round-heeled bitch."

"Look who's talking, whore. Floozy. Skank."

"Gold digger."

"Slut."

"You already said that."

"Don't forget. I want a shot at him if you fuck this up. I have to run, Walter is pinging me. Lunch?"

"No, I'd better run home and check on things. See ya."

Gerusha turned her attention to the man standing patiently in front of her. The front doors unlocked automatically at 8:00 and he was already waiting. He wore a large gold watch and a navy suit jacket over a turtleneck sweater. His smile was bright and well-practiced.

"Good morning, Miss Gerusha. My name is Don Poste with an 'e' on the end and I'm here to see Mr. Walter Crowley, please." He had a slight southern accent, a medium baritone timbre and a slightly hypnotic cadence. Gerusha felt her nipples perk up slightly. *Interesting,* she thought.

"Do you have an appointment?"

"Yes, my admin talked to his admin yesterday and we're all set."

"What time was your appointment? Mr. Crowley doesn't usually see anyone before 10:00."

"We didn't set a specific time or date, but he is expecting me, you can check upstairs with Paula."

"Have a seat, Mr. Poste, and I'll see if Mr. Crowley is available." Gerusha dialed Paula and whispered into the handset. "I have a Don Poste here for Walter…?"

"That's Poste with an 'e'?"

"That's the guy."

"I think he's sells supercomputers or office supplies or something, I don't remember. He's a creep, get rid of him."

"Will do."

She hung up the phone and called Poste back over.

"Excuse me, Mr. Poste, but Mr. Crowley's admin informs me that he will be in conference all day and will not be able to see you."

"Well then, I'll try back tomorrow, thank you very much."

"Get a confirmed time and date on Mr. Crowley's schedule, otherwise it's a wasted trip down here."

He produced a mega-watt smile. "I understand completely," he said. "See you tomorrow, young lady," he said as he pushed out through the entry doors.

Yes, I'm sure I will, she thought. Gerusha tried to fluff her blouse unobtrusively to dissipate perspiration between her breasts. *Pheromones,* she thought. She'd experienced the same effect from an atomizer Walter showed off one day. As he explained it, it was a new aphrodisiac spray developed by the clever chemists at Pfizer. Tricky bastards, she mumbled under her breath as the next salesman walked confidently up to her desk.

Glen and Mayor Harry Silverberg

Glen slowly achieved consciousness. He lay on a thin and lumpy mattress and collected his thoughts. Awakening in many odd places, he had a mental process; not knowing where he was didn't disorient or upset him so much anymore. He inspected the room, it was lightly furnished with austere blonde Scandinavian-style tables and chairs. His head felt better than he had any right to expect, but his mouth was dry and gummy. He heaved himself up and cursed at the cheerful sunlight that streamed in from outside. He was nude. He didn't remember having sex with anyone which was the sort of thing he usually remembered. He threw back the covers and looked for a sign, but there were no unexplained streaks or stains. His underwear, folded neatly on top of his clothes, lay on a rocking chair. His canvas bag sat beside the chair. Smelling coffee, he scratching his balls and allowed his nose to lead him. Clean dishes were arrayed on a drying rack. He took the most manly-looking cup he could find and poured coffee. From dinner, he had snapshot memories of standing and lecturing his friends, but he had no idea what he'd said to them. Nothing too shameful, he hoped. The girl: Gerusha, he remembered. She seemed nice enough, too damn young, but Glen could forgive that. He thought hard and could not remember any kind of sex and he wondered why. Did he pass out too soon? Did he do something rude to offend her? The way she was dressed and the way she allowed his hand to roam her thighs at the dinner table, he was sure it was a done deal. He put these thoughts aside to puzzle over later. He remembered that he had a job and decided there was no time for a shower, though he did brush his teeth with Gerusha's electric toothbrush. He rummaged through his canvas bag for the hand-written contract he'd drafted on the airplane and exited the apartment with Gerusha's coffee cup.

Out on the street, he asked for directions and set off on foot for the City Hall building. He was sweating profusely by the time he reached the high rise office building. He checked his wallet. He had almost all the fifty dollars left from his timeshare canvassing money, so he stopped at the latté stand in the lobby and bought a drip refill for his coffee cup. He searched the directory and walked to the elevator.

The City of Seattle government had an expansive entry and waiting room. This area was busy with well-dressed men and women carrying briefcases and umbrellas. Glen presented himself at the reception desk and put down his coffee cup, sloshing some. The receptionist, examining him, could not hide her disapproval. He was sweating, had gray stubbly whiskers and his hair was sticking up in spikes. He bore a slight odor of alcohol and vomitus; he looked like one of the chronic drunks that they tried to keep out of the building. A security guard hovered in case of trouble.

"Can I help you, sir?"

"I'm here to see Silverberg."

"You mean the Mayor? Mayor Silverberg?"

"Yeah, that Silverberg. My name is Wilson and he should be expecting me."

All the sudden the receptionist became brisk.

"Yes, he was looking for you yesterday, he's been driving us all crazy. I'm sorry, I was expecting—."

"Expecting what?"

"Um, I'll get him for you right away, sir."

Glen admired a painting on the wall for a few minutes while the receptionist tracked down the Mayor. Silverberg, who had been sitting on the toilet reading the Seattle PI, came out in a rush.

"Wilson, ya fuck, where in the hell have you been? Hanging out with your rich prick friends across town? Let me look at you."

He stood back to take him in. He was not impressed with Glen's state of dishevelment and the limp suit, but the Mayor didn't look much different himself with huge dark circles under his eyes and still wearing yesterday's clothes.

"You look like a walking corpse. Where have you been living, under an overpass? Let's get you inside, we need to talk."

Silverberg led the way into the elevator. When they reached the top floor and walked by the admin, he hissed: "Hold all calls."

In his office, Silverberg continued, "Have you heard about my son? No? It's simple enough, this city killed him and I want you to clean it up." Glen placed his hand-written contract on the Mayor's desk. "What's this?"

"Our contract. If you want me to work, you need to sign this contract."

"Bullshit. We agreed on a price and I transferred the money. Now it's time for you to get to out on the street and get to work."

Glen inspected his fingernails and began chewing on a hangnail. He stared around the room.

"Nice office," he commented.

"How are you going to do it? Hire some thugs? A private security force?"

"My contract says you don't get to ask any questions." Glen said idly.

"I never did like you." The Mayor produced his pen and scrawled his name on the last page of the contract.

"Initial all the pages, " Glen said.

The Mayor glared at him, but complied.

"Okay, now we have a contract, asshole. Do you need help from the police? The beat cops have offered full cooperation. I'll call the Chief and get him over here to coordinate your efforts." He picked up the telephone handset while Glen looked through the pages. He snagged the Mayor's pen and initialed and signed the thing himself. He stood up and slipped the contract and the Mayor's pen into his inside jacket pocket.

"Paragraph 17 says I work this job alone. Paragraph 23 says no meetings. See ya."

"Wait, Wilson, where are you going? We need to gather a team and work on the planning." Glen walked out of the room. The Mayor followed, blustering. "At least I should have a photocopy of that damn contract."

Glen pressed the button for the elevator which opened almost instantly to disgorge passengers.

"Wilson!" the Mayor sputtered.

Glen entered the elevator and turned around. The mayor grabbed a stapler off his admin's desk and hurled it. His aim was poor and it bounced off the wall, narrowly missing a trio of sleek lawyers. As the doors closed, Glen raised his coffee cup in salute and gave a small wry smile.

Gerusha Andersen

Gerusha stood in front of her apartment with her key in hand. She was nervous. Would Glen still be there? Deciding to stop being silly, she slipped in the key and found the door unlocked. She walked in and was instantly assaulted by a burning smell. Glen had left the coffee pot heater on and the coffee had completely boiled away. She turned it off and put the carafe on the stove to cool. She turned and inspected the room. The covers were tossed off the sofa bed and there were bread crumbs and streaks of raspberry jam on the kitchen counter. It looked like Glen had helped himself to her 12-grain bread. She didn't mind, but he could have cleaned up after himself. In the bathroom, he'd left the head screwed on the electric toothbrush and it was still damp. *Gross,* she thought. There were curly gray pubic hairs on the rim of the toilet. She daintily used a swath of toilet paper to clean them up and flush them away. Her eyes were damp and it took a moment for her to figure out why. He wasn't here and she didn't know if he'd be back.

Looking around the living room, she saw no sign of his canvas bag. She'd got it from Paula and brought it home in anticipation of Glen spending the night. She got on her hands and knees and looked under the pullout bed. The canvas bag was stuffed underneath. She felt flooded with relief. He'd be coming back, even if it was only to get his bag. *The game was still in play.* She sat on the bed and sobbed. She hadn't realized she cared so much, but apparently she did. After making up the bed, she went into the kitchen to scrub out the coffee pot. This consumed the rest of her lunch hour so she walked back to the bus stop hungry, but, for the moment, happy.

Glen

Glen walked west down Olive Street toward the waterfront. The sidewalks were busy with professional people walking briskly, doing their part to rotate the big wheel of commerce. The closer he got to the water, the city changed. X-rated theaters were interleaved with seedy bars and exotic dance halls. The pace slowed and people idled in alleys and shuffled along with their worldly belongings stuffed into plastic garbage bags. At the waterfront, Glen watched the ferries arrive and depart. The sun was hot and Glen's shirt plastered to his body. He decided to start his new job by having lunch and a few beers. He walked up First Avenue to the Central Tavern and ordered a pitcher of Rainier and a cheeseburger. A girl sat on the adjoining stool and asked if he had a light. Glen motioned for the bartender to give him a pack of matches.

The bartender, a barrel of a man with tattoos crawling up his arms, shook his head 'no' and said: "There is no smoking allowed in here." Glen shrugged and the girl tucked the cigarette behind her ear. "Is this lady bothering you, sir?"

Glen rotated on his stool and looked her over. She was short, maybe five-foot if she wore high heels, with very bad complexion. Her hair was oily and matted. She wore long sleeves in the hot weather so Glen assumed she was a junky.

"Nah, she's okay. Set her up a glass, will ya?"

The bartender, frowning his disapproval, slowly set out a schooner. Glen poured her beer and topped off his own glass.

"Long life to our friends and death to our enemies," he said.

"To making it through another shitty-ass day," the girl replied before she drained the glass. She looked longingly at the pitcher, but Glen made no move for it.

"What's your name, dear?" he asked.

"Lucy, though my friends call me Half-size and you can too if you fill me up again."

"We'll see about that. I used to live in Seattle but I've been away for a while. How are things around here?"

"Okay, I guess."

"Where are you from?"

"Chicago area. You want to sit around here and talk all day? Buy me another beer."

"Let's suppose you had a job cleaning up this city?"

"Like a garbage man? Picking up trash?"

"Something like that. However, I'm talking about human trash. The bums and dope addicts. If you were supposed to run out the undesirables, how would you do it?"

"Ha! There ain't nothing you can do. Besides, they are people like you. They have *humane* rights."

"They have a right to shit in the parks, sleep in the doorways and harass the tourists?"

"We, I mean they, wouldn't do all that stuff if there were better public facilities. These people need help."

"I don't give a shit about any of that, it's not my problem. I have a job cleaning up the streets, so that's what I'm going to do."

"Look, you want a date, or what? Are you a cop?"

"No, I'm not cop. Can you believe I haven't had a *date* in over three years?"

"No shit? You must be carrying a load. I can help with that problem for a hundred bucks, mister." She bent her head and tried to look coy, but the effect was ruined by a volcanic pimple on her chin that was weeping a tendril of bloody puss.

"A hundred bucks, you must be kidding. I can get an out-call escort for that."

"You must have been gone a long time, they charge at least 300 dollars now. I know some of the girls and I can tell you that even $300 doesn't get you much. I used to do that work before I got sick."

Before you became a junkie, Glen thought. The bartender placed a large plate covered with a cheeseburger and a mound of home-cut fries in front of Glen, who noisily squeezed a large puddle of catsup from a plastic bottle onto the plate.

"You don't have to pay for a room. I can get you off in an alley for thirty bucks, show you a real good time."

"How about twenty," Glen suggested while cutting his burger in half.

She considered this offer while staring pointedly at the pile of French fries. "Okay, twenty for a man who hasn't had a woman for a long time. Can I have some of your fries?"

"Help yourself." She grabbed a handful while Glen filled her glass. "As tempting an offer that is, I think I'll pass. You looking for a job? I could use help."

She drained her glass again in short order. "What's with you, anyway? We made a deal for twenty bucks, so when you're ready we'll go, okay? But for twenty, I'll tell you now, I'm not doing anything weird. You're an old guy, I'm not going to stick my finger up your ass. I know some of you old fogies like that. Twenty gets you off and that's it. No kissing and you don't get to lick my boobs. As far as a job goes, I've never been much good at work."

He dipped a messy hunk in catsup and finished the first half of his burger. "Man, that's a good burger, I haven't had one that good in a long time. Filled me right up." He wiped his mouth on a paper napkin and got off his stool. "Let me ask you something. If I bought you a one-way ticket to San Francisco, what would it cost me to get you on the bus?"

"For two hundred I'd leave town if you paid for the ticket."

"How about a hundred bucks? They are real good to the street people down there in Frisco."

She thought about it. "Okay, for a hundred, I'd go."

Glen laughed. He waved twenty dollars at the bartender, who walked over. "Let the lady finish her lunch before you throw her out?"

"Sure, Mister, whatever you say."

Glen handed him the twenty. "Keep the change. That was a great burger, my compliments to the chef."

"Sure, whatever," the bartender said.

Half-size Lucy stuffed food in her face.

"Hey, what about our deal? What about the job?" she asked through a mouthful of food.

"I'll see you out on the street, Lucy, and we'll talk," Glen said as he pushed through the door and walked outside.

Fortified by beer and beef, Glen drifted along First Avenue. He idly glanced at the window displays at the bookstore, antique and art shops. Occasionally, transients would hit him up for spare change, but Glen ignored them. It occurred to him that it would be nice to have some idea of how many bums were on the street. He arrived at the Seahawks Stadium and noticed that the team shop was open. He browsed the goods and saw a box of hideous green wristbands. He took the box to the checkstand.

"Don't look like you've sold too many of these," he commented.

The clerk looked up from his unfurled copy of the Seattle Weekly. "They been out for a month or two. I've never sold any on my shift. Things will get busier when the season starts."

"Is there more stock in back?"

"Yes, there is another case."

"Go get it, I'll take them all."

"All? Okay. I don't care, buy one or all of them, I'm not on commission, so I don't give a flying funk. You gotta pay the $3.95, there ain't no discount here."

"Fine," Glen said, brandishing his debit card. "But I want you to count them. And sell me a duffel to carry them in, if you please."

"Can I ask what you're going to use these for?" the clerk asked as they counted the wristbands.

"Nope," Glen replied. The count came to 497, plus 500 in the un-opened case. Glen looked at his receipt. "338.81 for sales tax?"

"Yeah, the Teacher's Union pushed through a referendum, they just added a half a point for schools. A lot of people are mad about that. It don't seem like much until you notice how it adds up."

They packed the wristbands into the duffel bag and Glen walked back onto the street. He needed cash, so he walked to the Bank of America. Because of his ragged appearance and the duffel bag, the security guards watched him closely, but they did not detain him. *Good thing I don't look like an Arab,* he thought. He presented the card at the counter and asked for twenty thousand dollars in cash with half in five-dollar bills. The teller called her supervisor and they talked for a few minutes. They asked for identification, but Glen argued that having the PIN was enough for them to complete the transaction. They called the branch in Sarasota and finally agreed, then it took another 15 minutes to gather up enough five-dollar bills. At some point, it was determined that Glen was a VIP so they seated him in an office and brought him a cold Vanilla Coke. By the time the banking was done and money was stuffed in his pockets and the duffel, Glen was exhausted. *This fucking social work is hard,* he thought.

He walked to Occidental Park and found a bench for home base. He motioned to a group of blacks that were sitting nearby.

"Yo, motherfucker, what you want w'us?"

The speaker was missing a few teeth, so his speech was nearly unintelligible.

"Here's the deal, guys. I'm with the Seahawks and we're doing some promotion. I'll pay you five bucks if you'll wear a wristband." He pulled out some of the bands and showed them off.

"Those motherfuckers are ugly."

"I don't give a shit, for five bucks, I'll wear your momma's underwear on my head, man. Gimme one."

Glen pulled the band back and said, "That's one per customer and I have a good memory for faces, got it?"

"Yeah man, gimme one."

"Spread the word, guys. I'll be here everyday."

Glen busily handed out money and wristbands all afternoon. Yelling, he turned away a few people for trying to double-dip. He noted bums streaming from a Vietnamese grocery store carrying bottles of malt liquor in paper bags. A couple of cops, wearing silly-looking aerodynamic helmets, rode up on bicycles.

"Excuse me sir, can I ask what you think you're doing?"

"Yes officers, I'm doing unofficial promotion for the Seahawks, I'm paying five dollars to the transients willing to wear our wristbands."

The officers conferred between themselves.

"This is going to cause a lot of problems, it's bad enough when these guys get their checks at the end of the month and we have extra cops on the street to handle it. We'd rather you didn't do this now."

"Respectfully, sir, I'd like to continue my job."

The cops called in on the radio.

"Do you have a permit for this activity?"

"I don't need a permit to hand out free promotional material."

"You're creating a public disturbance."

"No, I am not."

"Cripes, he's right. We'd better call in for overtime, this is going to be ugly. Some of these bums won't make it through the night. Just know, we'll be keeping an eye on you, sir."

"I certainly hope so," Glen replied.

Half-size Lucy wandered by. Glen called her over and recruited her to help with distribution. She was good with the bums, cursing them when they tried to get more than one wristband (most of the double-dippers were falling down drunk, so they were easy to identify) and urged them to find more scattered transients camping under the Alaska

Way Viaduct, in Battery Park and in the campsites hidden in the woods by I-5. Some bums came from as far away as the Broadway area. When the trickle dwindled Glen gathered his bag. He handed Lucy $25.

"Come back tomorrow, I'll have more work for you," Glen told her.

"Ain't got anything better to do," she replied after counting the money and stuffing it in her greasy jeans.

Bone-tired, Glen walked north on First Avenue. A couple of ragged characters, sitting on the sidewalk with donation cans and cardboard signs, asked if he was the wristband guy. Even the blind man sitting by the old Bon Marche' store knew him.

"Hey man, a blind guy can wear a wristband," he called out.

"That's the truth, brother," Glen said. "Here you go."

It was almost 7:00 when Glen arrived at Gerusha's apartment. He opened the door with the key she'd left out for him and startled her while she was watching TV. The apartment smelled like brownies, she'd done baking to take her mind off her anticipation and loneliness. She was dressed comfortably in jeans and a t-shirt.

Glen dropped the duffel at her feet. "Hey, Gerusha," he said.

"Hey yourself," she replied while putting the TV on mute with the remote.

"Help me count these things," he said.

He unzipped the bag and dumped out the remaining wristbands and cash. She looked at the stuff with curiosity, but dived in and counted.

"If you started with 997, then you sold 226 of them."

"I didn't sell them, I gave them away to bums."

"Why?"

"Because I want to get an idea how many bums are out there."

"Why?"

"You're like a five-year-old. Why-why-why. Why don't you get me a beer, there's a why for you."

Barefoot, Gerusha padded to the kitchen.

"Want that in a glass?" she asked over her shoulder.

"Sure," Glen replied, leaning back on the couch and resting his eyes.

"Want dinner? I can heat up spaghetti real quick and toss up a salad."

"Can we order Chinese or something?"

"There's a Thai place down the block that will deliver."

"Good."

"What do you want?"

"I don't care. Some Phad Thai, not too spicy. Maybe some Swimming Rama too."

"Okay."

After making the phone call, Gerusha brought Glen's beer.

"How was your day?"

"Is that what we're going to do? Talk about our days? My day was alright, it started with a meeting with the Mayor, I had lunch with a Skid Row whore, argued with the bank until they coughed up my own damn money, then spent the rest of the day handing out wristbands to lost souls in Occidental Park. That was my day. Now I guess I'm supposed to ask about yours?"

"You don't have to be a dick about it. My day was alright, I fended off salespeople, cleaned up the mess you made in my kitchen, tossed you a salad and made up brownie mix, all the time wondering if and when you were coming back."

"Now that we have that out of the way, we can relax and watch the boob tube." He grabbed the remote and started flipping through the channels. "Don't you have cable?"

When the Thai food arrived, Gerusha tried to serve it on a plate, but Glen grabbed a take-out box and a fork and shoveled noodles into his mouth. Gerusha offered him chopsticks, but he waved them away. He'd settled on a TV show about WW2 submarines, and try as she might, Gerusha could not understand the fascination. He drank three of her beers in quick succession, then belched his approval. When the submarine show was over, Glen yawned, clicked the TV off and threw off his clothes. His chest, covered with gray hair, was slightly concave. He looked like a Siberian concentration camp intern. His grayish skin hung in folds as if he had been much heavier in the past.

"Where do you put the dirty laundry?"

Gerusha waved at the bathroom. "Throw it in there and I'll take it down to the laundry room." After he launched the dirty clothes in the general direction of the bathroom, he flopped back on the couch. Gerusha was not exactly shocked, but she thought his behavior was odd. *Was he mentally ill?* She examined him with sidelong glances. His cock seemed smallish, but she didn't know, maybe it was in the normal range. *Does he expect me to cast off my clothes too?* He leaned over and rubbed his feet. His hairy legs were scrawny and his knees were lumpy and knobby.

"I gotta get a motorbike or something, I'm too old to be walking all over town all day. Do you have a bicycle?"

"It's in the storage room downstairs, the front door key opens it. Hey, Paul Allen was in the office today. He and Walter had lunch catered for a meeting."

"Hmmph," Glen grunted.

"Paul has a 757 jet and a yacht over 100 feet long that used to belong to Craig McCaw. They say that the Immortality IPO will be the biggest since Google and will create more instant millionaires than Microsoft. All the engineers and marketing people got stock options. I was hired through a contract agency, so I don't get anything."

Glen was casually scratching his pubic hair. "You going to serve up those brownies? I'll bet they'd be good with skim milk, got any? Whole milk upsets my delicate stomach."

"I'm not asking for much. If I could talk privately with Walter or Bennie, I'm sure they'd offer me a better job if you put in a good word for me."

"Look, I remember talking to Bennie a few years ago. He asked me how to make money and I told him that there is a huge economic wheel turning, just figure out a way to push in the right direction and the money will flow your way. However, all this talk about money is dull. What matters is what you do with your money and power. I don't give a damn about Paul Allen's yacht. You don't need me to get you an audience with Walter. Find out something he needs or come up with an idea that excites his warped mind. He'll see you."

"That's what I need help with. I need good ideas."

"My mind comes up with good stuff after sex. I do my best thinking in the afterglow of athletic fucking with beautiful young ladies."

"You're a filthy-minded old fart. When things were quiet in the lobby, I would look at your statue and imagine what kind of great man you must be for our founders to idolize you so. I would imagine the grand thoughts you would think and the immense ideas you would conceive."

Glen got up and walked to the kitchen. Gerusha tried, unsuccessfully, to ignore the couch seams imprinted on his flabby ass cheeks. He found a spoon and took the pan of brownies from the oven. He walked back, then stood in front of her while spooning brownies into his mouth. She turned her head so she wouldn't have to look directly at his flaccid penis.

"Why do you think I invited you to join us for dinner last night?"

"Because you haven't been laid in three years and you thought I'd be an easy fuck."

"Yes, there was that part. But there was something else. Think of what that might have been and we'll have a real conversation." He dropped the brownie pan on the carpet and the spoon bounced a few feet. "Right now, let's get you out of those clothes and taking care of my needs, I've been saving myself for you for three long years. It's time to make sure the plumbing still works and get my pipes flushed, if you follow my meaning."

She pushed him away and stood up. "I'll fuck you when the world stops spinning, when the stars fall from the skies, when the seas boil dry after the flames of hell engulf us all. Until then, goodnight, Mister Wilson." With that, she stomped into her bedroom and slammed the door.

Glen thought for a moment. The 'flames of hell' comment stirred something in his mind. He remembered a left-over cigar in his jacket pocket. He lighted it on a stove burner and walked out on her small balcony, smoking and watching the Belltown traffic stream by.

Truth is Stranger than Fiction, Item 5

Medical prescription of heroin to treatment resistant heroin addicts: two randomised controlled trials

Wim van den Brink, *professor*, Vincent M Hendriks, *senior researcher*, Peter Blanken, *researcher*, Maarten W J Koeter, *assistant professor*, Barbara J van Zwieten, *delegate to CPMP*, Jan M van Ree, *professor*

Article Accepted May 23, 2003 by British Medical Journal (BMJ, www.bmj.com)

Abstract

Objective To determine whether supervised medical prescription of heroin can successfully treat addicts who do not sufficiently benefit from methadone maintenance treatment.

Design Two open label randomised controlled trials.

Setting Methadone maintenance programmes in six cities in the Netherlands.

Participants 549 heroin addicts.

Interventions Inhalable heroin (n = 375) or injectable heroin (n = 174) prescribed over 12 months. Heroin (maximum 1000 mg per day) plus methadone (maximum 150 mg per day) compared with methadone alone (maximum 150 mg per day). Psychosocial treatment was offered throughout.

Main outcome measures Dichotomous, multidomain response index, including validated indicators of physical health, mental status, and social functioning.

Results Adherence was excellent with 12 month outcome data available for 94% of the randomised participants. With intention to treat analysis, 12 month treatment with heroin plus methadone was significantly more effective than treatment with methadone alone in the trial of inhalable heroin (response rate 49.7% *v* 26.9%; difference 22.8%, 95% confidence interval 11.0% to 34.6%) and in the trial of injectable heroin (55.5% *v* 31.2%; difference 24.3%, 9.6% to 39.0%). Discontinuation of the coprescribed heroin resulted in a rapid deterioration in 82% (94/115) of those who responded to the coprescribed heroin. The incidence of serious adverse events was similar across treatment conditions.

Conclusions Supervised coprescription of heroin is feasible, more effective, and probably as safe as methadone alone in reducing the many physical, mental, and social problems of treatment resistant heroin addicts.

CHAPTER SEVEN

Gerusha Andersen

Hours passed before Gerusha fell asleep, then the alarm clock went off five minutes later. In spite of the noise she made in the kitchen, Glen slept solidly. This irritated Gerusha all the more. She slammed the door when she left to catch her bus to work. She was a little late getting to her desk, the first time since she landed this job. What she lacked in schooling and talent, she tried to make with promptness and she hoped someone would notice her discipline. Sitting at her desk, while she tried to rescue her hasty makeup job, it occurred to her that the plan to use Glen for access to the Immortality insiders was perhaps backward. Walter came in and walked quickly to the elevator.

On impulse, she called out, "Mr. Crowley, is this a good time to speak to you for a moment?" Walter glanced at his watch and a brief expression of exasperation crossed his face, but he quickly hid it with a pleasant smile.

"Sure, Gerusha." He leaned over the reception desk. "What is it?"

She gestured toward the bust in the corner. "Glen," she said flatly. "It seems like the inspirational idea of Glen is one thing, but the reality of him is something quite different. To be frank, Mr. Crowley," she whispered and Walter leaned close to catch her words, "I find him quite crude."

Walter burst out with a volley of laughter. He couldn't catch his breath; tears streamed down his face. "I'm sorry, Gerusha, I shouldn't laugh," he said as he stood straight and tried to regain his composure. At this instant, the front door lock clicked and three salespeople hovering outside pushed through. Walter looked over his shoulder with concern. "Oh, I have to run," he managed to say, still laughing. He pressed the elevator button and entered. He pressed his hand to his belly. "Don't worry, dear, I will assist you," he called out as the doors slid closed. "We'll do lunch."

She took a deep breath and smiled professionally at the first salesman.

"Can I help you?"

"I'm here to see Mr. Benjamin Jackson."

"Do you have an appointment, sir?" Gerusha asked.

Glen

After foraging a breakfast of stale brownies and beer, Glen felt ready to face the day. He found the storage room and rolled out Gerusha's shiny 21-speed mountain bike. He examined the goofy-looking aerodynamic helmet, then tossed it aside. After throwing his duffel over his shoulder, he rolled up Eighth to the Greyhound bus station and waited impatiently in the ticket line.

"How much is a one-way ticket to San Francisco?" he asked.

"186 dollars, sir."

"Can I buy a block of passes?"

"No sir, you have to buy tickets for specific busses. You can buy gift certificates."

"But those are refundable, right? They can be cashed back in?" The clerk nodded 'yes'. "Crap. Okay, give me 10 tickets for each bus starting tomorrow, for five days. Wait a minute. Can I charter a bus?"

"Yes, it's expensive, but we offer that service."

"Great, I want a bus standing by and ready to roll to San Francisco every day for the next week."

The clerk examined Glen. "How will you be paying, sir?"

"Debit card."

"Very well, sir."

After completing the transaction, Glen stuffed the paperwork into his duffel. Outside, he was accosted by a Hispanic man who Glen guessed was from Honduras or Nicaragua. He waved a plastic card and slips of blue paper.

"Okay, what do you have?" Glen asked.

"Food stamp card with $25 credit and grocery slips."

Glen opened one of the grocery slips, it was marked as one-dollar, on the back it said it could be exchanged for food only. Glen looked at the man questioningly.

"People have been handing them out instead of spare change because they think it will keep us from drinking and smoking," the man said, laughing.

"I hate those naïve do-gooders," Glen commented while handing the slip back.

"Me too," the man replied. "It's ten bucks for the card and fifty cents for as many of the food slips as you want."

"Nah, I'll pass. However, I will give *you* five bucks if you you'll wear my Seahawks wristband."

The man brightened. "You're the bandman, sure gimme one of those."

After handing out a dozen more wristbands to the men and women that gathered, Glen announced that he would be doing more business in Occidental Park, then mounted his bike and rolled toward Pioneer Square. As he traveled, he noted that most, but not all, of the transients wore the wristbands. He staked out a bench and found a few fresh street people to do wristband business with. There were about 15 of the prior day's customers hanging around to see what Glen was offering. Half-size Lisa came over and Glen put her to work with the wristbands. He stood on a bench and addressed the crowd.

"Ladies and gentlemen. I have chartered a bus to San Francisco, meet me at the bus station at eight AM tomorrow and I'll pay $200 in cash to each person who gets on the bus and leaves town. They have great programs for street people down there, they even pay you a few hundred bucks in cash."

"We'll get thirsty, that's a long ride."

"Okay, I'll throw in a quart of beer. This offer goes all week, meet me at the bus station and you can get on your way out of here. Things are going to get ugly on the streets, I hope you'll take me up on this opportunity."

"What do you mean, ugly?"

"Bad karma."

Glen left Half-size Lisa in charge. "Line people up, I'll be back early in the afternoon. And no godammed double-dippers!" he told her.

He pushed the bike uphill toward the Harbor View hospital. After stashing the bike in a clump of bushes, he studied the hospital layout. He walked to the south side, arriving in time to watch a hearse pull smoothly away from a loading dock. Walking to an informal smoking area, he joined clumps of people puffing cigarettes and chatting around picnic tables. A tubby young man, dressed in stained hospital greens, sat in the shade reading a Bukowski novel and nursing his cigarette. His nametag said Bill. Glen sat down.

"Hollywood, eh? Post Office was my favorite. No matter how fucked up my life gets, Bukowski makes me feel better because his characters fuck things up more and have things worse."

"Word."

"Well, Bill, I'm curious, how was business last night? How many bums checked in and didn't check out, if you follow me."

"We had a couple."

Glen pulled out a wristband. "Were any of them wearing one of these wristbands?"

Bill put his book down. "Yeah, one was, why do you ask?"

"It doesn't really matter, I'm just curious." He pulled a spiral-bound notebook from his pocket and made notes. "When you say a couple, do you mean a pair or three?"

Bill sucked his cigarette down to the last fraction and stubbed it out. "Three," he said. "Are you a reporter?"

"No, I'm a social worker on contract with the city." Glen looked around like he was going to share a big secret. "I work for the Mayor," he whispered.

"The Mayor is a mess right now, they're burying his son today, that's a fucking bummer. Well, back to the grind."

"See ya," Glen said.

Glen retrieved the bike and coasted down the long hill back into Seattle. He checked on Lucy, she'd gathered a half-dozen bums and Glen issued them wristbands. Lucy was cheerful and moving slowly. Clearly, she'd shot up recently.

"I need to meet your pusher," he said.

"Oh honey, I'm not using."

"Right. Keep lining them up. Tell your dealer I have a deal for him."

Glen walked into the Vietnamese grocery store.

"How's business?" he asked.

The clerk was a tiny brown man with imperfectly-cropped white whiskers. He wore a yellow jumpsuit. Glen met men like this before, often they were Viet Cong officers who bribed their way onto a US helicopter in Saigon. Communists or American collaborators, depending on which way the political or financial winds were blowing.

"Somewhere between bad and shitty," the old man replied. Glen picked a bottle of Heineken from a groaning and clanking cooler.

"Can I eat one of these sandwiches without getting E. coli or food poisoning?"

"The turkey ones are fresh from this morning."

"Sure they are. Give me one and I need one of those prepaid cell phones."

He pulled money out of the duffel bag.

"You're the band-man."

"That's me. You hear things in here, do you?"

The old man shrugged. "Not much else to do."

Back on the street, Glen, chewed on his sandwich and drank beer from a paper bag. He decided to do an experiment. He rolled his bike through the park and handed out $200 to each conscious bum he saw wearing a wristband. The count was eight. He jumped on the bike and peddled quickly along Third Avenue. The money was already causing a ruckus behind him, but the bums couldn't move fast enough to catch him. He found an isolated spot near the ferry terminal and pulled the cell phone out of its packaging. After some cussing and angry moments, he managed to get the phone activated. With operator assistance, he connected to Immortality, LLC.

"I need to speak with Bennie," he said.

"Who might I say is calling?" Gerusha asked professionally.

"Goddam it, Gerusha, it's me. Make the connection, will you?"

"Oh hi, Glen. What are you doing?"

"I'm trying to fix Seattle, but you're wasting my time by gabbing. Let me speak to Bennie."

"I don't know, Glen. I'm under strict instructions not to bother him."

"If you don't connect me now, I'm going to come over, reach down your throat, rip out your spine, and beat innocent puppies to death with it."

"Alright, you don't have to be so melodramatic. Will I see you tonight?"

"Arghh," Glen roared.

Gerusha winced and pushed buttons on her computer to route the call to Bennie's extension. Bennie's admin forwarded the call to the proper lab.

"This is Bennie, how can I help you?"

"Hi Bennie, this Glen. I need Ethanol, quite a bit. How about fifty gallons?"

"Ethyl Alcohol, I think that comes in four-liter plastic bottles. We can get some in from Baxter. What do you want it for?"

"Mixed drinks."

"Ha, you're funny. Okay, I will get this on order, it will take a day or two. Where do you want it delivered?"

"Hold it at the receiving dock, I'll come get it."

"Anything else?"

Yes, I can use Diacetylmorphineis, I don't know how it comes, I could use a kilogram or so."

"Hey, that's heroin. We can't get that, there's no medical or industrial use."

"Shit. How about Roxinal?"

"Morphine? Yes, we can get that from Pharma. This must be some party you're planning."

"Right, get me a kilogram," Glen said before ending the call.

Peter Harris

Peter, taking a break, filled a bowl with tomato soup and joined a group of men loitering around one of the Homeless Solutions picnic tables. He nodded to Red, Dusty and Tiger. The day was perfect, the sun streamed through leaves of the adjoining green belt. He noticed broken syringes and hypodermic needles strewn along the brick wall and felt a wave of black depression. He nodded at a Seattle cop riding by on a bicycle, then crushed soda crackers and sprinkled them on his soup. The men wore multiple layers of smelly clothing, but a slight breeze from Elliot Bay made the odor tolerable. All three were wore green wristbands.

"Hey Red, what's with the Seahawks advertising?" he asked.

"A crazy dude is handing them out in Pioneer Square. He's paying 5 bucks."

"Some fool is paying five dollars to take a wristband? Point him out, I could use the scratch too. What is this loon up to?"

"We don't know, but all the street is talking about him. He's offering two hundred dollars if we get on a bus to Frisco."

Peter laughed. "I hope you guys hang around or I'll be out of business."

"I'm going," Dusty said. He was tearing strips of newspaper and lining the inside of his shoes. "For two hundred bucks, I'd get on a bus to hell-and-gone. I can always hitch a ride back."

"You can't hitch back from hell," Tiger commented.

"You know what I meant, piss-meat. They got better AIDS clinics down there. In San Francisco, you can get all kinds of help if you got AIDS."

"You positive? How'd you get it? Needle or ass?"

"I ain't no fag, shit-breath. You can get AIDS from a bad transfusion."

"No you can't, not no more. They test the blood for it."

"You're a hater."

"Guys," Peter said soothingly, "I don't want bum-fighting around here."

"Don't call us bums, we're homeless persons of color."

"Hey, I'm not homeless, I'm a poet," Red said. "All poets is poor."

"You're no poet."

"Listen. I used to teach English in a high school. Check this out.

My backpack is my pillow
In the futility of utility
When I sleep in the ER
The nurse is cool
As long as I don't cuss her."

"That don't rhyme," Tiger complained.

"Sure it does, sort of." Red said, offended. "Besides, poems don't need to rhyme anymore."

Peter slurped up the last of his soup and stood. "I'd like to meet the band-man, tell him to stop by if you see him, okay?"

"He's a crazy motherfucker, I don't like the look of him," Red said, carefully shredding cigarette butts and rolling up a home-made. "Mad Maxwell had that same look in his eye before he waved that sword and the cops killed him."

"It wasn't a sword, it was a machete. Those cops violated his syllable rights."

"Civil rights, ya moron, and I don't give a shit what it was, if a nigger waves a big fucking knife around the cops will blow him away and no one will give a shit. Anyway, you're all mixed up, you're thinking of Herb Roland, he was the one with a samurai sword the Seattle cops offed."

"Why are we talking about cranked-out niggers with swords? The band-man, as long as he's passing out green, he's alright with me," Tiger replied. "Gimme one of those ciggies, will ya?"

"Fuck off, it took me all day to gather these butts."

"In San Francisco, they pay enough that you can afford both likker and ciggies," Tiger lamented dreamily, "and the ho's are prettier."

Glen

It was a long ride up James Street. Glen was out of shape, so, panting, he had to push the bike most of the way up until he could turn north onto the relative flatness of Broadway Avenue. He enjoyed the gays, goths and anarchists that decorated the First/Capital Hill neighborhoods. Glen rode in circles almost 20 minutes before he found the Lakeview Cemetery. By the time he arrived at the Mayor's son's funeral site, he was sweaty and grumpy. A substantial crowd had gathered and Glen felt bad for nearly a microsecond for his sloppy attire; the atmosphere was very formal with dark-suited men and black-veiled women standing around. A camera crew filmed a talking head. Glen was late, but it looked like the service had not started yet.

"What's going on?" Glen whispered to a worker standing by a backhoe smoking a cigarette.

"The fucking Mayor won't come out of his car."

"For shit's sake," Glen muttered. "I don't have time for this. Which limo is it?"

The worker gestured. Glen propped his bike against a pine tree and walked over. A group of police officers chatted near their parked motorbikes. They gave Glen a hard look, but did not move to stop him. A security officer, wearing a dark suit and headset intercepted him.

"Excuse me, sir, but this is a restricted area."

"I'm a friend of Harry's, he'll see me."

"They have asked not to be disturbed."

"Get out of my way and let me talk to him, I'll get him to come out of there."

The officer looked around for guidance, but no help came from the uncomfortable-looking bystanders.

"Are you sure you're the Mayor's friend? I remember your visit at City Hall."

Glen shrugged. The officer did not stop him as he slipped around and opened the limousine door. The interior was dark. Mayor Harry Silverberg and his wife, Evelyn, leaned against opposite sides. Both hid teary eyes behind dark glasses. Glen studied them, then gently removed Evelyn's. Her make-up was smeared and she looked barely conscious.

"What have you guys been taking?"

Harry slowly raised a glass. "Fuck you," he said quietly.

Glen opened Evelyn's purse and pulled out pill bottles and looked at the labels. Xanax, Halcion, Restoril and others. Glen put his finger on the rim of Harry's glass and pulled it out of his hand. It spilled on his suit and Harry instinctively reached for the bottle of Jim Beam to refill it.

"This could be fun," Glen commented slyly. "Do you mind if I fuck your wife while she kills herself? You're both walking corpses, so what difference does it make?" He scooted on the car seat and began opening the buttons of Evelyn's blouse. "Looks like she has nice big tits, I like that."

With shaking hands, Harry filled his glass. "What are you doing?"

"I'm going to fuck your wife. I haven't been laid for a good while, this could be fun. She's kept herself in pretty good shape, I'll bet she's a good lay."

"Get your hands off her," Harry sputtered.

"What the fuck are you going to do about it! Do you know how dangerous it is to mix alcohol with these goddam sedatives? I might as well have my pleasure, but do you mind if I wake her up a bit first." Glen lifted Evelyn's chin and slapped her lightly on the cheek. "Pay attention sweetie, we're going to party it up here in the limo."

Harry dropped the glass on the floor. "I said take your hands off her."

Glen worked Evelyn's breasts free of her silk bra and squeezed.

"Look at these nice titties. I'll bet they taste great."

Harry took a swing a Glen, but he was slow and Glen evaded it easily. He grabbed the Mayor by the lapels. "That's right, get angry now, you useless fuck."

"You goddam bastard. Leave my wife alone."

"That's the spirit. Feed the fury, you son-of-a-bitch."

"I'll kill you."

"Now we're talking about something worth living for, aren't we? But you couldn't kill a mouse in your condition. Get goddam good and mad, then get your wife together and get out there and bury your son."

Breathing heavily, the Mayor stared at Glen with immense hatred.

"If you leave, we'll come out."

"And get your son in the ground?"

Harry deflated. "Yes."

Evelyn, with clumsy fingers, tried to button her blouse. Harry leaned over to help her.

"Okay, I'll give you a few minutes. If you don't come out, I'll come back and finish the job."

"Just go." Harry said.

Glen slid over and put his hand on the door handle. "Get her into treatment, okay? This is no good way to be."

"Get out."

"Okay," Glen said brightly. "See ya later."

He got out of the car and stood blinking in the blinding sunlight. The security man stood nearby.

"What's going on? I heard shouting."

"Nothing, they'll be out in a minute." Glen picked a dandelion blossom and worked his way through the crowd around the grave. He laid the yellow flower on the casket and walked back toward his bike. He felt drained. Under the tree, he stopped and watched the Mayor and his wife come out of the car.

"Pretty fucked up thing to lose a child, ain't it?" The worker commented.

"You got that right," Glen replied.

He pushed the bike until he was off the grounds, then climbed on and pedaled away.

Gerusha Andersen

Walter escorted Gerusha to a reserved table near the front windows of Julia's in Wallingford. The restaurant was crowded. Gerusha had never been in before though it was quite nearby work. The staff knew and liked Walter, ice water was served quickly and menus were pressed into their hands. Hummus was placed on the table and Walter immediately started dipping pita bread in it.

"I talked to your boss, you've been doing a good job in the lobby. I can't remember where I found you, was it at Burger King?"

"Don't play, you know perfectly well we met at Starbucks. Triple espresso with a shot of licorice."

"Of course dear, you're right, I should not play dumb with such a bright young lady."

The waitress intruded and Gerusha ordered Gorgonzola walnut ravioli and Walter ordered a turkey-sausage-biscuit platter.

"Have you seen Glen recently?" Walter continued.

"He's been staying at my place."

"Well now, that must be interesting. Has he told you what he's up to?"

"Can I confide in you?"

"Certainly, my dear," Walter said, covering her hand with his. Gerusha noticed how smooth his palms were. It appeared as if he shaved the backs of his hands. His nails were trimmed into perfect crescents, buffed and shiny. His hands looked like a surgeon's. Precision tools immaculately maintained. For an instant she visualized them traveling over her naked body. He seemed like the kind of man who took his time and could please a woman properly. She felt something twitch in her womb and she hoped Walter could not read her mind.

"I hope you won't be offended, but I must tell the truth. Glen seems like a dumb pig. From all the stories and gossip, I expected superman but I have the King of Slobs living with me."

"Are you saying he's inconsiderate in bed? He's not addressing your needs? He's probably out of practice, perhaps more time will help. Have you communicated your preferences and desires?"

"There hasn't been any sex."

Walter looked surprised. He leaned back in his chair and considered this information.

"Well now, that puts a twist on things. I wonder what they might have done to him the last few years," Walter mused. "I'm sorry dear, I assumed Glen would be on you like a starving jackal if you'll excuse my crude imagery. Making up for lost time, so to speak. What has he said about our little business venture?"

"Nothing. He's doing a job for the Mayor, but he won't talk about it. What is it about this guy? His bust decorates the lobby, for cripe's sake. There must be something I'm missing."

"We talk about this a lot. Bennie thinks in terms of physics, so he will use different similes. I'm more of a chemist, so I will use the word catalyst. Is that a word you're comfortable with?"

After an instant's hesitation, Gerusha decided not to bluff. She shook her head. "Only vaguely."

"You'll simply have to crack a book or two if you want to get anywhere in life, my dear. Your beautiful face and trim figure will only take you so far. Anyway, catalyst is something used in small amounts to initiate a reaction without being consumed in the process. A trigger, so to speak. The catalyst might be a very innocuous substance on its own, but it can wield great power when mixed with the right reactants. Do you follow my allusion?"

"I think so. You're saying that a catalyst might appear useless or ineffectual, but may hold great power."

"My dear, you have a few fully-functional brains cells in that pretty head of yours, too bad they appear underutilized to date. So, we agree that our Mr. Wilson may be tuned into events and potentialities that are not readily apparent. So, what shall we do with this hypotheses?"

"Well, Mr. Crowley, I want to join the inner circle. I'd like a better job inside the company, a job that includes stock options."

"I see. And in return?"

"I will keep tabs on Glen and report everything. I'll be your spy, if you will."

Walter laughed. "I'm sorry, dear, I shouldn't make light of your ambitions. How can I educate you? How about a check for 1 billion dollars, right now, made out to cash. Would you like that?"

A rosy flush appeared on Gerusha's cheeks. "You would do that for me?"

"You misunderstand me, young lady. Okay, I'll do it, just to emphasize my point."

Walter pulled his checkbook from his jacket pocket and filled out a check with a ballpoint pen. "What's your last name, young lady?"

Gerusha could hardly speak. "Andersen with an 'e'", she said.

"Very well," he said as he double-checked the digits. He waved the check at her. "What would you do for me in exchange for this?"

"Anything."

"You'd sleep with me and let me perform unspeakable acts of perversion and depravity? You'd poke out an eye with one of these inexpensive Chinese forks? You'd allow me to surgically remove your ovaries or amputate a limb? You'd swallow a gallon of slugs or swim in sewage? You'd kill some random innocent?"

Gerusha swallowed and thought it over. "Yes, anything."

Walter chuckled. "Very well, it's yours." Gerusha held the check and counted the zeroes for herself. "Now, let me tell you something. Beyond a certain novelty related to my signature which might win you a few dollars on Ebay, that check is worthless. You traded an unspeakable act of my choice for nothing. I don't have anywhere near that amount of money in my bank account, almost all my wealth is on paper. I may at some future date be able to make good on a check of that magnitude, but I will certainly be using a different bank account at that time. So, what enlightenment have you derived from this amusing thought experiment?"

"You are a manipulative bastard with a sick sense of humor?"

"Yes, that goes without saying. All successful people share certain traits of questionable honesty and exploitive manipulation. With regard to your situation, it is my inclination to not grant your request for a better job. Let's look at things, you are a moderately bright and ambitious young woman with a job at a hot up-and-coming biotech company. You are assailed all day long by the best and brightest salespeople walking through the front door. You can enjoy a private lunch with the internationally famous Doctor Zalooq. You have an oddball supposed-catalytic loser named Glen Wilson living with you. You have everything you need to improve your situation on your own. To paraphrase the Holy Bible, give a man ten dollars worth of charity and he can feed himself for the day, but give him a knife, the smarts, and the will, and he can rule the world. That little speech was a bit clumsy, but I'm sure you follow the concept."

Gerusha folded the check slowly and placed it in her handbag.

"You said you would assist me."

"Which is precisely what I'm doing by teaching you a valuable lesson about the cold world."

"I don't think you are a very nice man."

"And what value do you derive from your certainty of that knowledge? Don't answer right away, dear. Eat your ravioli before it gets any colder."

They ate in silence. Gerusha's head felt like it might explode like an unbalanced flywheel. Her thoughts whirled and left her feeling dizzy. When they finished, Walter stood and took her hand.

"Just so you know, I have every intention of collecting on your promise. You said you'd do anything. I did my part and one day you will be called upon to do yours."

"I don't see how you could possibly expect me to honor that deal in exchange for your worthless check."

"Then you are displaying yet another objectionable limitation in your imagination, my dear," Walter said with a perverse little smile on his face. "Mull over what you've heard and perhaps a certain manner of sense can be discerned."

Truth is Stranger than Fiction, Item 6

The Puppy Dog Close

A sale is emotional and to peak [sic] emotional responses, you must let the prospect see, touch, feel, smell, hear the benefits of your product or service. That's why it's imperative, whenever possible, to place your product in the hands of the prospect so he can experience, first hand, the emotional values.

In the vacation ownership industry, they invite you for a "free complimentary, no obligation weekend" to decide if owning a share in a condominium fits your philosophy and lifestyle. You arrive, the salespeople greet you with a bottle of wine and show you a luxury, two-bedroom villa, complete with Jacuzzi and huge, wall-to-wall mirrors in the master bedroom. Prior to meeting your representative, you enjoy the health club while the children are at the pool. The representative meets with you and really doesn't attempt to close, but says, "Now isn't this what you deserve? Wouldn't it be nice to treat your family like this forever? By the way, I have a very special home just like this one. Why don't you give it a try?"

If you sell automobiles, let them test drive the car. If you represent real estate, get them in the home and on the property. If you market boats, put them in the water. The Puppy Dog Close is so overwhelmingly appealing, the salesperson does little work to conclude the sale. The buyers close themselves, because experiencing the product makes them feel like an owner even before they commit to saying yes.

- From *Closing Strong, the Super Sales Handbook* by Myers Barnes

CHAPTER EIGHT

Gerusha Andersen

All afternoon, Gerusha was distracted. She could not get the image of Walter's crooked smile out of her mind. *What kind of people do I work for? Was he serious in thinking I would honor our deal? I would really put a fork in my eye for a worthless slip of paper? What other insane assignment might he invent?* Her reverie was interrupted by sales person she was familiar with, Paul Butler, who appeared before her desk.

"Hey Gerusha, how's it going?"

"I'm okay, I guess," she said. She remembered what Walter said about the sales people that appeared before her in this lobby. *Did he mean that she could get more from them than a free lunch and a corporate logo pen?*

"Would you see if Mr. Jackson has a few minutes for me?"

"You come in here every week and you say the same thing every time. You know I'm not going to let you see Bennie Jackson without an appointment and you know that you're never going to get an appointment. Why do you keep trying?"

Paul looked surprised. "Okay, I'll tell you. I learn something each time I come in. I learned Mr. Benjamin Jackson goes by 'Bennie'. From the visitor's log, I see that my competitor, April Alexander, came in to see a B. Thomas. April mainly sells RAID storage systems, so I'll call in tomorrow, see if I can figure out what the 'B' stands for and try to land an appointment to give *my* RAID pitch. You're getting FedEx envelopes from International Biomech, so I look them up on the web and see what they do. You're buying something from them, I want to know what it is. When you think I'm leaning over and looking down your blouse, though I find your cleavage is very fetching, I peek at your email and scan the subject lines. In my business, knowledge is power and information is currency. As long as this is the hottest company in town, I will keep coming until I get my message across and make a sale. That's just the way things work."

"Information is currency…"

"I just said that."

"I know. I'm trying to get my mind around the concept. I have been a silly girl." She shook her head. "Maybe I *am* sitting on a goldmine," she mumbled.

"Excuse me?"

"Alright, Paul. If you had sixty seconds with Bennie Jackson what would you do?"

"That's easy, I'd get his attention with a comment about a bleeding-edge research subject or a scientific curiosity and still have fifteen seconds to give my standard elevator pitch and exchange business cards."

"A scientific curiosity? What do you mean?"

"Well, I know Mr. Jackson is interested in physics, so I might ask a provocative question like 'How sure are we that Newton was right and gravity force is proportional to mass and not diameter, like some curious sort of surface tension?' I have a friend at the UW that is looking into heretical questions like that."

"I'll write that down, mass versus diameter. I want that one, you use another. Now, what would sixty seconds be worth to you?"

"A lot. What do you want?"

"How about a pair of Seahawks tickets?"

"Would Charter A seats on the forty yard line for the LA game do you? If you aren't interested in football yourself, you can easily scalp the ticket."

"Wow. I really thought you were peeking down my blouse."

Paul shrugged. "You asked, I told you. Now, let's talk about my sixty seconds with Mr. Jackson."

Glen and Gerusha

Riding the bus on her way home, Gerusha's mind was a muddle. She realized that listening to her iPod isolated her from the world. She took out the earbuds, looked out the window and eavesdropped on a man talking to his boss on his cell phone. Computational Dynamics was buying Herman Miller conference room chairs for almost a grand a pop. *Business must be good.* She stopped at a convenience store and bought groceries.

When she got to her apartment, she changed into shorts and a t-shirt. After a while, Glen threw open the door and blew in like a whirlwind. He threw his duffel on the floor.

"Don't try to talk to me, I've had a tough day," he growled before she greeted him. She shrugged and tossed him a bottle of Red Hook beer. He looked surprised as he snatched it out of the air. He barely held it as he caught the bottle opener she tossed. He opened the beer and flopped on the couch.

"Great, now I'm going to get the silent treatment?" he complained.

Gerusha smiled to herself. *Catalyst,* she thought.

"I landed a pair of tickets for a Seahawks game."

"Fuck me, isn't that wonderful. Now we can crowd ourselves in with fifty thousand other morons and watch oversized men knock each other over. It used to be that religion was the opiate of the masses, now it's sports and reality television. And Prozac, that's a new opiate for the masses. You'd think people would be more discerning about what they allow into their brains."

"Gosh, you are Mister Grumpy Pants today. How about this, doctors used to think human health was defined by the balance of four fluid humours: blood, phlegm, yellow bile choler and black bile," Gerusha commented for no particular reason.

"I liked you better when you were sane," Glen said, "can we order in pizza?"

On the couch, Glen fell asleep with a partially-eaten hunk of cold pizza on his lap. Gerusha muted the TV and studied Glen in its shifting light. His head was tilted back and he was breathing noisily though his mouth. Wild hairs grew out of his nose and gray hairs created a stubbly patchwork on his neck. She leaned over and examined his mutilated hand; the finger stubs were grotesque and oily from the pizza. Leaning back herself, she felt heavy and sodden from overeating. Gravity was pulling her toward the center of the earth. Or was it? Did it feel more like something was pressing on her from space? She got up and gathered the pizza box and soiled napkins. She washed her hands under the kitchen faucet and examined them. A drop of water formed, but did not fall because it was in static balance between the drop-forming surface tension and the pull of gravity. *Am I losing it? Am I drunk? I only had the one beer, right? Plus a couple of sips of one of Glen's. I'm not stupid, I took physics in high school. I know about electrons and the laws of thermodynamics.* Setting these thoughts aside, she went in the bathroom. She put her fingers down her throat. The pizza and beer erupted into a gross mess in the toilet bowl. After flushing it away, she rinsed her mouth with mouthwash and brushed her teeth with her electric toothbrush. She felt a lot better, she could never sleep with all that greasy food lying heavily in her stomach. She slipped a nightgown over her panties, but then changed her mind and discarded it. She left her bedroom door partially open as an invitation, if he wanted to come in and join her, then he would. If he didn't, then he wouldn't. The assorted potentials of the universe would sit and wait for the catalyst to create whatever came next. *Gravity is a form of destiny,* she thought absurdly as her conscious mind drifted into a comfortable dreamy slumber.

Mary Swanson

At Emerald Hills, the nurse's shift change occurred at 3:00 in the afternoon. For over an hour, the paperwork was reviewed as the day shift handed off to the evening shift. During that time the hallways were quiet and unsupervised. Mary slipped into Peter Carson's room. Peter had cancer of the colon metastasized into his lower intestine. He was tired of surgery and the embarrassing use of his colostomy bag. Mary ordered Pentobarbital Napental from an Eastern European Pharmacy website.

"If we're going to do this, we'd better hurry," Mary said.

"We have time for one last roll in the hay, don't we? One last game of 'hide the sausage'?"

"Knock it off, Peter. You haven't had an erection in twenty years. The hair dresser is coming to touch up my tint and I don't have time to mess around with you. Did you take your Dramamine? I don't want you barfing up the dope before it does the job. I mixed the sleeping pills with a half cup of vodka, you're weak enough that 10 grams ought to do it."

"I'm scared, Mary. I wish I could go out with a little more style. One last screw and a cigar. It don't seem right to end this way, with my guts hanging out, forgotten by my kids and ex-wives." Mary sighed and sat down. She swirled the liquid in the glass and held it up to the light to see how the drug dissolved.

"In your day, you were quite the swinging dick. Remember when you said you had three different women in one weekend?"

"That's nothing, when I was on furlough in Thailand, I lost count of the young gook pootie I got. Sitting in a bar in Phuket with all the whiskey and cigarettes I wanted and a twelve-year-old girl on my lap. Did I tell you about the twins I bought in Manila?"

"I heard about it. But now it's time to take one last drink and say goodbye."

"If I'd known I would live this long, I would have taken better care of myself."

"Yes, I've heard that one before too." *Too many times,* she thought. "Drink up."

He took a big sip and looked at the glass with a pained and sour look on his face. "That's good," he said sarcastically. He drained the glass and Mary took it to make sure it got washed out.

"Sit with me?"

"Sure," Mary said, glancing at her watch. After a minute or two, his eyes drifted closed and his breathing slowed.

About damned time, Mary thought. *Was this job ever going to get easier? It needed to be done or many of the old folks would live in useless pain forever. Why me? The nurses don't do it anymore because they are afraid of getting sued and losing their licenses. I hate this. I'd rather read a large-print romance novel and sip hot tea in the garden while the weather is warm. It just isn't fair.*

Mayor Harry Silverberg

The taxicab idled before the gates of the detox center. Many of the local rich did their penance at this expensive North Seattle facility. Evelyn was crying and clutching her overnight bag to her chest.

"I can kick on my own. You don't have to leave me here."

"Baby, it has to be this way. I can come see you in a couple of weeks, you'll be out of isolation by then. If we keep drinking and taking pills we'll both be dead. Be strong for me, will you?"

"I don't see how you can leave me here alone when we have the same problem. We should do this together."

"Just go, honey."

He watched as the interns took her bag. She didn't turn and wave goodbye, but one of the interns made a brief gesture. Harry tapped the driver on the shoulder and they turned around and headed back toward town.

At his house, Harry grabbed a couple of bottles of cold water, then stripped down and slipped on spandex running shorts. He pressed the buttons on his treadmill and inclined the machine to 15 degrees. Running, he imagined the poisons sweating out of his body. He ran until he was out of breath (this took about five minutes), then kept running another few minutes until his legs were rubbery and his mind was clear. He was shocked at how quickly he'd lost his conditioning, he should have been able to run twice as long. Exhausted, he felt like he could almost accept his son's death. He took a long cool shower and fell into bed. His thoughts turned toward Glen. He felt a pure and cleansing hatred. He'd enjoy strangling Glen slowly after burning his flesh with hot irons or breaking his kneecaps with a hammer. For a few minutes, he stared at a bottle of rum and he could feel his body strain toward it with a fierce force, like the force that inevitably draws water down a drain. Deep inside, he decided to do the world a service and kill Glen Wilson. This decision was crude and uncivilized. *One day, when the time was right, he was doing to rid the world of this demon.*

He couldn't wait to get back to the office and fire Glen. It occurred to him, maybe he should have read the stupid hand-written contract before signing it. He made a mental note to do that in the morning after another run. The city had plenty of lawyers, he was sure he could dispense with Glen's services easily enough. *Fire the bastard first, then murder him.* That would be the grand plan.

Truth is Stranger than Fiction, Item 7

Patient H. had been a passionate smoker for decades. Even when his family doctor strongly advised him to give up smoking he paid no attention. Nothing could keep him from indulging in this passion.
The diagnosis of endangitis obliterans had been confirmed radiologically and angiologically.
The assisted suicide was arranged for May 22nd. The 'playboy' Mr. H. received a suicide assistant and myself with extreme friendliness, even somewhat euphorically, while his wife appeared rather reserved. Mr. H. entertained everyone present (his wife, son, brother, a couple they were friendly with, the suicide assistant, who was relatively inexperienced at that time and myself) to a goodbye party at his home bar.
After taking an 'antiemetic' the patient's last wish was to smoke a final cigarette. Fifteen minutes after taking the barbiturate, J.H. died peacefully among his friends and family of a respiratory and cardiac arrest.

- From the Euthanasia in Practice website, www.finalexit.org

CHAPTER NINE

Gerusha Andersen

It was a new day in the lobby of Immortality, LLC. Outside, it was raining a peculiar Seattle rain, the kind that dribbles gently out of the sky like it will never stop.

"Well Paul, your offer of Seahawks tickets is interesting. What else do you have?"

"You can always sell them, it would be easy to get a few hundred bucks."

"No, think of something else."

"How about shoes from Nordstrom's? You get the receipt so you can exchange them."

"That sounds good, but how about a future undefined favor?"

Paul thought it over. He put out his hand to shake on it.

"Done," he said.

"I'll give you a temporary badge. Go up and come right back down. If you cause me any trouble at all, you'll be banished from this lobby. Got it?" Paul nodded in agreement. "You're going to have to give your elevator pitch on the stairs because Bennie never takes the elevator."

"What does Bennie look like?"

"You've seen him a few times, in fact, here he comes."

"That black kid? He looks like he's twelve. You gotta be kidding me."

"Don't make an ass of yourself."

Bennie walked quickly through the lobby with his head down, watching the floor as if it might disappear from under his feet.

"Hey Bennie," Gerusha called out. "Do you ever feel like gravity is a pushing force instead of a pulling force proportional to mass."

Bennie looked up. He looked confused for a moment as if his brain had trouble embracing a new topic.

"We haven't explained gravity well yet because it is a mix of at least three forces, an attractive force, a spinning repulsive force and a binding force, a sort of cumulative acceleration against the fabric of space. I haven't quite worked it out yet, but there is interesting data being published. I have enough of an idea that I could create a rather spectacular imploding gravity bomb. Are you a quantum mechanic? I'm a collective electrodynamic wave guy, myself."

"No, not me, I'm trying to figure things out."

"Me too," Bennie replied. He turned and walked quickly to the stairway. "Hey Gerusha, buzz me in, will you? I forgot my badge again."

Gerusha gestured with her head. "Go," she whispered. Paul picked up his briefcase and hurried to join Bennie. Walking up the stairs together, on the second floor landing, Paul made his pitch.

"Mr. Jackson, is there anything interesting about the number 146,137?"

Bennie stopped. His forehead creased with concentration. "You can call me Bennie. Um, it's not a prime number. Oh, I get it, its one of those funny vampyre numbers, it's the product of 317 and 461 which are called fangs. Those component multiplicands are rearranged and hidden inside. Of course, this is all maximal horse poo. Vampyre numbers? Pure nonsense. I'm not a competent numerologist, is that what you meant? If I think about it, I might be able to discover a more interesting characteristic, I do like numbers."

It was actually the current balance of his mortgage loan, but Paul nodded yes. "That's it, very good," he said.

"Thanks," Bennie replied.

"Let me give you one of my business cards."

"I recognize you from the lobby. What products do you sell?"

"Well, for example, we have high speed fibre channel MADD disk systems, massive arrays of disk drives…"

"Cool, look, call Jeannette in Information Systems and tell her I said to buy some of your stuff. It was nice chatting to you." With that, Bennie ascended the stairs and disappeared.

Paul walked back down the stairs and entered the lobby.

"Well…" she said.

"What's Jeannette's last name?"

"In the I-S department? Her last name is Wong."

"Please give her a call and tell her that Paul Butler is here to see her."

"Do you have an appointment?

"Absolutely, tell her that Bennie asked me to contact her about an important disk storage matter," he replied.

"You dog," Gerusha whispered. She made the call and Jeannette agreed to come out in a few minutes. Glancing at the other sales people loitering in the lobby, there was electricity in the air. A new force rippling the fabric of the universe.

Glen

Glen leaned his bike against the wall of the Greyhound bus station where he could keep an eye on it. Sweaty from lugging plastic bags filled with cans of Keystone beer, he found his charter bus. The driver walked around inspecting the tires by beating on them with a crowbar.

"Where do you usually stop?"

"Portland, Eugene, Medford, Redding. We'll change drivers in Medford."

"Well, I don't want *this* bus to stop at all if possible."

"It's your charter, so I guess it's your call. I gotta piss sometime and the passengers will get restless."

"Fuck them, don't let them out until you get to San Francisco, got it?"

Glen pulled out a wad of cash and started counting out bills.

"I'm not allowed to accept tips," the driver said.

"This is not a tip, it's a bonus and believe me, you'll earn it with this load."

The driver looked around to see who was watching. "Okay, it's your charter."

Glen walked up Virginia Street and stood near a parking lot. He recognized some of his passengers and waved them over. He soon had a group of eight.

"Look guys, here's the deal. I'm going to give the money to the driver and he'll pay you when you get to San Francisco."

"Bullshit, man. You said you'd pay us to get on the bus."

"That was a bad idea. You guys would take my money then refuse to get on or sneak off behind my back."

"Fuck you honky," a dark-skinned man scoffed. He looked more like a Native American than a black, but Glen did not comment. The man left the group and strode back toward Pioneer Square. That left seven.

"I'll show you the money, but the driver will hold it until you get to Frisco. Got it?"

"What about the beer?"

"No problem, I have it right here." The remaining men grumbled but did not leave. "I also have sleeping pills if you want, it might make the long ride go faster for you."

Glen herded them toward the bus station. He made a show of handing the bus driver the seven envelopes.

"Due to company policy, I can't let them have beer."

"Yes you can."

"Alright, but I'd better not get fired."

"Whatever," Glen replied disinterestedly. "If they get out of hand, give them another pill."

"What kind of drug is it?"

Glen grinned like a ghoul. "Horse tranquilizers. Who gives a shit if we lose one or two?"

"Not me. Look, you can save money by buying an old bus. I know some guys. We could make a few runs for you."

"Great, after you get back in town, come back and see me, I'll be hanging around Pioneer Square. I appreciate your ambitious and creative thinking."

"Not much else a man can do when he's driving a goddam bus except think about things."

"I read you, brother."

The Bus Driver – Part One

I didn't like the look of the client, who reminded me of a hatchet-faced barracuda I saw in a Florida aquarium tour, but I did like the color of his money. I'd been trying to save up to fix the damn transmission in my Econoline van, so I didn't have much choice, a guy hands me 500 extra bucks and I'm going to do the job. It was early enough in the morning that my asshole supervisor was not around to witness the transaction, he liked to sleep in. The bums stank so bad that my eyes watered, but they were pretty busy draining their liter cans of beer. They didn't cause much trouble. I broke the pills in half and handed them out. I don't know what they were, but they looked like very bad medicine. The client might not care, but I did not want a stiff on my bus. Too much paperwork. I could probably find a quiet spot to dump one or two, but who needs the aggravation? These guys slept so hard, they didn't even move, they lay back in their seats and pissed themselves. I felt sorry for the cleaning crew who'd have to deal with this mess. Lucky for me the windows in the cab opened, or I would have died from asphyxiation. This was worse than driving chickens to the slaughter house. I rolled hard down I-5, and once I got out of the traffic gridlock in Tacoma, I set the cruise control to

5-over-the-limit, pissed into a plastic pop bottle and got to Medford without a single stop.

I handed off the bus at the diesel pump. The fresh driver was not happy about what I was leaving him, but Wilson's money settled him right down. He'd given me $500 for the replacement driver, but I got his undivided attention with only $200. With the Greyhound money, I was going to clear over $1,000 for tolerating a bus-full of stink for eight hours. Not bad, another two hundred or so and I could get my van ransomed from the transmission shop. Life was looking up. I deadheaded back on a milkrun bus, these things take forever to get anywhere, but I took a quarter of one of Wilson's pills and slept most of the way, so I didn't care.

Paul Butler

Jeannette Wong occupied a small office on the third floor. Leading Paul through a maze of corridors and cubicles, they stopped by the kitchen to pick up complimentary bottles of cranberry juice. Once settled into her office, they performed the 'exchanging business cards' ritual.

"Mister Butler, to what do I owe the honor of your visit?"

"I represent Wavefront and we make optical and magnetic storage libraries. We do software development and offer maintenance services which could be valuable for an advanced company like Immortality."

Jeannette sighed. "We do business with Microsoft and EMC. We have all bases covered by partnering with the major network storage vendors."

"I understand and I assure you we have unique proprietary technology that supports open standards on a very competitive and cost-effective basis. We also work with the big companies, but add value in system architecture and software providing 24 by 7 uptime and support."

"You'll pardon me, but I get three or four calls every day from people offering exactly the same thing. I don't want to count the emails that slip through the firewall and spam filters." She stood and offered her hand. "So, if you'll excuse me, I have to get back to work. I thank you for your time."

"Bennie told me to tell you to buy something."

Jeanette sat back down. "Not this again. Alright, very well. I don't suppose a blank purchase order would get you off my back?"

Paul shook his head no. "Show me your current architecture drawings and I'll offer a solution that will make your life easier and enable faster data access for your engineers and scientists."

She leaned back in her chair and took a deep breath. "Okay." She pulled out a sheaf of drawings and rolled them up. "I love Bennie to death but he's always pulling stuff like this. I don't have time for it."

"Have you thought about outsourcing yourself?"

"What do you mean?"

"We provide personal assistant services from India. A 24-hour team is assigned to read your email and filter out the fluff. They handle the routine stuff and with your guidance, an expert system is developed that assists with decision-making and follow-up. They do research and act as a buffer between you and the outside world. We provide in-person surrogates that will attend meetings in your stead and document and guide project teams. I have a client that moved to Mazatlán and runs her team from the beach via high speed satellite link."

"Sounds expensive."

"Not as expensive as you might think. We can work within whatever budget you define."

"Won't the company decide they don't need me?"

"We build in poison-pill defenses for that. It rarely comes to that because the company is thrilled. Your output increases and the intelligence of your decisions increases exponentially. The results are quite good. Its very cost-effective and you could have a personal life again."

"Okay, you got me on that one. Go ahead and build up a quote. This is going to cost a bundle, isn't it?"

"Regardless of the total project investment, you'll find the cost-to-benefit ratio very attractive."

"I thought so. We have lots of money, so I guess we can afford it. Let me assure you, Mr. Butler, we don't mind writing big checks, but the customer care and equipment performance had better be world class."

"I understand completely. I will have a proposal on your desk in a week. If you'll clear a spot on your calendar, I will bring in our technical and marketing team and we'll go over all the details."

Jeannette pulled up her schedule on her computer. "I'll give you two hours on the 26th at eleven."

"I will see you then."

Paul gathered up his briefcase and the drawings. "I can find my way out and let you get back to work."

Jeanette looked at the unread email on her screen and the message light flashing on her telephone. "Alright, but go straight out and don't cause any trouble for me."

"I understand completely and I appreciate the time you've spent with me. Hey, while I'm on a roll here, you wouldn't be available for dinner, would you?"

She stared at him for a long moment. "You noticed I'm not wearing any rings, you're very clever. However, I don't have time to date right now, but when the time is right, I'm sure I will meet the right *Asian* man. Just so you understand my personal boundaries, I find your question to be unprofessional and borderline offensive."

"For my lapse of judgment, I apologize. Please consider it a temporary insanity induced by your overwhelming charm and loveliness."

For this, Paul was rewarded with a small smile which Jeannette tried to hide.

"You're smooth, I'll grant you that," she said. She waved her hand to usher him out.

Paul had perfected a sort of salesman moonwalk that looked brisk but gave him time to glance at computer screens and listen into cubicle conversations as he weaved toward the exit. He wasn't seeking anything in particular, it was force of habit to get a feel for the company and try to uncover unmet business opportunities. It took about ten minutes to get back to the lobby and turn in his badge.

"How did it go?" Gerusha asked.

"Better than great. I'll be needing a partner's badge, could you fill out a form for me?"

"Sure, I guess. Jeannette will authorize it?"

"Yes, she will." He glanced at the salespeople seated in the waiting area. "What would it take to make our little arrangement completely exclusive?"

"A lot, the offers have been getting very sweet."

"I was afraid of that. What have I created?"

"A monster," Gerusha replied, "but I shall be *your* monster until I land a better deal. You owe me a big one, don't forget."

"I shall not," Paul responded sincerely as he strolled toward the door. There was no time to waste, he had a lot of work in preparing for the meeting next week.

Immortality, LLC Executive Meeting

The executive meeting room was equipped with teleconferencing cameras, microphones, and large video screens on three walls. A pitcher of ice water sweated in the middle of a large walnut table. Emma, with her hair hanging beside her face in braids, was dressed in a navy blue jumper with white leggings, she looked like a grade school girl on picture day. Walter was dressed immaculately in a jazzy suit wearing a bright red tie adorned with the Immortality, LLC logo.

"How are things going with your classes, Emma?"

"If you cared about my schooling, you'd remember that I'm only taking one class this semester."

"You're right. I was just making small talk."

"Well, let's not. You called me here to discuss something specific, let's get to it."

"It's Bennie. He's supposed to be working on minor glitches in the t-cell infusions, but he's always in one of the fusion labs. I don't know how many labs he has, if I didn't accidentally see invoices for new equipment in Building 11, I wouldn't even know we have a Building 11. The invoices were rather breathtaking, by the way. What exactly is a muon imager and why is it worth 48 million dollars? Does he look at price tags before he buys things?"

"Those are a lot of questions. Do you expect me to answer or are you just venting?"

"I guess I'm venting. I feel like we're losing focus and control. Our successful IPO requires continued breakthroughs in longevity and the money will dry up if we don't stay with our core business plan. Without cash pouring in, we're nowhere. We've worked miracles so far and we need that pace to carry on for another year or so. We don't want to be last year's fashion show. Is there anything you can do to guide Bennie toward his maximum productivity?"

"He's done so much and is working so hard, I'm not sure what more you expect. If he started sweating blood, would that satisfy you?"

"Emma, don't get me wrong. I love Bennie more than life itself. I'm just telling you there will not be cash to run the company and buy muon imagers if Bennie does not zero in on our corporate requirements. If there is anything you can think of that can be done, then I urge you to do it, that's all I'm saying."

"I'm sorry, Walter, I understand, I really do. We don't understand the mystery of his intellect and he's not going to be led around by the nose like an ox, but I'll try. I really will. Did you know he's been playing bongo drums? He's gotten very good at it."

"Bongos? Why?"

"He says he likes it because it helps him think, but I think he's copying that Nobel Prize guy, Feynman. Personally, I think it's kind of cute."

"Honest to God, Emma, we can't afford any *cute* right now. The company is hanging by a thread. If there is anything you can do to get him to work on the t-cells instead of his bongo drums, I would greatly appreciate it."

"Yes, Walter," Emma sighed, "I'm with you, don't worry, I'll do what I can."

"Thank you."

"You're very welcome. Now, what about Glen, is he joining us? Maybe he can guide Bennie. Bennie will listen to him."

"I don't know what Glen is doing. As far as I know, he's staying with Gerusha, let's get her up here and see what she has to say."

Walter made the phone call and after Gerusha got her backup to cover the lobby, she came up to the conference room. She was wearing a sheer silk blouse with a pair of lime green culottes, accessorized with the wireless telephone headset. On impulse, she kissed Emma's cheek. Emma blushed and patted her shoulder.

"Hello Gerusha. We were sitting here chatting and the 'Glen' topic came up. Can you tell us what he's been doing?"

"I'm not exactly sure. He uses my bicycle to roll Seattle with a duffel bag full of wristbands and quite a lot of cash. He says he has a job working for the Mayor, but I can't figure it out."

"A duffel bag full of cash? I hate to speculate, a guy like Glen could be up to nearly any damn thing. We have a job for him here, has he said anything about wrapping things up for the Mayor and coming to join us?"

"Not a word."

"Alright dear," Emma said. "Would you press him and find out? We need his help to keep things going."

"I'll see what I can do, but I can't promise anything."

"We understand. Tell me Gerusha, out of idle curiosity, has there been any movement on the, uh, intimacy side of things?" Walter asked delicately.

"No, he's sleeping on the pull-out couch. Nothing."

"That seems very odd."

"I agree. Since we're being so confessional, tell me, Emma, are you and Bennie lovers?"

"No, we're waiting until we are married. Bennie says the statistics are clear about this. I'm not so sure myself, but of course, my parents are thrilled."

"Like Bennie, perhaps Glen has embraced a new moral code?"

There was a moment where they considered this before all three burst out laughing. Emma passed out tissues and they dabbed their eyes.

Glen

Sipping coffee from a paper cup, Glen watched the employee area outside the hospital morgue until his friend Bill came out. He walked over and dropped a copy of the novel Post Office on the picnic table.

"You can borrow this if you wish."

"Great, I've been meaning to see if I could find it at the used bookstore. I remember you, you were asking about the expired bums."

"Yes, I'm curious, how was business last night?"

"There is something going on, we had five alky's come in on gurneys. We usually don't get that many until the first of the month when the disability and welfare checks come out. Occasionally we'll get a few extra in the middle of the month, because a few government checks come out then. Where did they get the money for all that booze? It takes a lot to kill those old guys. I got in some overtime, which comes in handy now and then, I'm trying to save up and buy a little house with my girlfriend."

"I have no idea," Glen lied.

"If it keeps up, I'll have the down payment in a couple of weeks."

"I think it's safe to consider last night's traffic to be a leading business indicator," Glen said obscurely.

"Huh?"

Glen patted him on the shoulder. "After you get the house, she's going to want kids."

"She has a couple from a prior relationship, they're great."

"Good luck to you, my friend," Glen said. He waved over his shoulder and walked back to his bike.

Glen rode down Broadway and found a hippy café. He ordered a Western omelet and perused a discarded Seattle Times. A homeless man was stabbed to death in an apparent robbery under the Alaskan Way

Viaduct. Street gangs, the mobile packs of rats that preyed on the vagrants, were an interesting problem. It was going to take out-of-the-box thinking to handle them. Some would dissipate when their victims evaporated, but the hardcore would simply move up the food chain to prey on civilians. *All problems will yield to my work ethic and creativity,* Glen mused.

After breakfast, he made his rounds and handed out a few more wristbands. He had a good idea how many bums there were, somewhere north of 500, so he wasn't so interested in the wristband thing anymore. He made cash grants to about 20 transients but rolled away on Third Avenue before they could mob him. $200 cash grants worked, but were expensive. Glen didn't want to go overboard with spending. He was known for hand-outs and could hardly maneuver in the Pioneer Square area without drawing a crowd. Looking up, he did a double-take when he saw Red sitting on a bench on Fifth Avenue. He rolled the bike up to see if his eyes were deceiving him.

"Hey Red, I paid you to leave town!"

Red was drunk. "I decided to come back, so I hitched a ride. I need money, how about helping me out?"

"Goddam it, you were supposed to stay in San Francisco."

"They wouldn't let me panhandle, the streets are run by a bunch of thugs. Things are easier up here."

That's what I get for trying to be a nice guy, Glen thought bitterly.

CHAPTER TEN

Bennie and Emma

The company supplied Bennie with a cell phone that included a GPS tracking device, so Emma knew his coordinates, but it still took her twenty minutes to find the right floor, corridor and room. Wearing headphones, he hunched over and stared intently at a large high-resolution monochrome computer screen with images flashing at a rate of about one per second. Occasionally he would freeze an image and gaze at it with his nose three inches away. As Emma watched, she could hear rock music squawking, he must have the volume cranked. She put her hands over his eyes and he froze the screen and turned to scoop her into his arms. They kissed and Bennie nuzzled her neck and tickled her with the soft fuzz on his cheeks.

"Hey Bennie, what are you doing?"

"I've invented something I call Oceanic Archeology."

"That sounds like an oxymoron. Do you mean studying civilizations that became submerged like Atlantis?"

"A little like that, you won't believe it when I publish my findings. I've been looking at photographs of stones, there are millions of pictures on the web."

"I know there are millions of pictures but most of them are European porn and you're looking at rocks? I thought all black guys were horny?"

"Oh, I'm horny all right, but these pictures are really something. Here, I'll show you some I've archived." He pressed a few keys and blotches appeared on the screen. "Take a close look at this," he said.

Emma looked, but beyond random speckles, she didn't see anything. It looked like an ordinary piece of granite.

"It looks like granite. We have a lot of that in Alaska. If you like it we can get kitchen counters made from it."

"There is a pattern. I think its intelligence. Can't you see it? I have software analyzing it."

"So what if it is a pattern?"

"Well, it's over 150,000 years old for one thing. For another, it was found in the Mariana Trench about 30,000 feet below sea level. You know that over 70% of the Earth's surface is covered by water? And you know evidence of human life dates back three million years or so, depending on who you believe."

"All this is very interesting Bennie, but could you get to the punch line please?"

"Okay, what it means is—. No, I'll tell you later when I'm more sure. You found me for some reason, is it dinner time? I don't think I've eaten for a while, what time is it?"

"I came down to see what is going on with the t-cell infusion testing."

"Oh yeah, I'm supposed to get regressions done and define test protocols. I get easily distracted."

"Yeah, sometimes."

"Why don't you wriggle out of that pretty little dress and I'll make a woman of you?"

"Because we decided we want our wedding night to be special. Besides, my dad would eviscerate you if you violated his little girl. We don't want any of that."

"You're right, might be painful. I can hardly wait, my sweet."

"Me either, but we're not wild animals, we can exercise discipline for the greater good."

"Alright, I suppose. I'd better get back to work. I'm hungry, send out for barbeque, will you? I need beef."

"Whatever you want, baby." Giggling, she slapped away his wandering hand. "Except that, for that you have to wait."

"'Wait'. That has to be my least favorite word."

"Shut up and get to work. I'll order your barbeque." Standing and smoothing her skirt, she turned off his screen and waggled her index finger at him. "Not this, the t-cells."

"Okay, babe," Bennie promised.

Mayor Harry Silverberg

Wearing leather gloves and wrestling boots, the Mayor landed blows with his feet and jabbed his kick boxing bag with his fists until he could hardly lift his arms. His stamina was already starting to come back, but his hatred did not diminish. He imagined smashing Glen's face and kicking his groin. He flopped onto a weight-lifting bench, wiped his forehead with a damp towel and guzzled water from a sport bottle. Trying to calm his mind, he could still see his son's grave and the helpless look on his wife's face. He thought of the five Kubler-Ross stages of grief. Was anger first? He was bitterly angry. As his body cooled, his heart rate settled and his mind began to function. He remembered. The first stage was denial, then bargaining followed by anger. At the hospital, he refused to believe what his eyes were telling him. The bargaining, that was the deal with the devil himself, Glen Wilson. Now he was angry, but feeling the effects of the next stage, despair. *What kind of world is it if I can accept my son's death and carry on with my life?* On impulse, he grabbed a kitchen knife sitting by his chair. He stabbed the boxing bag again and again until plastic pellets scattered around in a giant mess. Dropping the knife, he kicked at the pellets on the floor. *Glen Wilson did not kill my son. So why does it feel so good to imagine his face on that bag when I ripped its guts out?* He unhooked the bag and, trailing a cascade of pellets, took it into the backyard and threw it into his swimming pool. *That was irrational,* he thought, *but it sure as fuck felt good.* The maid and the landscaping crew could clean up the mess.

He tore off his clothes and walked naked through his house. Grabbing a bottle of Johnny Walker Red Label, he carried it into the shower. Discarding the cap, cool water cascaded over him. Looking at the whiskey with great need, he cursed bitterly under his breath. The drink promised a temporary peace and he craved that peace with every molecule of his body. Slightly deranged, he poured the whiskey on his head and rinsed it off under the shower head. *What a goddam insane and hopeless world*, he thought.

Glen and Bennie

Glen helped himself to a cup of free coffee from the Immortality employee kitchen. He was supposed to meet Bennie in a conference room, but Glen was early and Bennie had not turned up yet. As he studied advertisements on the community cork board, he noticed a lot of traffic through the area. He supposed employees were coming around to check him out. He'd been issued a red-outlined VIP badge with employee number 0001, a singular honor. A slovenly young man, wearing a plaid shirt over a huge protruding belly, had hairy toes protruding from a pair of well-worn Birkenstocks. He grabbed a free Diet Coke and looked Glen over.

"You don't look like much," he said.

"That may be true," Glen responded, "but I'm wearing badge 'One' and you're wearing badge '112', so get back to work before I have your ass in a sling."

"Whatever," Badge 112 replied, before wandering off with insolent slowness.

"Software engineers," Glen grumbled to himself.

Bennie finally walked by and Glen followed him into their reserved conference room. Bennie was carrying a rumpled sheaf of papers and had lint stuck in his nappy hair. He looked like he'd been sleeping in his clothes.

"Hi Glen, I got your voicemail about wanting weapons and I'm very excited. I have some awesome ideas. Don't tell Walter I'm working on this because I'm supposed to be working on minor issues in our immortality project, but this is much more intriguing. Your timing is perfect, I've been doing simulations on a gravity bomb, this could be a real breakthrough, a kind of black hole implosion device, very compact and powerful, you could eradicate New York with a device the size of a grape."

"Out of curiosity, you mean New York City?"

"No, the whole of New York State, this technology is really elegant and efficient. No radioactive fallout. There may be problems with stopping the reaction once it starts, but the chances of that are slim, no more than one in fourteen thousand. My analysis has turned up interesting hypotheses, for example, I think there is a tiny black hole in the center of each planet and a white hole in the center of each star. Einstein would have gone nuts with the experimental data we've collected. In addition…"

"Look Bennie, my dear friend, this all fascinating, but I was clear. I'm looking for small non-lethal weapons that can be wielded by civilians, not doomsday bombs that might suck the guts out of the earth and kill us all."

"No, that's not it. The new black hole might be attracted to the one at the center of the earth and section us like an orange, chop the world into octants and —"

"Bennie, I don't care. Focus for me, will you?"

"But the G-bomb…"

"I know, it's great work, truly it is, but I need non-lethal weapons."

"Okay, okay, I get it," Bennie said, miffed. "Fine. There's boring ultra-slick low friction polymer. Spray this stuff then wet it down and it's slicker than ice, you can't get enough traction to stand up."

"That's more like it, but not what I'm looking for. What else?"

"There are ultra-sonic weapons, you focus a pair of them on a victim and an interference pattern is created that creates severe disorientation, vertigo and nausea that will last a few hours. That will incapacitate a person quickly and wouldn't generally be fatal."

"That might be alright. Anything else?"

"I could make a neat Kevlar web thrower like an old-fashioned bolero. It would shoot rubber bullets with a netting between them, they would wrap around legs and the perp will go down fast and hard. A bola entangler. I could make them shoot at different strengths, at full power they would pull the Kevlar tight and could even chop off a limb. With a little grit on the web, they would cut right through bone lickety-split, slick as you please. Boom, down they go. At long distance, say 20 meters, the net would be fully spread out and would cause a nice tangle."

"That sounds like a good one, though I don't know about the amputation part. I want a relatively untrained person to take down a bad guy."

"Oh, I have a good one. We create a CO_2-powered spitwad thrower like a miniature paintball gun and use it to deliver a stink projectile. This stuff creates a stench worse than any skunk and it's hard to wash off. Or, there is a hormone extract that will give a person a permanent horrible body odor, but it takes a few hours to take effect. You'd have to be careful with that one, the effect is irreversible, the victim would never be able to mingle with others unless they were wearing gas masks. Then there are more traditional weapons like beanbag guns or guns that emit compressed air bursts, they can knock a person off their feet. Or, guns that shoot a glop of instant-drying adhesive, you can glue a person against a wall or stick their feet to the ground. We can shoot tranquilizers or make a high voltage stun gun, this will stop someone in their tracks real quick. Or vomiting agents, we could create a veritable barforama." Bennie was getting excited with all the possibilities. "We could shoot flechettes that would barely break the skin, but deliver a concentrated wasp venom. Or, we could..."

"Alright Bennie, that's enough, let me think a minute. That bolo net thing would work for me. But I like the glue gun too. How long would it take to make me a hundred prototypes of the bolo gun and the glue gun?"

"We have most of the stuff here already. I could put a team on it and get some milled out tomorrow. They wouldn't be pretty, but they would work okay."

"Good, do it. And make me up some of the Skunk Guns in your spare time, they might be fun to play with."

"Sure Glen, I'll get right on it and thanks for the mission, I was getting real bored."

"No problem, Bennie, anytime. Out of curiosity, if I wanted to maim someone, what would you suggest?"

"That's easy, I can make a burst laser gun or flash-bang grenade that would blind a man. In a fraction of a second it would fry the rods and cones, the wavelengths are so narrow we could make safety sunglasses. The light does not have to be visible, it could be infrared. The intensity could be so high that a reflection could cause permanent blindness. It wouldn't matter of your eyes were closed if the infrared beam was strong enough."

"What could you build it into? A watch or a ring?"

"With some time I could design it that small, but it would get real hot, we'd have to figure out how to cool it. A better form-factor would be something like a flashlight. As I sit here and think about it, this would be a very cruel weapon. Permanent blindness? That's like a death sentence, isn't it? I hadn't considered the moral and ethical aspects of a weapon like this."

"You build it. Make me the protective glasses and I'll worry about the morals and ethics, alright?"

"Sure, Glen," Bennie said with relief, "consider it done."

Gerusha Andersen

Watching the clock, Gerusha willed it to move faster. Walter came in shaking rain from his umbrella. She gestured for him to come over and led him over to the corner by the Glen Wilson bust.

"Can I speak to you for a moment, sir?"

"I have a meeting in a few minutes, can you make it quick?"

Gerusha nodded. She had not previously noticed how intense his gray eyes could be, they pierced like carbide drill bits. Her words came out in a rush. "There was a sales man. He offered me expensive Seahawks tickets in exchange for an audience with Bennie. I set this up the meeting, but now I'm wondering if I made a mistake. I didn't take the tickets."

"Did Bennie complain?"

"No. In fact, I think we might buy some of the salesman's equipment, there is a big proposal in work. Bennie basically told Jeannette to buy something, I think he liked the guy. Do you think I screwed up?"

Walter stared at her. Gerusha felt like he was X-raying through her bones and finding her inadequate in every way. It was a similar feeling to spreading her legs on the gynecologist's table.

"Hmmph," he grunted. Gerusha could not discern a tone from it. He walked to the elevator and left her standing by the bust. Once he'd disappeared into the elevator, she leaned down and looked into Glen's bronze eyes. She had not noticed a disapproving scowl in his expression before, but his cold eyes mocked and scolded her. She was startled by a touch on her arm. A lady salesperson dressed in a tailored pantsuit. She smelled of an exotic perfume that was reminiscent of bug spray. Her designer glasses and wristwatch probably cost more than Gerusha grossed in a year. She exuded a classy and expensive aura.

"I'm sorry to bother you, but could you check and see if Mr. Crowley has a few minutes for Tanya Prescott?"

"I'm sorry," Gerusha replied, "but he's in meetings all afternoon and has asked not to be disturbed."

"Very well, I'll give him a try tomorrow."

"Make an appointment with his admin or he won't see you."

"I've talked to her a dozen times, this time I thought I'd fly up in person and try to get an audience. It's a short hop from San Jose, we're in the same time zone and everything, so I thought it would be worth a try. I'm flying back on Friday. If there is anything you can do to get me a few minutes between now and then, I would be rather infinitely grateful."

Gerusha noticed Tanya's hand was on her arm and applying subtle pressure.

"We're under strict orders."

"I understand, I wanted to make sure you knew how important it is to chat briefly with Mr. Crowley. I'll see you tomorrow, dear."

Gerusha walked back to her desk and covered her face in her hands.

Walter probably went right up to Human Resources to start the paperwork to get me fired. I blew it, it's back to Starbucks for sure. Why did I confess my unethical behavior? Am I insane or just stupid? I'm in over my head trying to work with these people, they are such a mystery. I should throw Glen out on his ass, what has he done for me except drive me mad? I should coax Martin back, offer him sex in an elevator or something, he'd come back in a flash. He will be a lawyer when he finishes school and passes the bar exam. I have to lock in my future before my hair gets thin and my ass gets fat sitting at this chair all day. How long could I survive without a job? If I get fired, can I draw unemployment insurance? I've become accustomed to the money I make here, I have a credit card balance hanging over my head like a battle axe. If I don't start acting smart I'm going to blow everything and end up with nothing.

"Excuse me, Miss Gerusha." Her thoughts were interrupted by a commercial real estate agent she did not like because he was pushy and poorly groomed. "I'm here to see Mr. Crowley about property for lease up in Fremont. Have you heard any rumors about needing more space?"

"You don't have an appointment and without an appointment, you will not be seeing anyone that works here, I've told you this many times."

"I talked to Wendy on the phone yesterday —"

"I'm sure you did, but you do not have an appointment. In fact, I will lay it out for you. For as long as I am sitting here (*which may not be long,* she neglected to mention) you will never see anyone in this building, so fuck off and die, do you get it?"

"You don't have to be crude, I can take a hint."

"Liar, you work in sales, you *can't* take a hint. The only thing you understand is a baseball bat upside your thick damn head. Take your pitch down the street, there is nothing for you here. And, for some additional free advice, when the teenager at Burger King asks if you want onions on your Whopper, tell them no! I'm tired of your onion breath on me. Now beat it and don't come back."

"I'll see you tomorrow, Miss Gerusha, perhaps you'll be in a better mood then."

She sighed. *Was there no way to be rid of these pests?*

He turned and stomped off. She heard him mumble something to the next salesperson.

"Good afternoon, Ms. Andersen," her next customer said.

"What did he say to you?"

He thought for an instant before deciding to respond with brutal honesty. Gerusha was impressed with this quick and decisive thinking. "He said 'the bitch is in a snit'."

Gerusha laughed. It occurred to her, if she was going to be fired, perhaps she could extract some small benefit before it was too late to take advantage of her situation.

"Alright, Mr. Perkin, what are you slinging today?"

"I represent a Taiwanese company that produces a line of precision laboratory equipment that I think Mr. Jackson would find very attractive in terms of features and price."

"How do you know Mr. Jackson's name?"

"From a newspaper article."

"Let me ask, if you order a hamburger, do you ask for onions?"

"No, the odor is hard to avoid and will be offensive to many."

"Is that something they cover in sales school?"

"No, that's something you figure out for yourself in the field. However, I don't care for onions anyway and I haven't eaten a burger in many years, as they are filled with carbohydrates, hormones and saturated fat. Unhealthy. Bad for the complexion. Low class."

"Alright, Mr. Perkin. Let's get down to business. What is it worth to you for a short audience with Bennie Jackson?"

"I have complimentary tickets to the ballet. If that does not pique your interest, then perhaps I could bury something for you in my expense account, like a weekend in Las Vegas. An airline and hotel package, for example."

"What if all I care about is cold hard cash?"

"That would require creativity. I could expense a nice handbag that you could return for a refund."

"I understand. I'm not comfortable with pushing the envelope, we're just talking here, right?"

"I understand completely."

"I think I can arrange an audience, but I want a future undefined favor in exchange."

"Done."

"You won't forget?"

"Upon that, you can rest assured."

Gerusha laughed. "I guess I'm not in a snit anymore," she said.

"Please forgive me for the unprofessional question, but would you care to join me for a quiet dinner sometime? I'm told I'm pleasant company once I take off my necktie and put aside my sales persona."

"I can't accept right now, but if you give me your business card, I'd be pleased to call you if my home situation changes."

"I couldn't ask for anything more," Mr. Perkin said as he extended his card with a flourish.

Truth is Stranger than Fiction, Item 8

Psychotherapy, from the tuberose.com website.
The depressed person lacks hope and usually suffers from dreadful, self-punishing, self-blaming ideas. If the therapist can inspire hope and, at the same time, help dissipate the feelings of guilt — the worst aspects of severe depressions can often be speedily overcome through psychotherapy. This is much more true for depression than for a whole variety of other difficulties, especially those where the individual tends to blame someone else as the source of the problem, or where the feelings of emotional pain are locked inside obsessions and compulsions, or suppressed by addictions. Psychiatric propaganda about the superiority of drugs over psychotherapy is wholly misleading. Clinicians need to learn to resist the urge to deliver the quick fix in the form of a pill despite considerable pressure from the medical establishment, the media, and even the patient to do so. One cannot heal the soul with a medication. We tend to overlook the power of a caring psychotherapeutic relationship in the treatment of depression. There are so many kinds of psychotherapy that it can be misleading to speak of "psychotherapy" as if it were a single kind of human service. There are a variety of *Twelve-Step programs*, inspirational religions, and psycho-spiritual workshops and retreats. A variety of life experiences, including time itself, will heal depression. Each person, hopefully with the support of loved ones, must find ways to make life meaningful.

CHAPTER ELEVEN

Glen

After a tough slog up Aurora Avenue toward Lynnwood, I was nearly turned into lunchmeat by a huge yellow H2 Hummer. The driver steered with her elbows while juggling a cell phone and an insulated mug; she didn't have a free hand to give the polite Seattle wave, all I got was a shrug of the shoulders and an apologetic smile. Pretty little thing, about 13, probably had Daddy's lawyer on speed dial in case of minor incidents like vehicular homicide. I made a motion indicating that I'd like to wring her exquisite neck and she showed me a little pink tongue between perfectly formed white teeth before accelerating out of sight. I added her to the list of enemies I would petition the great father to punish, perhaps to roast in hell forever turning on a rotisserie with a steel rod rammed up her anus, we'll see how she liked that. However, if I understand the universe correctly, she'd float on clouds eating strawberries and cream while honorable and useful men like me endure eternal torment. Now that I consider the matter, my private Hell would surely look like this stretch of Hwy 99; all used appliance stores, run-down linoleum purveyors with carpet remnants 75% off and used car dealers where your job is your credit.

I finally reached the area near the Costco where my mother's house had stood. Just as Elke said, it was now a Jack in the Box restaurant. I leaned the bicycle against a light pole and walked around the parking lot seeking inspiration or feeling sorry for myself, it's hard to tell the difference sometimes. Mom's ashes were scattered on the grounds, so this fast food joint was a crass monument. Irrationally, I imagined her spirit rising from the earth and infiltrating burger patties. I couldn't remember my father at all and I wasn't close to my mother, to be honest she was not a very warm or nice person. Stubborn. Unpleasant. Still, I suppose I loved her as much as could be.

What was I doing here? I don't believe in afterlife, I'd be a much happier person if I could manage this leap of faith. The spirit of my mother is not lingering around this stupid parking lot, so why did I risk death and leg cramps to ride all the way out here? Dumb, that's what this was, just plain dumb. The fact is, I am stuck. The bum plan was oiled up and running smoothly, but what about the gangs? There is no simple solution to this problem, law enforcement had been trying programs for years, nothing seemed to work when you had dissatisfied idle youth banding together in roving artificial-family units. They needed money for their low-rider cars and decking out their girlfriends in jewelry and clothes, more money than they could make slinging hamburgers, so they hit the streets to sell crack and rob civilians. It would take someone meaner than me, in great numbers, to make a dent. An army. I could take the Mayor's remaining money and hit the road, but I signed on to clean up the streets of Seattle and I didn't feel right about abdicating my job, no matter how impossible. Mom would run out in the yard and chase the bangers with a broom, they would laugh at her but would move it down the street. She was fearless when her ire was invoked, besides, what did she have to lose? I was morosely thinking these thoughts and kicking an empty soda cup across the parking lot when it hit me. A plan popped, fully-formed, into my mind. A thing of beauty, sheer genius. I was so happy I treated myself to a chemical milkshake spit out of Jack in the Box machinery. It tasted good and I wasn't worried that it would stimulate my lactose intolerance, if you catch my drift. Happy, I got back on the bike and headed back toward town.

Somewhere around 145th, the goddam rear bike tire went flat. I heaved the wretched traitor over a chainlink fence into a wetland reserve area (swamp) and cursed my bad luck. My brain was operating in fine fashion as I walked by a used car lot. Of course! Immortality could buy a company car to prevent a dignified and esteemed corporate mucky-muck from walking the streets like a penniless transient. I looked over the inventory at First Quality Pre-Owned Auto Sales Company, but I was not impressed. A lot of imperfectly-repaired decade-old domestic cars, these would never do for an eminent man like me. There was a Cadillac Seville that had a certain appeal and the salesman assured me the low mileage on the odometer was accurate, but I didn't like the puddle of oil and antifreeze that decorated the parking lot underneath. I was about to continue my hike when I caught a glimpse of something bright and emerald green hiding behind a hedge. 'What's that?' I asked. 'That's mine', the sales-creep said, 'and it's not for sale'. 'Well', says I, 'it sure wouldn't hurt to take a little look-see, now would it?'

It was a '68 Chevelle all tricked out with chrome bumpers, dual exhaust pipes and metal-flake paint. The interior smelled like new vinyl. I liked it.

'Start this sucker up,' I said.

'No,' he replied.

I wasn't in the mood for a lot of dialog, so I walked around and found a landscaping brick. My intent must have been evident, though I didn't know myself whether I was going to threaten the salesman or the car. It didn't matter, because, though very angry, he produced his keys and fired up the beast. It started right up and emitted a satisfying rumble though its glass-pack exhaust system.

'How much?' I asked.

'I have 15 grand in it and it used to belong to my uncle. It's been in the family since it rolled off the assembly line.'

'I'll give you twenty via cashier's check in an hour.'

'Goddam you, I said it ain't for sale.'

'Look genius, are you in the business of selling cars or what? Nothing seems to be flying off the lot, are you sure you have next month's lease payment covered?'

This broke him and we had ourselves a deal. I used his phone to call Walter and he agreed to messenger over a cashier's check. I was proud of him, he didn't even ask too many annoying questions.

While we were waiting, the sales-creep cleaned out the trunk and I suggested that he should be happy driving the Cadillac with twenty grand in his pocket.

'That Caddie is a piece of shit,' he said dejectedly.

Soon I was rumbling down Aurora, blasting out classic rock on the stereo in my shiny new ride. Life can be good when it isn't squeezing your balls in a vise. Seattle traffic really stinks, there were some places I could get around more quickly on the bike, but all-in-all, life seemed to be worth living again.

Glen and Gerusha

Gerusha walked into her apartment and surveyed the mess. Glen's underwear was hanging on the shower curtain rod to dry. As far as she knew, he had only one pair, so she assumed he was running around town without any. He'd left a gallon of milk on the counter, it was warm and already starting to reek, so, sighing, she poured it down the sink and ran rinse water after it. He'd scrambled the last of her organic brown eggs and left the dirty pan on the stove. *The lousy bastard was too damn lazy to run water into it to make it easier to wash.* She took a shower and scrubbed off her makeup, then wandered around her house in one of her father's old bathrobes and her mom's fluffy pink slippers, picking up pizza boxes and newspapers and allowing her hair to air dry. She caught a glimpse in a mirror and realized she looked a wreck, but she was too tired and depressed to care. *I'm off-duty, anyone that doesn't like how I look can shit on a stick and eat it.* Watching TV and eating low-fat popcorn from a microwave bag, she was startled when Glen rushed into her apartment like a whirlwind.

"What are you doing?" Glen shouted.

"I'm relaxing and watching television, you goddam pig," she replied around a handful of popcorn.

"There is no time to waste, get your panties on, we're going out."

"No, we're not. I'm tired, I'm going to bed."

"Yes, we are," Glen yelled. He threw open her bedroom door and started sorting through her clothes, examining and tossing aside rejects. He threw black underwear at her with a matching black silk blouse and blue jeans. "Nothing fancy, you have two minutes."

"I'm exhausted!"

"You have no idea the day I've had. If an old man can dredge up the energy to party, then so can you."

"I need time to put my face on."

"Bullshit! Pull your hair back in a ponytail and lets hit the street. Move it!"

She put the popcorn aside and stood. Glen swatted her on the butt hard enough to sting.

"Do that again and I'll break your nose," she threatened with a barely controlled rage.

"That's the spirit," Glen said, "now you have ninety seconds."

It took three minutes, but soon they were on the street. Glen ushered her to an illegally parked shiny green muscle car.

"What's this?"

"My new car, jump in and I'll take you for a ride."

She slid onto the seat. "Hey, what happened to my bike?"

"Don't worry about it," Glen said, "I'll buy you a new one someday."

"You are such a goddam prick, how did I get stuck with you?"

"You invited me in, remember," Glen said, grinning as he kicked over the motor. The car was loud, a deep rumble penetrated every nook of Gerusha's body.

"Do you like classic rock?" Glen asked.

"Not really."

"Great!" He turned the stereo up until Deep Purple performing Highway Star could be heard over the exhaust noise. "This will be pure torture," he said as he squealed the tires and cut off a screaming Chinese man driving a minivan. Any evening that starts off with an Asian man cussing at you will inevitably be a good one.

Gerusha was angry about her bike, the mess at the apartment and being swatted on the butt, so she was determined to give Glen the passive-aggressive silent treatment. However, she could hardly resist the warm throbbing of the engine coming through her seat and the feel of the cool wind whipping through her hair. He took her to the 13 Coins Restaurant and they enjoyed large bloody cuts of beef Glen insisted on ordering. It turned out that he knew the owner, though exactly how was not clear. Gerusha could only eat a small section, but it was delicious and cooked to perfection with sautéed onions and mushrooms. She lost count of the martinis and soon her head was spinning out of control while Glen grinned at her and nursed a pint of microbrew through the whole meal. He got directions to an R&B club and soon they were driving on Broadway near the University. Glen gave a black kid twenty bucks to watch the car and soon they were packed into a tiny sardine can club she'd never heard of. The music was pulsating. After staking a claim on a table, Glen pulled her onto the dance floor and started undulating. She was frozen for a moment, it seemed like he could really dance by doing something inexplicable, though with enough grace and confidence that it worked. She shut down the higher functions of her brain and let herself be carried away by the alcohol, the crowd, the music and the night.

When the band went on break, Glen led her back to their table and ordered Baileys and coffee drinks. She noticed he did not let go of her hand and she realized that she was not angry with him anymore, not even slightly.

"You are a man of many talents, I would never have guessed you could dance so well."

"I have many hidden skills, maybe one day you'll be blessed enough to observe them all."

"You are completely full of shit."

"Yes, that's one of my specialties."

"Okay, tell me something nobody knows."

"Well, for example, I wield a mighty righteous blues riff on electric guitar."

"No way."

"It's the gospel word, I hereby testify," Glen said, placing his hand on his heart.

"I don't believe you. Prove it."

A flash of anger sparked across his face, then vanished.

"Very well, but it will cost you. If I blow you away with my guitar work, you'll owe me something."

"What?"

"What do guys usually want? A night of uninhibited sex. Nothing held back and no territory left unexplored."

This sounded like a high price to pay, a night of sex with this old man. But, she could not visualize Glen with a guitar in his mutilated hands, so she decided to call his bluff. He didn't even have enough fingers to do a real chord. Impossible.

"Done," she said.

"Alright," he said. He released her hand and went over to talk to the guitar player. He was enjoying a drink and the company of friends in a corner. She saw money exchange hands as they arrived at some sort of agreement. Immediately, the guitar player got back on stage and started fiddling with his Stratocaster.

"I have a special guest guitarist I'd like to introduce," the singer announced over the PA. "Glen Wilson." The band assembled and Glen shouted out instructions. They started playing a medium tempo blues sequence as Glen manipulated the knobs and switches on the guitar until he heard what he was looking for. With his back to the crowd, he started out slowly, seeking out notes. Then he turned with his eyes closed and started hammering out tones with a look of extreme concentration on his face. He played for a few minutes, slowly increasing the intensity and the frequency of his sputtering strumming. The crowd crammed against the stage urging him on. He started doing his strange dance and his body writhed like a python. Down on his knees, he wrung out anguished notes. The energy was infectious, then Glen began stroking the neck with a mike stand and a beer bottle taken from an onlooker. The song ended with Glen rubbing the guitar on the amplifier and creating a storm of howling feedback. It was one of the most remarkable things Gerusha had ever experienced. He made his way through the crowd, enjoying handshakes and pats on the back. He stood before Gerusha with sweat pouring off his body.

"I win?"

"Yes, Glen, you most certainly win this one, I shall be yours for the night. I never would have guessed you could play."

Seating himself, Glen said with a twisty smile on his face, "Well, I don't know how to play the guitar."

"Excuse me? What do you mean?"

"I know some tricks, that's all. I told the guitarist to tune his guitar to E Minor, then asked the band to play a medium-tempo blues shuffle in A. With that, you can play any kind of interesting looking patterns or hold a finger straight down over the strings and it will all sound alright. Make it look good on stage and you got it licked. See, it's easy, if you have the courage to stand in front of a crowd and try it. A lot of things in life are like that, hard to master but easy to fake for short periods if you have the guts to hang it all out on the line."

Gerusha stared at him and felt like she'd had a glimpse of what his friends saw in this old man with the balls to roll the dice and the fortitude to make the best of the result. *It wasn't magic, but how many men could do it?*

"Let's take this party home," Gerusha whispered into his ear.

The ride back to the apartment was relatively quiet, though her ears were ringing from the assault of the club sound system. Glen turned off the car stereo and they idled through town enjoying the low thunder of the mufflers. In the apartment, Gerusha left all the lights off, but opened the drapes to let the reflected light of the city illuminate the room. She pulled the elastic band from her hair and ran her fingers through as a crude comb. She discarded the blouse and bra and unzipped her jeans. The cool air made her nipples pop out. She held out her arms.

"Alright Glen, do with me what you will."

He gave her a kiss on the cheek. "I didn't mean we're screwing tonight."

"You won the wager. I'm all yours."

"I didn't say when. I'm going to save you for later."

"Bullshit, let's do it now. I'm ready."

Glen shook his head. "You young girls know nothing about men. We don't want what is easy, we want what we may never get. You allow yourselves to be exploited too easily. I'm tired, tonight I will sleep and when I'm ready, then I will collect my winnings."

"What the hell are you talking about? If you don't take me now, then the deal's off and you can fuck your fist for the rest of your life as far as I'm concerned."

"Later," Glen said neutrally.

"You're impossible, you can go straight to hell!" she shouted before running to her room and slamming the door.

Glen smiled as he peeled off his trousers. *Any evening that begins with Oriental curses and ends with angry screaming from a frustrated woman is a memorable and interesting one. I ask for nothing more.*

Still grinning, he pulled up the covers on his makeshift bed and went to sleep.

Truth is Stranger than Fiction, Item 9

NCH Housing Justice Project: Core Principles Guiding Housing Justice Goals and Objectives

- Every member of society, including people experiencing homelessness, has a right to basic economic and social entitlements of which safe, decent, accessible, affordable, and permanent housing is a definitive component.
- It is a societal responsibility to provide safe, decent, accessible, affordable, and permanent housing for all people, including people experiencing homelessness, who are unable to secure such housing through their own means.
- All people, including people experiencing homelessness, who are able to secure safe, decent, accessible, affordable, and permanent housing through their own means need economic and social supports to enable them to do so.
- People experiencing homelessness deserve access to safe, decent, accessible, affordable, and permanent housing through the same systems and programs available to people with housing.
- People experiencing homelessness have unique needs and life circumstances that may be addressed through housing programs designed specifically for them.
- All people should have equal access to safe, decent, accessible, affordable, and permanent housing regardless of their unique needs or life circumstances.
- Universal access to safe, decent, accessible, affordable, and permanent housing is a measure of a truly just society.

- From the National Coalition for the Homeless website, www.nationalhomeless.org

If you want more of something, subsidize it. If you want less of it, tax it.
- Ronald Reagan

CHAPTER TWELVE

Glen and Mary Swanson

Glen stood on the sidewalk in front of the Emerald Hill Retirement Community. The grounds were perfectly maintained and several old ladies sat and gossiped on shady benches. After walking to the nurse's station, "I'm looking for Mary Swanson," he said.

The nurse looked him up and down. She was not impressed by his dirty suit. "You must be the man she talked about meeting. From the Mayor's office?"

"That would be correct," Glen said.

"Alright," the nurse replied as she picked up the phone to call Mary.

Glen watched the hallway, a very old man shuffled along with a walker and rack with IV pouch and oxygen bottle.

"Hey son, you got a cigarette?" he whispered.

"Nah, I quit," Glen said, patting his jacket. He felt a lump in his inside pocket. "How about a stogie?" He held it down so it was out of sight of the nurse.

"Thank God for fine men like you," the old man whispered gratefully.

Glen saw an old woman, wearing orthopedic sneakers, support stockings and a mid-calf yellow muumuu, stride forcefully down the corridor toward him.

"You must be Mary Swanson. I'm Glen Wilson."

"I'm pleased to meet you, Mr. Wilson. Please step into our foyer where we can talk privately." Glen followed her into a small room which held a radio and a chess set. "If you don't mind me saying, you don't look like you work for the Mayor."

"It's not a direct relationship, I'm a subcontractor of sorts." He slowly and carefully went over the gist of his plan.

"Sounds dangerous," Mary said after rocking in her chair and thinking for a few minutes.

"I don't mean to be offensive, but what have you got to lose? At this stage of your life, there's a choice between dying quietly in front of the TV or going out in a blaze of glory in service to your city. You may not like your options, but you can take that issue up with your God, not with me."

"I think we'll need a catchy name."

"Guardian Grannies? How about the Granny Gang?"

"The Granny Gang? That's insipid. We'll call ourselves the Gray Brigade and to the blazes with you if you don't like it."

Glen held out his mutilated claw to shake on the deal. Mary extended her skeletal hand and Glen shook it gently. "I'll gather the weapons and schedule a training session, we'll see how it goes."

"Very well," Mary replied.

Gerusha Andersen

After sleepwalking to work, Gerusha found herself at her desk. Checking her clock, she was surprised to note that, running on auto-pilot, she caught the bus and arrived on time. She knew nothing about the state of her hair and makeup and was afraid to find out if her blouse matched her skirt. She was tired, but inexplicably, not as hung-over and headachy as she should be. Her only concern was making it to 4:30 to drag herself home for a shower and a nap. The sales people had better be nice today or they would taste her wrath. Startled by a tap on her shoulder, she looked up. Tanya looked pert and carefully groomed and Gerusha choked back an instinctive jealousy.

"Hey Tanya, good morning to you, I think."

"Late one last night? Tie one on?"

"Yeah, I danced the night away and had a few too many martinis. What's up?"

"I'm here to spell you, Jeannette wants to see you in her office."

Uh-oh, my bosses' boss, this can't be good, she thought.

She stood and smoothed her skirt. It was neutral beige and matched up fine with her peach blouse. *I have good fashion sense even when I'm unconscious. That skill should be useful somewhere around town.* She felt detached from her body. For some reason, the half-expected summons did not upset her, whatever would be, then so it would be. She'd make it somehow.

Impulsively, she gave Tanya a hug.

"If I get fired, well, it was great working with you."

Tanya teared up. "Don't talk like that, everyone knows you're the best when it comes to dealing with the sales creeps that come in the front door." The loud click echoed in the lobby. "Oh shit, here they come," Tanya said. She settled behind the reception station and took a deep breath. Gerusha watched as Tanya greeted the first visitor.

"Good morning, sir. How may I help you?"

"I understand that the co-founder, Mr. Wilson is visiting? Would you check and see if he will see me for a few minutes, please?"

Tanya gave a little wave to Gerusha who could not hide a slight smile.

"Do you have an appointment, sir?" Tanya asked politely.

Gerusha walked through the building. It was early, so most of the engineers had not arrived yet, they usually rode in on their roller blades, mountain bikes and Segway machines starting about 10:00 or so. A few tousled heads, wearing headphones, bobbed in front of their workstations, but they concentrated on their screens and did not notice Gerusha as she walked by. This might be her last stroll through the building, so she wanted to remember all of it, the ethnic smells escaping the microwave oven, the tinkle of music seeping through tiny earbud headphones and the tiny Japanese girl sleeping in her cubicle clutching a precious Hello Kitty stuffed doll. She eventually made her way to Jeannette's office. Jeannette poked listlessly at keyboard keys with an index finger. She looked tired.

"Pull the door closed behind you, will you, Gerusha? I'm goddam exhausted, management runs around spending money like there's no tomorrow and we worker bees have to save their asses and ensure productive work gets done around here to deliver milestones close to the schedule we promised the investors. But, not your problem, am I right?"

"Do I collect unemployment checks if I get fired?"

"What are you talking about? We don't have time to worry about minutiae like that. After the IPO we can chat about counterproductive government services, okay? Here, I had these printed up at an overnight printer, what do you think?"

She passed over a box of embossed business cards. Gerusha looked at one.

Gerusha Andersen
Director of Vendor Relations

"What's this?"

"You've been assigned a new job. If you don't like the title, then pick another and print new cards. Your office is five doors down the hall and you have a window, but it overlooks the parking garage, too bad for you. Basically, we've been overrun by equipment and service vendors and we can't afford to consume engineering or senior management's time in sorting them out. Vendors have stuff we need, but it's too much effort to filter them. The receptionist will turn away everyone she can, but your job will be company gatekeeper. All vendors will see you before they get an audience with anyone else and you'll act as a second level of screening. If they can get by you, then maybe they have something worthy of higher-level attention. Got it? Let too many through and you're fired. Scare away the ones we need and you're fired. Life's tough, eh?"

"I think I understand what you're saying. But how am I supposed to know what we need around here?"

"That's your job, figure it out. We'll send an all-company email around. People with requirements can route specifications to you to create a database or just scribble them on a white board. I don't give a shit how you do it, as long as you don't bother me. I'm completely slammed and I don't have time to babysit you, nothing personal. Any further questions? I didn't think so. There's no furniture in your office, so go buy something, but don't go crazy, we're on a tight budget. You have signature authority up to five thousand dollars, but between you and me, no one around here has any time to argue, you could probably go up the 25 grand and get away with it. Use your best professional judgment, but no hinky stuff, all right? There should be a cell phone in your office, check with the IT department if the damn thing doesn't work. Oh, here's the HR paperwork, we didn't know what to pay you, so we picked a number. If you don't like it, you can argue with HR during review time. Sign by the X's and drop them in company mail, we'll pay retroactively, but it will take a couple of weeks for payroll to catch up. No whining, I don't want to hear it. Why are you hanging out here? You must have a ton of work, please close the door behind you, thanks ever so much, dear."

Dazed, Gerusha walked to her new office. As described, it held no furniture and the parking garage dominated the westward view, but, she could see silvery slivers of rippling Puget Sound through an emerald patch of evergreens. She had no time to admire the scene, her new cell phone sat in the middle of the floor, bleeping and vibrating with urgency.

CHAPTER THIRTEEN

Gerusha Andersen

Through her doorway, Gerusha could see a wall clock across the work area and realized that she'd been standing and fielding calls on her new cell phone for an hour. She poked her head into Toni Painter's next-door office and got her attention.

"Excuse me, Ms. Painter, I'm your new neighbor, could I please borrow your guest's chair until my furniture arrives? I have nothing."

Toni put her hand over the receiver of her phone and leaned over her desk to shake Gerusha's hand. "I heard you'd be starting soon, congratulations on your promotion. Nothing personal, but if you touch my furniture, I'll tear off your head and tinkle down your neck. It's hard to get necessities around here." She motioned at the phone. "Nice to see you, but if you'll excuse me, I'm slammed…"

Gerusha raised her hands in surrender and escaped back to her office. She had exactly one business card in her handbag, Paul Butler's, the Wavefront sales rep. She decided to call him.

"Hello Paul, I don't know if you remember me…"

"Hi Gerusha, of course I remember you, congratulations on your promotion."

"How did you know? I just found out myself."

"I heard it through rumor central. Things are going well with my proposal to supply Immortality with optical storage equipment, I owe you one for letting me talk with Bennie."

"Well, I could use help right now. I have an office with no furniture, not even a damn stapler or chair to sit on. I can sign a purchase order up to five grand."

"Cherry, oak or walnut?"

"Excuse me?"

"Do you have a preference for wood or style? Most people at Immortality are going with oak in a traditional style. Plywood, not the cheap pressboard stuff. I know people, I can put a package together, charge it to my credit card and invoice you."

"Sure, oak is fine. Can I get this stuff in the next few days? I'm going nuts sitting on the floor."

"You're a funny girl. Don't worry about a thing, I will take care of it. I can get you a wireless connection using a directional antenna pointed at the Starbucks Wifi server down the street, that will get you online until I-T gets you on your company's VPN. Let me make a few calls and I'll get back with you, fair enough?"

"Sure, I guess," Gerusha replied. Walter appeared in her doorway. Nervously, Gerusha pushed the terminate button on her phone. "Hello Walter."

"Congratulations on your promotion."

"I owe you a huge thank you, I suppose."

"Ha! We'll see. Besides, I didn't have much to do with it, I didn't veto the idea when it crossed my desk, that's all."

"Okay." Her phone was bleeping. She pressed the button to make the call go directly to voicemail.

"I can see you're busy. I sent you an email about selecting chemical and pharmaceutical vendors. I'd appreciate it if you'd give that your highest priority. We have a quote package to put on the street, but I don't want to mess with more than a couple of key vendors. You know the drill."

"I don't have a PC to get email yet."

Walter laughed heartily. "You were selected because the management team believes you are a woman who can get things done. I suppose we'll find out the truth of that hypothesis soon. About my vendor selection, I know you're going to have many first priorities, I'm counting on you to put mine on the top of the list. Don't disappoint me." With that, he winked at her and strolled quickly away.

She turned off the cell phone, closed her office door and sat in the corner of her office with her back against the wall. Overwhelmed, she felt like crying. She'd nervously rolled the HR paperwork into a solid cylinder. Flattening the roll, she signed the areas marked. Through watery eyes, she thought she was taking a huge pay cut, from 30 grand to 12, but her mind slipped a decimal place. She was getting almost four times as much and the package included stock grants vesting over a four year period with a bonus program. *If I survive long enough, I'm going to make great money.* She didn't read all the details, she just signed. After a knock on her door, a young man poked in his head. He looked nervous and jittery.

"I'm sorry to bother you, Miss Andersen, but we're trying to reach you on your cell phone. There is a truck at the back loading dock, we need you to come down and sign for a delivery."

"What is it?"

"I don't know, a bunch of stuff. Mostly furniture, I think. The truck is in the way and holding up our parcel service shipments, could you come down right away please?"

On impulse, she held out her hand. He courteously offered his hand. He seemed like a nice young man and wasn't blatant about looking up her skirt while helping her stand. Following him to the back of the building, they took the freight elevator to the receiving area, and then led the moving crew back to her office. Within fifteen minutes, her furniture was arranged and a technician was booting and configuring a rented tablet PC. Thoughtfully, Paul sent over a large framed photograph of the Seattle waterfront to hang on the wall and a vase filled with dried daisies and ferns for her desk. She scribbled on the paperwork and soon sat in her new leather chair and checked her email with the wireless connection on the PC. She had 17 emails from vendors congratulating her on her promotion and asking for appointments to stop by for short introductory visits. She opened Walter's incoming email and scanned the list of supplies he was looking for.

Toni, from next door, poked her head in. "How'd you get all this stuff so fast? I had to wait a week for my furniture to arrive."

"I called in a favor," Gerusha replied.

"Look, I hate to ask after being rude this morning, but can I borrow your tape dispenser?"

"No," Gerusha said firmly, "and scat, I'm buried."

Glen

Glen admired the fine threadwork of the Emerald Hills Retirement Community Corridor C 9-11 memorial quilt. The ladies brought their quilt to the empty warehouse that Glen rented for their training session.

"Very beautiful work, ladies," he said. They beamed and jostled among themselves to serve him tea and almond cookies. "I'd like to introduce you to my associate, Red." Red was busy stuffing cookies in the pockets of his grimy jean jacket. "Stand by the wall, would you please, Red." To the ladies he said, "Red is being paid to help me demonstrate equipment I think you will appreciate. Okay Red, please walk toward me."

Red pushed off the wall and ambled toward them. Glen pulled a canister-on-a-handle from his bag. He aimed it at Red's feet and pulled the trigger. There were two loud pops in quick succession. A pair of rubber bullets, with a webbing stretched between them, tangled around Red's feet and he went down in a heap. "Ow, that hurt," he said.

Glen pulled a box cutter out of his pocket and cut the cords so Red could regain his feet. He handed Red a ten dollar bill. "A deal is a deal, so shut up. Walk away until I say stop, then come back." Red, rubbing his shoulder, did as instructed.

"Now watch carefully, ladies, here's how this works from a longer distance." He fired at a distance of about 35 feet and the webbing between the rubber billets expanded into a spider-like web. Red did not fall down right away, but his arms were wrapped tightly around his body. He lost his balance and toppled over. Glen walked up, cut off the webbing and handed him another ten dollar bill. Red sat on the floor and pressed his hands to his head.

"I hit my head," he complained.

"Shut up and be a man," Glen responded. He helped Red to his feet. "Now stand there." Glen walked over to his backpack and pulled out another canister weapon. He fired at Red's feet. A white glop popped out of the barrel and spread out over Red's left foot.

"See if you can break it," Glen suggested.

"I'm stuck," Red shouted. His foot was glued to the floor.

Glen got an aerosol can from his bag and sprayed it on the glop. After a few moments, Red was able to unstick his foot from the floor. Glen handed him another 10 dollar bill. "The aerosol dissolves the glue, otherwise it is tough and strong. It will stop a bear. Now stand by the wall and lift your hand like you have a gun," he ordered.

Glen aimed and fired, this time the glop hit Red's hand and glued it to the wall. "This stuff is hot, it's burning me," he said.

"Good," Glen replied. "Now ladies, I want you to divide into pairs. We're going to have glob gals and bologun gals. Don't fight. Let's get good practice in and make sure Red gets his ten bucks for each lesson."

"You didn't tell me it would hurt this bad."

"You should have stayed in San Francisco, so clam up."

Glen sat down with Mary and they watched the ladies shoot glop and trip Red with the bolo guns. They started out rough, but slowly their aim and technique improved. Red looked more and more unhappy with purple bruises appearing on his face and wearing plaster-like gobs of glue all over. The warehouse was becoming a real mess with left-over webbing and glue splattered on the floor and walls.

Glen handed Mary a cell phone. "We're going to use these direct-connect walkie-talkie phones to call in backup. The ladies are going to come across gangs too large for a pair to handle. When the call goes out, Code Red, everyone converges to get the scene under control."

"I like it. Can we get t-shirts printed up? Maybe a beret, like that vigilante guy from New York?"

"Sure, no problem," Glen laughed. "Can I leave it to you to gather and train the ladies from Corridors A, B and D?"

"Absolutely, I'd love to," Mary replied.

Glen stood by a stoplight near the James Street on-ramp. He'd made his own cardboard sign, it said 'Vietnam Vet, Stranded, need gas for car. Will work, anything will help, God Bless.' Not sure how the punctuation for a sign like this should work, he did the best he could. He wanted to experience the panhandling scheme for himself. Most of the drivers would not make eye contact and pretended he did not exist. Some of the drivers were scary, their eyes bored into him and their lips moved with curses and threats. However, it was busy intersection and a few kind souls offered a dollar or two and Glen pulled in 11 dollars in just over an hour. It wasn't much, but it was a lot more than he would make running a burger machine at a fast food joint. He didn't have to punch a clock, shave or clean himself up. All in all, with the fringe benefits of tax-free income and with no expenses like laundry or soap, it was a good gig. He was approached by a competitor.

"Hey man, this is my corner, get the fuck out of here."

"Chill man, I'm working here, let me see your sign." It said 'Vietnam Vet, three hungry kids, will work for food, God bless you'. "Not bad," Glen commented. "The kid thing is good, I didn't think of that."

"Hugh is going to fuck you up. This is my corner."

"Who is this Hugh? Are you saying someone assigns you guys to a location?"

"You can see for yourself, here he comes."

Glen turned and saw three men get out of a Black Chevy Tahoe parked in the lot under I-5. Two of the men were large and dressed in leather jackets. The obvious leader was a small Hispanic man with a razor-trimmed goatee and tiny sunglasses. His shoes were black and polished to a mirror finish. All three moved with muscle-bound tightness which only came from daily gym workouts.

"Hey Tommy," the leader said as they exchanged a complicated handshake. "How are you doing out here?"

"Hello, Hugh. This guy is gypping my spot."

Glen held out his hand for a shake. "I'm Glen Wilson and I'm pleased to meet you."

Hugh looked at his hand with an amused interest until Glen withdrew it.

"We get funny guys like you coming through town all the time. You think you can make yourself a sign and stand on any corner you want, but that's not the way things happen around here. That would be chaos and chaos is inefficient. I'm going to go easy on you because I'm in a good mood today. I will assign you a corner. We meet in Denny Park as dusk, pool the money and I get my cut and the rest gets divided up. You'll work at least 8 hours on your corner and if you hold out any of the money, I will know about it and you'll get disciplined. Until I know you, you will work the AM/PM parking lot down by the old Sears store. It's a shitty location, I know and I don't want to hear about it. You'll get your cut from the pool so don't sweat it. Now, do you understand the business? Are you going to irritate me by asking any annoying questions?" He cupped Glen's chin in his hand and stared into his eyes. He sucked on his teeth. "I've seen you around. Are you the wristband man?"

"That's me," Glen replied, staring deeply into Hugh's eyes.

"What is your game? Some of my best canvassers got on the bus. I don't like people messing with my business. I'm going to give you the benefit of the doubt. You didn't know I run things around here. I get my cut and the people I work for get their cut. Everybody makes out. Are you stupid? Can you follow the layout?"

Glen did feel stupid. He didn't figure the streets would be run by organized crime. No money-making scheme exists without someone pulling the strings and taking a cut. This was fundamental physics and Glen should have known. Now he was sure he'd get the crap beat out of him by these goons.

"I get it," he said.

"I don't care for the look in your eyes, but I'm going easy on you. Knock it off with the bus stuff, it's too much trouble training new people all the time. I'm not going to tell you twice."

He motioned for his associates to take Glen. They dragged him into a dark area between two huge concrete pillars that held up the freeway. They took turns holding him while they pulled on black leather gloves. They didn't unleash everything on him, but did batter him, face and body, until he could not stand.

Hugh walked over and threw Glen's sign at him. He lifted Glen's bloody chin. "This sign is not bad, you are approved to use it. Stay at the AM/PM station until I promote you to a better location. And don't forget to bring your cash to Denny Park."

They walked back to their SUV. Glen sat up with his back against the pillar and did an inventory. He was bleeding and had a loose tooth, otherwise he seemed to be in one piece. He'd gotten off easy, he knew it and he was thankful.

"Stupidity should always be this painful, then perhaps there'd be less of it, he thought. *They could have killed me and left me here and no one would care or find my body for a few days until it started stinking too much to ignore. To get this job done, I'm going to have to declare war. Not today, but soon. Blood will have to flow. If it was easy to make these streets safe and secure, then the cops and the social workers, with their huge budgets and unlimited manpower, could do it. This is not the part I was looking forward to, but I knew it would come to this. Why do I get myself into these tough spots? The time share gig was comfortable and safe, I could be back in Florida drinking beer and watching the hurricanes come and go.*

He struggled to his feet and stood for a while until his vision cleared. He didn't feel any broken ribs grinding, but decided to get an X-ray to be sure. Finding himself clutching his sign, he tossed it away with disgust, then walked up the hill toward Harborview hospital. The panhandler, working his freeway onramp, pointed at him and cackled.

The Harborview Emergency Room was not busy, so Glen only had to wait a few hours before a harried doctor would see him. He poked and prodded and clucked at Glen's bruises and wrapped tape and cotton batting around his chest.

"You'll live," he declared confidently. "I'm not going to prescribe you any painkillers, so don't ask. Aspirin is all you're getting."

A cop poked his head into the examining room. "Did you get a good look at the perps? Do you want to fill out a report?"

"I didn't see anything."

"The cop shrugged. "Suit yourself," he said. "I get paid the same either way."

Glen walked downhill toward his car. He felt a little better, but was moving gingerly because his body was throbbing and tender. On Second Avenue, Half-size Lucy talked to a man leaning against the wall of God's Infinite Love Mission. Glen wanted to get his car out of the parking garage and didn't want to talk to anyone, but was moving slowly. They caught up with him.

"Shit Glen, what happened to you?" Lucy asked.

"I fell down. I'll be okay once the aspirin kicks in."

"Wait a minute. My friend, Peter Harris, wants to meet you."

"That's right, I've been hearing a lot about you. I run God's Infinite Love Mission on Pike Street," Peter said.

"That's grand. I'm sure you do plenty of good work there. Now, if you'll excuse me, I need to go home and rest my fractures."

"I won't take much of your time, sir." Peter licked his lips and looked uncomfortable and nervous. "Your busses are starting to have an effect. We are not running a business, but our funding depends on how many we feed and house. We're already running on a shoestring. All the care providers and missions are talking about this, if this keeps up, we'll have to close down."

Glen was impatient. "And this is my problem how?"

"I guess it's not your problem if you don't care about the homeless."

"Well, you nailed that one. I *don't* care about the lowlife scum that infest these streets like vermin. I have a job to do too, and if you don't like it, you can take your case to the Mayor. I took this job and I will see it through to the end if it kills me. Now get out of my face."

Glen pushed Peter aside, walked into the parking garage and slowly climbed the stairs toward his car. He opened the door and fell into the plush seats with relief. The soft vinyl was a comfort to his aching body. He sat for twenty minutes until his breathing and heart rate settled. *Heaven,* he thought. *Blessed sanctuary.*

CHAPTER FOURTEEN

The Bus Driver – Part Two, the Last Run of Bluebird Bus 17

My girlfriend didn't understand why I was willing to give up the Greyhound job to drive a bus for Wilson. I shouldn't worry about her so much, after all, she stuck with me when I was busted for possession with intent to traffic. Fortunately, my lawyer got lucky and I skated. No conviction and nothing on my record. She stayed after I dropped out of college. I'm not sure what use an English major is in the hard world anyway, but she was right, I should have pulled those 11 credits and got the official paper. She put up with the string of jobs that never seem to quite cover the rent. Convenience store clerk, a hot-sheet motel desk clerk and taxi driver. What a resume. From all that, the Greyhound job was a real step up, it even had benefits like a health insurance plan and 401k retirement fund matching. I didn't have the guts to tell her I'd been selected for a random drug test that I was certain to fail; marijuana stays in the piss for a long time, or so I've been told. I was bored with driving gray-heads and their insulated buckets of cola and paper bags filled with bologna sandwiches and Cheese Nips. A man can only take so much.

I'd like to say something about my first impression of Wilson. He wasn't much to look at, his clothes were old; more ragged and smelling worse than many of the bums he asked me to drive. Still, there was something about him, the power of his will, the fierce intensity of his eyes if you ever received his full attention. Of course, there was the ease with which he peeled money out of his sport bag from bundles that seemed like they would never end. He had cash to make things happen, there's no discounting that aspect of things. Perhaps I should have popped him upside the head and absconded with his bag, but I didn't.

The first charter bum-run to San Francisco was an ordeal. Mainly the smell. Wilson paid me to skip the first few rest stops, and I did, but I had to stop eventually and some of the bums got off in Eugene. I had about half a load when I got to San Francisco and then I had to kick a few to rouse them and get them out. I felt sorry for the detailing crew, the bus was gross with vomit, piss and even a few turds left behind. These bums lived like wild animals.

When I got back to town, I stopped at home, gave my girlfriend some of the money and screwed her a couple of times. She cooked me fried chicken, which was really good. Sex, greasy food and beer, life doesn't get better than that. But, Wilson gave me a job and I was determined to do it. There's a truck lot near the freeway by Tacoma, I stopped in there and looked around at the surplus busses. I was surprised how low the dealer came down when I flashed cash, must not be a huge market for these tired old Bluebirds. This bus had relatively low mileage, just over 100K and the diesel engine seemed solid enough. It sounded like a coffee can full of rusty bolts in a clothes dryer, but all diesels sound like that to me. I took it to a friend, an ex-biker junkie that had a chop shop in a seedy section of town off of Martin Luther King Way. I'd learned a few things from my bum-run to San Francisco to add to the modifications that Wilson suggested. This run was going to be fully self contained. We put a pair of porta-potties in the back and built up a cage system that would lock the bums in. All the windows were locked open about six inches, enough to keep the air flowing, but closed enough to keep any of the livestock from escaping. I was proud of my mechanic friend, he had too many scars and tattoos to ever get a good job at one of the car dealers, but he wielded the welding torch like an artist. We almost tripled the fuel capacity with huge tanks in the rear and installed a motorbike rack. The cockpit area was decked out nice, we outfitted a refrigerator and a mesh barrier to keep the bums off me. I'd have to trust one of the more reliable passengers to do some driving or take a break at some point along the way, otherwise, it would be smooth sailing. I stuffed the refrigerator with malt liquor and ham sandwiches, staples for a long road trip.

We loaded up the bus. Glen shoved them in like cattle, they were happy to take his money and the beer he handed out. We had a full load of 27 bums, mostly men, but there were a couple of women and a couple that were bundled up in rags so completely that it was impossible to tell. Not that it mattered. Finally we were ready to go and Glen gave me my money. I have to hand it to him, he didn't try to short me; he paid up promptly for the bus, the repairs, the modifications and my fee. I was eager to get rolling, I really like going. You can never leave your troubles behind, but it always seems worth trying. The bums started out very quiet, I drove all through the afternoon and most of the night before I stopped at a rest stop near Yreka, just across the border in California, to catch a bit of sleep. After a couple of hours of rest, I was good to go again.

The border crossing we picked was in New Mexico, and the route was a bit circuitous. I-5 to Bakersfield, where we turned East on 58 to Barstow. We passed a lot of signs pointing toward Las Vegas. The bums were up at this point and raised hell about stopping, but there was no way. These guys had money in their pockets and the dream of Vegas exerted a magnetic pull on their cash and their souls. I had to bat at their grasping hands with the billy club before they settled back down. I didn't want to break any more arms than necessary, but they needed to learn that trying to grab me through the mesh of the cage would be painful. We took Route 66 through the endless desert of Kingman and Flagstaff. For several hours in the Arizona desert, they cursed and threw empty liquor cans at me. They were used to sleeping through the hottest parts of the day, soon they were either napping or glaring at me with impotent murderous intent. The miles melted away steadily and seemed to stretch into infinity. I installed a good satellite radio and could tune in talk radio and religious stations along the way, this helped pass the time. We turned South on 17 and caught 10 at Phoenix and passed through Tucson. Nogales would have been a natural place to try to cross, but apparently Glen had a bad time there once, so we continued on to Deming, then South on a pot-holed and narrow strip of pavement called Highway 11. We arrived in Columbus ahead of schedule, so I found a grove of trees and parked the bus in the shade and we waited. Glen suggested I cross a half-hour before the border guard shift change, the Federales would be tired and ready to make a last bit of money before getting off work. Glen seemed to know what he was talking about; I wasn't going to argue, so we waited. The bums pissed and moaned, but I put on my headphones and ignored them.

We were waved through the American side without a sideways look. Getting out of the USA is no problem, if there would be any hitch, it would be getting into Mexico. The bored-looking border guards didn't miss anything, they certainly noticed the bums locked up like third-world prisoners. We quickly arrived at an understanding with them. A group of four walked around the bus and pointed out safety violations like the tire with a nearly-shredded recap (each got a hundred dollar bill), a broken lens on a tail light (worth another hundred dollar bill) and cracks on the windshield (more hundred dollar bills). I expressed my impatience when they started nit-picking, I grumbled at them when they hovered around a dribble of sewage that leaked out of the back. I handed out the last of my bills and showed them my empty wallet. They weren't convinced this was the end of my generosity and I showed them my empty pockets. They chattered among themselves for ten minutes, all the while looking at me expectantly, until finally, as the evening crew pulled into the parking lot in their shiny Chevy pickups, they waved me on. The next shift was gathering. I admired the timing of Glen's plan, it was perfect. No way were the afternoon amigos going to share their new-found wealth with the evening amigos. Soon we trundled southward through Las Palomas down a bumpy Mexican highway that linked up with Highway 2. The bus huffed and puffed as we skirted the Continental Divide, we slowed to 35 or so on the upgrades and observed a rude middle finger or two when Nissan dusty pickup trucks were finally able to pass.

I didn't think our fuel would take us to Nuevo Casas Grandes, but we rolled through as smoothly as you please. The bus sputtered for the first time near Buenaventura and stalled completely about 10 miles further down the road. The landscape was rough and dry, but I managed to get well off the road and parked in a dry creek bed. It was hot and quiet, siesta time. I unlocked the Honda 90 motor bike and wrestled it to the gravel roadway. I walked around the bus and shot out the tires with my .32 revolver; it settled onto its rims like a defeated prizefighter. The bums were screaming at me and rocking the bus on its springs. They had enough water to last a week and would eventually find something to break out a window with. Most would probably survive, but Glen was right, it seemed very remote that any of them would find their way back to Seattle from this god-forsaken stretch of Mexican wasteland. The Honda motorbike started right up and soon I was putt-putting away. Via con Dios, amigos.

Truth is Stranger than Fiction, Item 10

Most of the current prescriptive literature has focused on community-oriented tactics. Some have recommended that the police stop trying to eradicate gangs and that they communicate with gang youths in such a way as to demonstrate respect, acceptance, and concern for gang youths (Spergel 1995). The literature has also concluded that law enforcement alone cannot solve the gang problem—in fact, the typical police organization is ill-equipped and poorly structured to deal with gangs (Rush 1996). Dealing with gangs requires a comprehensive approach that involves all members of the criminal justice community, schools, community leaders, and the like (Owens and Wells 1993; Rush 1996). A fundamental problem with all of the aforementioned strategies, but especially the latter, has been the lack of reliable, well-documented, well-designed, empirical evaluations of the strategies and tactics employed (Klein 1993, 1995; Knox 1994; Spergel 1995). In fact, some of the evaluations of the tactics have been gleaned from newspapers (Freed 1986).

From: Gang Suppression Through Saturation Patrol, Aggressive Curfew, and Truancy Enforcement: A Quasi-Experimental Test of the Dallas Anti-Gang Initiative

From a report commissioned by the Dallas Police Department by: Eric J. Fritsch, Tory J. Caeti and Robert W. Taylor, 1996

CHAPTER FIFTEEN

The Powers that Be

Willie Thomas stood and shook Steve Stephen's huge hand. He gestured for Steve to seat himself.

"Hello Steve. How have you been? Is the DEA treating you well and keeping you busy?"

"Yes sir, There's black tar heroin from Afghanistan coming through, we're trying to stem the flood. Never a dull moment. The stronger the laws and the more we increase enforcement efforts, the dope gets stronger and importers get more creative. Sometimes I despair that we'll ever win this thing."

"Well, don't lose faith, we here in DC appreciate your efforts. To get to the reason I called you, I have a team in Seattle keeping an eye on your friend, Glen Wilson."

"What is he doing in Seattle?"

"We're not exactly sure. He's not doing much with his friends at that Immortality company. The treatment they came up with looks good. I may dig up the money and take advantage of it myself," he said, chuckling. "Give the old body a well-deserved tune-up. Anyway, to get back to our point, the Mayor is having a meltdown and Glen's doing something with the bums and street people. We don't understand it and don't care to. I have pictures you might enjoy."

He passed over a manila folder. Steve pulled out a bundle of 8X11 color prints. The first one showed Glen standing on the street with a cardboard sign.

"He's panhandling?" Steve asked, mystified.

"Apparently," Willie replied.

The next picture showed Glen playing guitar under colored lights on a small stage.

"I didn't know he played guitar."

"Blues. The agent said he was great, a crowd-pleaser."

The next picture showed a blond woman sitting at an expensive-looking reception desk. Willie leaned over to look. "That's his girlfriend."

"She's a knock-out."

"Isn't she though? Glen's a lucky guy. I think you'll enjoy the next series. The lighting was poor under the freeway, but we have low-light digital cameras."

The pictures series showed two large men beating Glen and leaving him slumped against a concrete pillar.

"They beat the crap out of him?"

"The medical record shows cracked ribs and a lot of bruises. The thugs were delivering a message, not laying him out. He'd be dead if they were serious."

"Who did he get crosswise with?"

"The local panhandler mafia." Willie's voice hardened. "We've spent serious money watching this clown run around the streets of Seattle. Everything I see makes me think we're wasting our time."

"I understand." Steve passed one of the pictures back to Willie. It was a close-up of Glen's face as he lay slumped and bleeding against the pillar. "See the look in his eyes?"

"Sure. He has a manic intensity."

"I've seen that look before. It means there's going to be trouble."

"With all due respect, Steve, this Wilson is a joke. He can't even keep himself from being thrashed by low-budget Seattle goons. I appreciate your coming to see me about him and we took a look, but I'm pulling the plug on the surveillance. We've wasted enough time and money on this dork."

"I'd like to register my objection. Stay on him for a while longer."

"Please, Steve. Enough is enough. We have terrorists we're tracking and other important work in Homeland Security. I can't justify spending another penny on this guy."

Steve sighed. "Okay. I tried. Do you mind if I keep this picture?"

"Sure," Willie replied, "no problem."

Steve stood and took a last look at the photograph. "Powderkeg," he mumbled.

"No. Loser with a capital 'L'," Willie commented. "My advice is: don't worry another minute about him."

Gerusha Andersen

Gerusha could not keep up with the phone calls. Her voice mailbox reported 19 messages. To escape, she walked out the back door and caught the first Metro bus that came by. It crossed the Fremont bridge and weaved through the downtown shopping district. On impulse, she got off near the flagship Nordstrom's store and window-shopped. She liked an outfit with a satin miniskirt and orange top decorated with an abstract and out-of-focus swirly pattern. The handbag and shoes were also cute. She walked toward the next window display, then stopped, suddenly understanding she could buy the outfit if she wanted. Even if the price tags added up to more than a thousand dollars, it was no problem. Then she realized she was too bone-weary and tired to make the purchase, an oppressive and overwhelming thought. She sat at a bus stop bench feeling sorry for herself as she watched the ebb and flow of the crowd. For an instant, across the busy street, she thought she saw Glen limp by and turn a corner. It couldn't be him because he was looking more ragged than usual and his face was covered with bruises and a white strip of bandage. Her cell phone chirped and she looked at the number, it was not one she recognized. She had not told many people the number, but it was printed on her new business cards.

"Good afternoon, this is Gerusha," she said.

"I hope you don't mind me calling on your cell phone, this is Jim Walker, I got your number from Marcia Clemons. Do you have a few minutes to chat?"

No! she thought. "Sure, what's on your mind?" she asked.

"I'd appreciate it if you could fit me into your schedule for a few minutes for a meeting with you and Mr. Crowley. I have information on a new automated spectroscope system that I'm sure he'd be excited to learn about."

I'm sure you do. "Send your brochures to my attention and I'll take a look at them."

"I sent a package last week, but I'll be happy to send it again if it did not make it to your desk."

"Yes, that would be the best thing. Have a great day, Mr. Walker."

She pressed the call-end key and turned off the phone, then dropped it back into her purse. Now all calls would be forwarded to voice mail so she could filter through them at her convenience. Sighing, she looked over at the Nordstrom's window display one last time before getting on the bus and making her way back to work.

Mayor Harry Silverberg

Harry spent a lot of time in the private exercise facility in the City Municipal Building. He watched a Mel Gibson movie on a DVD player and worked his legs on a stair climber until he could move them no more. He collapsed onto a weight bench and guzzled deeply from a bottle of spring water. Imagining toxins built up in his body being excreted in his sweat gave him great comfort. He wiped his face with a towel and ambled off toward the showers. After letting cool water pour on his head for nearly a half hour, he felt very nearly human. He dressed in a favorite navy blue suit and tied his necktie over and over until the knot met his precise standard of perfection. He created a sharp part in his hair and combed out his curls. His longish hair and gray roots needed touch-up. He made a mental note to have his executive assistant make a salon appointment. It was time to stop letting his appearance go. He was feeling chipper and energized when he rode the elevator and made the long walk to his office. He was careful to smile and greet the people he passed. His assistant looked frazzled and nervous. When she saw him, she came around his desk and whispered to him.

"I couldn't keep them out of your office, I'm so sorry."

"There's no problem, I'm ready for anything and I feel great."

His assistant looked suspicious. "They're very angry."

He patted her shoulder. "Don't worry about it, I'll see what's going on and deal with it." With that, he strode confidently into his office.

He recognized several city council members and social program activists milling around. His assistant was right, they looked angry. He walked around his desk and stood pointedly waiting until Councilman Spenser insolently got out of his chair. Harry settled behind his desk and waited for the throng to get to their point.

"I didn't see your entry on my calendar. I'm sorry if I kept you waiting, I had business to attend to downstairs."

"We couldn't wait for an appointment, this is urgent," Spenser said heatedly.

"That's fine. Perhaps you can clue me into the objective of your unscheduled visitation."

"You're upsetting our street outreach programs."

"I'm sorry? What is this about?"

"You have a guy on the street named Wilson. He's exporting our clients. We don't allow audits, but we have to have *some* customers for our programs. We have enough trouble justifying our budget increases every year without losing our patrons — our clientel."

Councilperson Meadows interrupted. "Stop it Spenser, we don't want to put things in crude terms." Addressing the Mayor, she said, "We have the utmost sympathy for the regrettable loss of your son, but we have a loose cannon running around our streets and it's derailing the good work we're accomplishing amidst our homeless citizens. If Wilson wants to work with us, then he can join up as a volunteer, observe our due processes, and follow our guidelines and regulations."

"This is no time for niceties! He's putting our disadvantaged citizens on busses and shipping them out of town."

"Let's settle down and dialog this," Harry said calmly. "I wasn't myself for a couple of weeks. I hired Glen Wilson without thinking the situation through completely. Let me assure you, I have made the decision to get rid of him, but I have to work through my options and consider all the ramifications."

"You should have worked with us, how are you paying this guy?"

"As mayor, I have some discretionary funds at my disposal."

"Well, if you're writing checks, we can use help at the Displaced Homemaker Temporary Care Facility over on Pike Street."

"We can use more funding at the Disadvantaged Youth Outreach Center…"

"The staff at the Gay/Lesbian/Bisexual/Transgendered Hispanics Shelter is losing their lease…"

"I understand," Harry said, raising his hand to stop the litany of agencies and programs that were perennially under-funded. "Believe me, I'm well aware of the unmet needs of our community. I'll figure out a way to pull the plug on Wilson and then we can get back to our serious work without his distraction, I promise. Okay?" He pointed his finger at every person in the room in turn. They all nodded sullenly before standing and filing out of the office. The last one to leave, Councilman Spenser, turned.

"If you have any more of those discretionary funds —"

"Just go, okay?"

"This isn't over," Spenser said.

It never is, Harry thought, waving Spenser away with a gesture like shooing a fly. Alone in his quiet office, Harry enjoyed a feeling of physical well-being, probably due to lingering endorphins from his exhausting workout. He analyzed his mood and opinion about Glen's disruption of the street life. He was upsetting the social services community, which was not a completely bad thing. Deciding not to decide, *I think I'll let this play out just a little longer,* he thought dreamily.

Glen

Glen collected an assortment of street people. He lined them up against a brick wall and looked them over, considering their suitability for his test. Three were blacks (two tough-looking men from Detroit, the third was a undocumented alien from Nigeria who spoke haltingly with a heavy accent), one was Salvadoran and the last was a young white who would not stop talking about converting to Islam while in prison. They seemed to mostly have their wits about them. One of the Motor City men was scary; he didn't say much but stared intelligently from under craggy eyebrows. All wore wristbands, which Glen noted with appreciation. Each and every one of them looked capable of gutting a junior high school girl for her latté money. He handed each a hundred dollar bill. "Are there any questions?" he asked.

"Just go in, grab the wigs off two old hags, bring them back and we get a thousand dollars? That's it?" the smart-looking black asked suspiciously. "There's only two of them? There aren't a bunch of cops in there waiting for us?"

"You understand the deal. The younger of the two ladies is 76, the other one says she's 79, but I don't think so. She's 85 or I'm no judge. I have the money right here. Grab the wigs off their heads and the money is yours. A thousand dollars for two minutes work, that's better than a trial lawyer, maybe not much, but you don't have to pass the bar exam."

"Do y'all always talk so fast?" the white guy asked. Glen placed his accent as pure Alabama Crimson Tide.

"Shut up and get going. I'll be here waiting."

The men pushed open a large sliding door and peered into the dim light of the warehouse. Beams of light passed through broken windows and created bright flooded areas in the gloom. Glen settled in a patch of shade to read his tattered paperback novel. His page marker was lost and Glen cursed as he tried to find where he'd left off. It made him grumpy when that happened. Things had been quiet inside the warehouse for a while, so he folded over the page to mark his place and went inside see what was going on.

Blinking in the dusty darkness, he walked around until he saw movement. Two ladies were teasing the southern man by standing just out of reach and crooning Yankee Doodle Dandy with surprisingly pure singing voices. The man was hanging by one arm glued to the wall; his useless feet were entangled with white webbing. One of the black men was writhing on the floor with his face covered by a blob of white epoxy. The other three wriggled like maggots on infested meat, they were wrapped up tightly in cocoons of webbing.

"How did it go?"

"One of the spooks almost snuck up behind us, but we got him before he got too close."

"You can't use the word 'spook' anymore, its racist."

"I don't care, he said he'd, uh, copulate my brains in my eye socket. You heard him, *that* was rude," she said, looking sideways at Glen to see if he'd be offended.

"It was rude, but it wasn't hateful, hate crimes are worse than regular crimes these days."

"Fooking my eye socket seems very hateful to me!" she complained.

"Ladies, there will be plenty of time for social commentary. For now, help me get my money out of their pockets. These fools don't deserve to keep anything."

"Should we cut them loose? They look pretty mad."

"Nah, let them lay here and consider the alternate paths they could have taken to avoid the unpleasant reality that they got their asses kicked by a couple of seasoned citizens."

"Please watch your language, young man."

"What did I say?"

"Asses," Mrs Clemson whispered.

"Oh, asses. I'm quite sorry," Glen laughed. "It won't fooking happen again. Okay, ladies. Here's the way this will work." He pulled out a bundle of gray ribbons. "The Gray Brigade is going to clean up the streets one block at a time. We'll start with the area just north of the stadiums. We'll mark controlled areas with these ribbons and it won't take long to convince the street scum to move on. As we gather women from the other old-folks homes, we'll expand the coverage area. We'll have zero tolerance. Take the creeps down hard and show no mercy. Any questions?"

A lady, leaning on a cane outfitted with four feet for added stability, raised a palsied hand hesitantly. "Shouldn't we wear a uniform?"

"Sure, why not? How about a pink floral-print dress with support hose and white orthopedic shoes? All that would look good with your gray berets."

The ladies talked among themselves and nodded their heads in agreement. Glen clapped his hands. "Okay, you know what to do, now get out there and get to it!"

Glen and Gerusha

Until Glen threw open the door and walked into her living room, Gerusha did not realize that she'd unconsciously eaten a whole pint of Ben and Jerry's Cherry Garcia ice cream while watching a show about spiders on the Discovery Channel. She was horrified.

"You didn't save me any, pig?" Glen accused.

"If I keep eating like this, I'm going to get fat. I don't have as much time to exercise and I'm always hungry. This is not good."

"It's stress. You body feels under attack and tries to lay in fat to prepare for the worst."

She undid the sash of her robe, then, watching Glen forage in the kitchen out of the corner of her eye to make sure he wasn't peeping, pinched some of the skin at her waist to see if there was any sign of flab piling on. She wasn't sure, but it did seem like she was already getting thicker. In the refrigerator, Glen found left-over peas in a plastic bowl, he walked back into the living room spooning the cold vegetables into his mouth.

"That's disgusting."

"I wouldn't have to stoop so low if you'd keep food in the house. Besides, I like canned peas, they're alright."

"I'm too busy to shop, why don't you take time out of your busy schedule doing nothing all day and buy your own damn groceries."

"Oh, touchy, are we? Pre-menstrual?"

"Screw you. How are your bruises? Do you want me to tape up your ribs again?"

"No, I'm fine. What are we watching?"

"Spiders."

"I hate spiders, give me the remote."

"Bullshit. This is my house. If I give you the remote we'll watch five minutes of 20 TV shows and never finish watching anything."

"You're cute when you're mad. How can I take you seriously when you have a dribble of ice cream on your chin like a toddler?" Setting the bowl of peas down, he reached out and rubbed the spot with his thumb. He stuck the thumb in his mouth. "You taste good," he commented. "By the way, you don't have to wear that bathrobe. If you're more comfortable running around here topless, I won't be offended."

"In your dreams. Anyway, I know you, you're trying to distract me so you can grab the remote."

Glen held it up. "I already have it," he said, grinning.

"Its mine, give it back."

"No," Glen said firmly. "You have a lot to learn about watching TV with a man and you can begin your lesson by shutting that pretty mouth."

"Shit," Gerusha complained, giving up. "Pick a program and watch the whole thing, okay?"

"Whatever," he said absently as he scanned through the channels.

The First Night of the Gray Brigade Patrols

The moon was near full and was visible only as a smudge through thick cloud cover. The women started out alert and ready for anything. They examined all pedestrians carefully and with great suspicion. They tied fancy knots in the gray ribbons attached to everything in reach, trees, street signs and telephone poles. A police cruiser happened by and the officer stopped to check them out.

"What are you ladies doing?" the officer asked after running the illumination of her flashlight over them.

"We're the Gray Brigade and we're taking back the streets to make them safe for families."

This caused a minor argument in the group. "I thought we were going to say 'we're striking a blow for decency in the inner city'."

"Too many words. We want to keep things simple."

"Fooey, I'm saying it anyway." To the cop, and using a firm voice, she said: "We're striking a blow for decency in the inner-city neighborhoods."

"It's not safe for you ladies out here."

A crone, leaning heavily on a walker adorned with streaming gray ribbons, said angrily: "If it were up to people like you we'd be rotting away in an old folks home, out of sight and dying useless deaths."

"Ladies, relax. I'm trying to do my job. I'm paid to serve and protect."

"Malarky," a lady scoffed, "go back to the donut shop until your shift is over. We can take care of ourselves."

"There's no need to be rude." To the officer, Mary said: "We're sorry, ma-am, we appreciate your efforts. Thank you for checking on us, but we're fine."

"I'll be on my way then," the officer said before turning back to her car. "Just take care, this can be a rough neighborhood at night, alright?"

"We understand."

The patrol car eased off into the night.

"There's no call for being mean to the police. They do the best they can with what they have. It's a tough enough job without taking flack from the public."

"Ha, the cops don't do nothing, that's why we're out here freezing our kiesters off and taking the law into our own hands."

They were interrupted by a low-rider pickup truck driving slowly past. It stopped and idled with steam emitting from its dual tailpipes.

Transcript, Police Interview with Pedro Gonzales

We were driving around, you know, drinking some beers and smoking pot, minding our own business, you see. We passed a group of old ladies and it looked funny, being late and what-all. Four or five old ladies standing around with these gray ribbons all over the place. I didn't want to stop, but Clarence insisted. What did he say? I don't got nothing to lose, I suppose I can tell you. He'd broken up with his girlfriend and hadn't hooked up with anyone yet, they were fighting about their kids or something, I don't know, I tune that stuff out, its always the same story, why can't we get a regular job and help more with the rent and school clothes, that sort of thing. Anyway, he's thinking that one of the old birds wasn't too fat and not all that old, you follow? He said 'Pull over, let me see if I can get me some of that.' I thought the idea was disgusting, but I can't judge a guy when he ain't getting any at home, I've got up in the morning with skanky old barflies myself, if you want to know the truth. So, we pile out of the car and start talking up these old-timers. The youngest was older than we thought, must have been at least 70. I was ready to call it quit, just get back in the truck and keep rolling, but the ladies were mouthing off. Telling us that the streets were not for vermin like us. I'm not sure what a vermin is exactly, like a rat or something? We can't be taking stuff like that off anyone if we want to have respect on the street, so we needed to shut them up and teach them to mind their manners. That's when they pulled these weird-looking cannons out of their bags and started shooting. It was this sticky stuff, once it was on you, it wouldn't come loose, it stuck us to the sidewalk and bound us all up. They were talking into their phones and next thing we know there are more of these old folks, 10 or 15, I don't know how many.

I couldn't reach my Mac-10, which was back in the truck, but I had a snubby .38 in an ankle holster. I wasn't planning to shoot anyone with it, just get their attention, know what I mean? Make them let us loose, that's all. Things were getting out of hand, I told you we'd been drinking, right? Maybe I wasn't thinking things through all the way. Did they think I carried a gun for fun? If you disrespect and embarrass a man, you gotta know things will get ugly. I admit it, I shot one of them. It was a mistake, I know that now, but I did it. I wasn't really scared until then. I expected they'd run off. They had to know I'd have five more shots and I was prepared to throw down. But they didn't run off, the next thing I know, the old bat I shot is blowing air bubbles out her chest and my hand is being burned by this hot goopy stuff. I can't move a muscle, I'm stuck, you see. And the ladies are arguing, some wanted to shoot the goop in my face and strangle me and some wanted to leave me and let the cops sort things out. Then the leader, I'll never forget her wrinkled old mug, she steps up with this funny looking little gun. 'I'm going to shoot him with the Skunk Gun' she says and the other ladies fall all quiet and move away. I've never heard of a Skunk Gun, but I didn't like the look in her eye. She shoots me with this needle thing, it hurts a little, stings some, but not too bad. By then, the lady I shot has stopped struggling, there is a lot of blood on the sidewalk and she's real dead, that's obvious. The ladies scatter and leave us. I was surprised when no one stopped, there were a few cars on the street, but it was real foggy and I guess they couldn't see too well. After a while, the glue dried and got brittle. I tore off some patches of skin, but I was able to get myself loose. I left my friends and got out of there. I figured to pack a few things and go south, I didn't want to hang around and catch a murder rap. I knew my posse would rat me out, I just wanted to be gone.

I got back to the crib and fell into bed, next thing I know, it's morning. My girlfriend is wrinkling her nose at me, asks me if I'd been screwing a pole cat and tells me to take a shower. She wraps my clothes in a garbage bag and throws the bundle in the dumpster out back. The funny thing is, I don't smell it, but I wash up real good and come back out. My girlfriend says I smell worse, like something rotten is seeping through my skin. I tell her to shut up and come to bed, I'm thinking I'll knock myself off a bit of morning delight, but she's choking and her eyes are watering and she can't stand to be near me. She throws a few things in a suitcase and runs out. I'm thinking she's trying to rag me out for being out late, but I'm getting a little scared. I throw on some jeans and go outside and everyone is pointing and moving away, like I'm a leper or something. My old lady takes my truck, the bus driver won't let me on the bus and people are screaming at me. It's like I woke up in some kind of hell. The cops are wearing gas masks and you say you don't know what's going on, how long this lasts. It might be permanent? How can that be? I don't know nothing and I don't want to know nothing about body odor chemistry. I always kept myself clean and wore good clothes. This ain't right. If my glands can squirt this out this stink, maybe something can be removed to stop it? The doctors didn't spend much time with me, maybe you can call specialists, I know my rights, as long as I'm in jail, I get free medical. Where's my lawyer? Come back here, I know what you're doing. You think I'm stupid, but I'm not!

These jail uniforms aren't supposed to have belts. Everyone knows that. You don't want the inmates hanging themselves because the busy-body people get all up in arms. Go find those old ladies and figure out what they did to me and how to turn it off. Don't leave me alone with a belt and expect me to solve your problem for you. You hear me? This is not my problem, it's yours! Call in more doctors and get this stink off me. I don't smell anything, just the harsh soap you gave me in the shower. Alright damn you, I am starting to get something. Like a dog food after the maggots have been after it. What are you doing? Trying to drive me mad? Well, it won't work, I know my rights. I want my lawyer now. And stop running the stink into the ventilation, I can't take it anymore, my god, it smells like death itself. Get me out of here!

Part Two

… conceals the hard world's iron fist.

From time to time they would pass a criminal who had been impaled on a javelin and left to die by the road-side, which only confirmed the impression that they were in a well-ordered place now, and had not taken any undue risks in sending their escort home.

- Neal Stephenson, the Confusion, Volume II of THE BAROQUE CYCLE

CHAPTER SIXTEEN

Glen and Gerusha

Glen sipped coffee on the apartment balcony. He watched early morning traffic flow on the street below. The weather had turned cool and thick fog had rolled in from Elliot Bay. Gerusha emerged from her bedroom with her hair in tangles, rubbing sleep from her eyes.

"Did you make coffee?"

"It's yesterday's, reheated," Glen replied. "I saved you some."

"Thanks," Gerusha said, looking ruefully at the half cup of black sludge in the bottom of the coffee pot. "I dreamed that my schedule got screwed up and I was triple-booked for appointments all day. How long have I had this job? A couple of weeks? It seems like forever."

"Today marks the next phase of my job out on the streets."

"That's nice for you," Gerusha said, yawning.

"I've been dreading this. Things are going to get ugly. I may be too old and too soft to pull this off. Maybe I should return what's left of the money and resign. The metaphorical shit is going to hit the allegorical fan."

"I'd love to share the trials of your job and help you over-extend the boundaries of literary imagery, but I have a full schedule this morning. You got problems and I got problems, life's a bitch. Whiners and losers need not apply. Leave your message at the beep. Have your people get with my people. Toss a penny over your shoulder and make a wish. Press '6-6-6' to hear this message again. You're the Glen Wilson of fable and legend. What do you want me to do?"

"I don't think you appreciate how intense things are going to get."

"Fine. Call my assistant, make an appointment and we'll talk things through. Alright?" She poured the coffee into the sink and rinsed out the pot. "I have to get my face on and get to work, I'll talk at you later."

Glen, with a cruel smile on his face, turned back to the traffic, muttering. "She's right, if the job was easy, they wouldn't need Glen Wilson to do it. I don't care if I live or die, so why do I give a shit about the scum on the street? Let's nuke them all and let the devil sort them out." He watched a group of kids on skateboards ride through plastering stickers on cars, newspaper boxes and utility poles. By squinting his eyes, he could see that they said 'War is not the answer'. *That depends on what fucking question you're asking,* he thought bitterly as he turned away from the balcony. He tipped his coffee cup into the sink and walked to the bathroom to grab a quick shower before hitting the streets.

Glen

Glen backed up the Chevelle to the loading dock at the rear of Immortality, LLC and popped open the trunk. He hopped up on the dock and waved at a kid driving a forklift. The kid made a rotating motion with his index finger that indicated he'd be right back. Glen leaned against the wall and while he waited, looked over the racks and shelves of incoming materials. A biohazard area was next to the radiation hazard area. It briefly occurred to him to wonder what exactly they were up to at Immortality, but this thought was displaced when the kid roared up and skidded the forklift's tires before stopping.

"You're Wilson?" he asked. Glen nodded. "I thought so, I've been expecting you. There is a lot for you to pick up." He waved toward a clipboard hanging on a nail. "I need your signature, then I'll help you load out. Cool car, by the way."

As they put the last case into the trunk, the kid whispered.

"Ethanol, ain't that the stuff the doctors drink? Everclear?"

"Yes," Glen replied.

"Look, could I have one of the gallons? I'm hosting a rave. I could pay you twenty bucks, cash money."

"No," Glen said, "but I don't blame you much for trying."

Soon, Glen pulled out. The rear of his car was nearly dragging with the weight and he had to slow down to avoid mangling the mufflers on rough areas of pavement. He stopped at a Fred Meyer store and bought a few cases of syrupy imitation orange juice, paper cups and rubber gloves. The clerk offered a discount if Glen would sign up for their shopper's card, and Glen laughed. *Like I want the Feds to follow this purchase back to me via the store's database. Ha!*

The plastic bottles of Ethanol were marked with lot numbers that could be easily traced, so, in the back of a deserted floor of a parking garage, he poured some of the orange drink into a storm drain and refilled the bottles with Ethanol. The empty traceable bottles went back in the trunk to be burned later. The fumes were overpowering and Glen had to take frequent breaks to breathe fresh air, but finally the job was done and Glen put the orange drink and re-packaged Ethanol back into his trunk. Sweating and light-headed, he looked over the concrete walkway at the bustle of Pioneer Square below until the cool air made him feel better. He recognized people on the street; shoppers and tourists weaved around and ignored the semi-permanent population of vagabonds, panhandlers, freeloaders and transients.

Just people, all of them, some functional and prospering, some working the streets for easy advantage. Some down on their luck, some addicted to booze and dope, some hopelessly deranged. All deserving of basic respect and a better fate. Life can be cruel, but take your complaints to customer service, it ain't my damn fault or responsibility. I'm trying to get a job done and earn my paycheck like everyone else.

Mayor Harry Silverberg

Harry read his morning copy of the Seattle Post-Intelligencer and enjoyed a fresh-brewed cup of coffee. He felt as good as he'd felt in years. His body was drained from working out, but his head was clear and he felt slightly cheerful about life. The death of his son weighed on him, but would not drag him down today. The staff at the rehab clinic reported that his wife was doing well and could be released in a couple of weeks with mild mood-modification medication and out-patient follow up visits. Leaning back in his leather executive chair with his feet on his desk, he skipped over a story about a murdered senior citizen as he skimmed through to get to the sports section. If the Seahawks continued to play well, most of the taxpayers would shut up about the Stadium that was rammed down their throat by the previous administration, which would be a great relief.

He heard a quiet knock at his door but ignored it. The phone was on mute and his cell phone was turned off, so he was enjoying rare peace and quiet. His admin was supposed to keep everyone out until noon, but after a few minutes, she poked her head in. She appeared ashamed to disturb him.

"I'm very sorry, Mayor."

"Yes dear, what is it?"

"The Chief is here and he insists he must see you."

Sighing, Harry folded up the newspaper and slipped it into a desk drawer. "Alright, give me a minute and then let him in." His admin nodded and closed the door quietly. Harry walked to his window. The weather had changed and rain was pouring from solid leaden skies. Police Chief Bart Standon came in and tossed his raincoat onto a spare chair.

"I'm sorry to disturb you Mayor, I know you've had a tough go of it recently."

"It's quite alright, Bart, I know you wouldn't be here unless you had something vital on your mind. Care for coffee?"

"Sure, I'd love a cup, black."

"Don't tell me how you want it, get up and pour it yourself."

The Mayor grinned as he said this, so Bart relaxed and grabbed a mug and filled it. He settled in a chair.

"I'll get right to the point. Did you see the story in the PI about the old woman that was killed last night?"

"I glanced at it. I have it right here, hold on, I'll take a closer look." He pulled the newspaper from his desk and riffled through it until he found the article on Page 7.

Senior Citizen Slain in South Seattle Mêlée

"Alright, I see that an old woman is shot and killed. Bystanders detained the thugs. What am I missing? Another sad murder among many."

"We have a good relationship with the news desk, we were able to keep some of the details out of the story. Here's the scoop: members of a street gang accosted a group of elderly women. There was a ruckus. All that is true. The complicating factor is in the details. The women had weapons I've never seen before, glue guns things and a bolo weapon. Let me show you pictures from the scene."

He unrolled a bundle of photos, they were high-resolution black and whites.

"These are the guns?" the mayor asked, pointing. Bart nodded.

"They are crude, made from extruded aluminum tubing spot welded together. The cartridges are very clever, the propellant and glue emitters are like big ink jet printer mechanisms, they only have to work a few times and are replaced when the weapon is reloaded."

"Any idea where they were manufactured?"

"No, there are no production markings. Just about any good machine shop around here could do the work."

"Are there any good machine shops left around here now that Boeing is outsourcing everything to China?"

"That's not funny."

"I know. I'm sorry. These guns, are they legal?"

"That's hard to say. There are general laws against weapons that might apply, but the gun nuts might be able to make a second amendment defense, we'll have to let the courts sort that out. They are non-lethal, though you might get some singed flesh because the glue comes out hot before it solidifies. You don't have to aim very well, just point and shoot, the stuff spreads out the farther it travels." He pointed at details in another picture. "This weapon shoots a bolo thing with a composite netting between rubber bullets. Again, you don't have to aim very well, just get close and they wrap around your legs and down you go. Very simple and very clever. Nearly foolproof. We'd love weapons like this for our people when the anti-globalists and anarchists take over the streets again."

"Fine, I'll help you slide it into the next budget cycle. Okay, so we have some odd weapons on the street. Anything else?"

"Yes, there are the people who wield them."

The mayor held up his hand to stop Bart. "Let me guess who the trouble-makers are." He closed his eyes and concentrated. "Jehovah's Witnesses. The bible-thumpers are riding in on their bicycles and are on the rampage."

"No."

"Okay, it's the MAD nags, the Mothers Against Drunks. They're driving their minivans in from the suburbs and giving the gang bangers what for."

"No."

"Okay, I give up, who is it?"

Bart slid a photograph face down across the desk. Harry took a deep breath, then flipped the picture over. "You gotta be shitting me? These old bags barely look alive."

"This group is from the Emerald Hills boneyard. They're a feisty group of biddies."

"This is funny. A bunch of old crones armed with bizarre weapons take down a street gang."

"Well, there is humor to the picture if you can ignore the old woman who died out there with a .38 slug embedded in her chest. But that's not the most troubling aspect."

"Go ahead, spit it out."

"As you said, these women have nothing to lose. They're just barely alive. We need the civilians to dial 911 and wait for the cops to show up. We'll lose control if people take the law into their own hands. The regular people toe the line because we can seize their homes and throw them in jail. We don't have any power over these old folks."

"I think you're over-reacting. They're just a few widows, after all."

"I'm afraid. I have a vision of hundreds of these hags roaming the streets with their glob guns tying gray ribbons on everything. Imagine it, everywhere you turn, another ancient grandma pointing a canister weapon in your face. What would we do about it? Put them in jail? Repossess their afghans and doilies?"

"Bart, have you been drinking? Don't let your imagination run you off a cliff here. You're talking crazy."

"I hope you're right, but in my heart, I don't think so."

"Where did they get these guns?"

"They're not talking. I know the city council has been talking to you. This guy you hired, Glen Wilson? Did he have something to do with this?"

"Wilson? I wouldn't think so. He has crazy ideas, but a conspiracy of coots? I don't think so."

"We have a balance of power on the streets. It's delicate. The crooks get out of hand and we come down on them hard. I don't think you understand how fragile the situation is. I'm telling you something like this could bollix things up."

"Maybe you need a vacation? Take a few days off and go fishing?"

"My official advice is to take this seriously. Pull the plug on your asshole friend Wilson. He has the downtown community up in arms. We don't need the disruption. Despite what you say, I smell Wilson's scent all over this. Oh, I almost forgot. We had a hoodlum commit suicide in one of our cells. We're going to have the Hispanic community all over our asses. Something was wrong with him, he reeked like a truck full of skunks. You couldn't stand to be in the same room with him. If he hadn't offed himself, I'm not sure what we'd do. We cremated him and the goddam ashes still stunk up the place, we had to bury them in a sealed bucket."

"I thought I smelled something on the wind, it was real nasty."

"Yeah, that was it. You have no idea, we almost had to evacuate the corrections building. We're going to pay a lot of disability and we're going to get sued up, down and sideways by the union guards."

"Weird things are happening."

"We think the stinky guy was part of the gang that attacked the old women."

"What do the women say?"

"They clammed up tight and refused to say anything. We haven't found any way they could do this. We talked to researchers at the UW, they say that a mutational hormone imbalance could be the cause. They studied people with horrible incurable body odor, but nothing at all like this. The bottom line is, there's too much chaos in our city."

"Are you implying that Wilson can make people stink? Along with creating an army of retirees?"

"I don't know anything. I have a bad feeling and this Wilson is a big unknown. You hired him, I'm suggesting it's time to run his ass out of here."

"Intuition?"

"Call it an old cop's instinct. I strongly urge you to get rid of that guy. I know the council has suggested the same thing, take their advice, please."

"Okay, you may be right. I'll think things over. My mind wasn't straight when I hired him, I'll do it. I'll fire him. Okay?"

"Thank you, Harry. I'm glad. Don't get me wrong, I'm real sorry about your son, but we have a city to run." He stood and shook hands with the Mayor. "Say hello to your wife for me, will you?"

"Sure," Harry replied. He swiveled in his chair and watched the rain pour out of the sky. He reached out without looking and his hand found his coffee cup. He leaned back and sipped the strong brew and tried to think about nothing.

Wilson is making enemies all over town. Maybe, if I wait long enough, someone on the street will kill him and solve all my problems all at once. But then I will be derived of that overdue and well-earned pleasure. I want to make sure he feels it and knows it was me. Something slow and painful, that's the only thing that will balance the scales and let me carry on my life in a positive direction. It should be easy to pin the blame on someone else, he's got everyone in Seattle angry. At the right time and at the right place, Wilson will feel my pain. The Mayor's lips twisted into a tight and cruel smile as he sipped his coffee.

At the right time and at the right place, we'll balance our accounting, yes we absolutely will.

Gerusha Andersen

"You simply must try the crabapple Martinis, they are out of this world delicious," Paul Butler said after they were seated at the Metropolitan Grill. The Met was a well-known steakhouse in downtown Seattle. Paul offered to take her anywhere for lunch and she immediately thought of asking him to take her to San Francisco, but decided it would take too much time away from her day. As it was, she could feel work piling up back at the office.

"I don't think it's a good idea to drink during business hours," Gerusha said.

"You're quite right, of course," Paul said, but he couldn't mask his disappointment.

Gerusha sipped ice water and told the waiter to bring her cranberry juice on the rocks with a sprig of mint.

"I'll take the same," Paul said.

"When you invited me to lunch, I thought for a moment about asking you to take me to San Francisco. What would you have done?"

"We'd be landing at SFO right about now, I imagine. My boss is pretty understanding when it comes to signing my expense reports. I was the only salesman in the territory to make budget last quarter."

"I see. I was just curious."

The waiter, wearing a starched white shirt and necktie took their lunch order. Paul ordered a salmon filet and Gerusha ordered a cobb salad. She was sad, she could have anything on the menu she wanted, Beef Wellington, lobster, prime rib, but she had gained three or four pounds and needed to exercise discipline or she'd balloon up like a sow.

"I wanted to talk with you, Paul. I'm in over my head. I didn't go to business school or anything, now I'm selecting vendors and reviewing proposals and contracts."

"You say you didn't go to B-school as if that's a bad thing. At least you don't have flawed notions of the world polluting your thought processes. You're an empty vessel ready to be filled with real-world wisdom and a very attractive vessel it is."

"If you think you're going to sit there and bullshit me, I'll get up and leave right now," Gerusha said, wadding her napkin and dropping it on the table.

Paul held up his hand to stop her. "You're right, I'm forgetting myself and I apologize."

Gerusha looked into his eyes for a long moment, then relaxed back into her chair.

"Alright, I forgive you."

"Thank you," Paul replied sincerely. "I may have expressed my point a bit crassly, but Biz school *can* fill a person's head with dumb and useless ideas. It can take time to cure this affliction. That was all I was trying to say."

"Okay. You're going to help me understand."

"Yes, I will." He took a sip of his cranberry juice and made a sour face. "But, you'll permit me to anoint my voice box with the right lubricant." To the waiter, he said: "Please take this away and bring me a double Ketel plum martini with an extra olive and feel free to replenish my glass when it becomes empty, if you please."

"First of all, taking me to lunch will cost a hundred bucks. I can't believe there is that much money to be made in sales to pay for such extravagance."

"First of all, we operate on good margins with proprietary precision equipment. You're right that it will take good sales numbers to cover the overhead, but there are a couple of things going on. For one, there are seven other companies that make this equipment, so there is value in selecting us instead of the other guys. Also, corporate mentality is very short term, I'm compensated and rewarded for making my budget this quarter. The Amex bill won't get paid until next quarter. I have enough to worry about now, next quarter will come along in its turn and that's not my problem now. It may not make sense, but that's how things work."

"Okay, I get it, I guess. What about the underside? Payoffs, kickbacks, blackmail, extortion, under the table backroom deals, the exchange of favors?"

Paul took a small sip of his martini. "Oh shit, Gerusha." He drained his glass and placed it on the side of the table where it was whisked away almost instantly. "These things happen, but we're not going to talk about it in public. Why don't you tell me what you want and I'll make it happen if I can." He sipped from a fresh martini and looked at her expectantly over the rim of his glass.

"You think I'm trying to squeeze you? I'm the curious type, that's all. I want to understand the landscape."

"You scared me for a moment. I apologize again," he said after taking another sip of his drink. "There's a sales meeting at the end of the month and I'm under budget for new customers, so I'm a bit touchy right now. There are things that go on, but I must warn you. If you get too greedy, then things can go bad. Any kind of excess asymmetry upsets the system, draws attention, and creates jealousy and envy."

"Greed? We're just talking. Let's change gears, what can I do to help you in exchange for this lovely lunch?" she asked sweetly.

"You could give me a list of projects that are funded and their budgets. I'm supposed to have intimate inside information about what is going on in my accounts."

Gerusha pulled a bundle of print-outs from her purse. "I came prepared. I'll show you, but you can't have a copy or make any notes, so don't even ask."

"Ah Gerusha, why did you let me drink? It plays hell with my memory."

"You're a salesman and a good one, so I'm told, I'm sure you'll do fine."

"Now you're blowing smoke up *my* ass, if you'll forgive the expression. I assume that someday you'll ask for a favor in return, something that will cost me big."

"Don't worry about it, Paul." Gerusha said with a tiny smile lying lightly on her lips. "Relax and enjoy another martini."

"Okay, while you're humoring me, what do you know about the statue guy? Glen Wilson? He must be a genuine company heavyweight."

"What about him?"

"Do you know him? Does he have budget or Purchase Order signature authority? Is he in charge of any of these projects?" Paul waved the sheaf of papers. "What's he like? Can you arrange an introduction?"

"Well, I know that Walter signed a check to get him a company car, twenty grand, no questions asked."

"Wow, so he is influential. Twenty grand is no big deal, a cheap car, but these days, perks like that are rare. Obviously, he's a key power player in the company. What else can you tell me?"

"He's living with me."

"Excuse me? Did you say you're shacking up with him? I'm sorry, that did not come out right. You're cohabitating with him?"

"Yes. Now you're probably thinking I got my promotion because I'm sleeping with the guy. I'll be perfectly frank, that thought is in error twice. First of all, we're not intimate. He's just a roommate, he crashes at my apartment. Second of all, I was promoted because the company saw raw talent in me I didn't know I had. I don't know if I have what they think they saw. I'm working hard and trying, but I may fall flat on my face. To answer the most significant of your questions, yes, I believe I can get you in front of him. In fact, that might be an interesting situation, so I'll set it up."

"When I think I've figured you out, you hit me with this. I wish I was sober so I could think properly. I have corporate visitors coming to town, they'd be thrilled to meet an important person like Glen. Immortality is a very important new account for us. Do you think he'd agree to meet with an executive team?"

"You'd better meet him yourself first. When you meet him, then you'll understand why I suggest this."

"Okay, Gerusha, I understand. Are there any other bombshells you want to throw at me? Tell me about Mr. Wilson, is he a new age Zen kind of executive or an old fashioned iron-fisted dictator type? A by-the-numbers accounting-oriented bean counter or a touchy-feely people person? Give me hints about how to approach him."

"He's none of the above, that's for sure. In fact, I don't understand him at all and I will be looking to you, with your experience with people, to figure him out for *me*."

"Ah, a mystery to be unraveled. I like that. I'm good at it." He seemed to hear what he just said. "Uh-oh, that was the drink talking, I should never make arrogant confessions like that with my customers."

"That's alright, Paul," Gerusha said, patting him on the hand. "You're very helpful to me and I appreciate it. About Glen, I don't see him as a mystery to be unraveled either. He's more of a 'what you see is what you get' kind of person, but apparently different people see different things. I will set up a meeting, all I want in return is your opinion on what kind of man Glen is."

"That will be easy, I've met all types and pride myself as quickly able to peer into their souls, so to speak. I'll unravel him and lay him out like a frog in a high school biology class. And dear, don't let me drink the next time we do lunch, okay? Obviously, I need to keep my wits about me when I'm around you."

"Obviously," Gerusha echoed, smiling and saluting him with her glass of cranberry juice. Their meals arrived and they ate in relative silence, both with thoughts to think through.

Glen

Glen parked his car in a loading zone and stashed a pair of the plastic bottles beside a smelly and overflowing dumpster. A rivulet of congealed grease flowed toward a drain in the alley pavement like the trail of the world's largest slug, but Glen tried to ignore it. He set out the orange drink, the Ethanol and paper cups. He was surprised by an old man buried in cardboard and old newspapers.

"What are you doing?" the old man croaked.

"Free killer screwdrivers," Glen replied. "I think I'll have the first one."

He poured a splash into his cup and took a sip. "Bad, but not too bad," he said wrinkling his nose, "but I hate this fake orange crap."

"Give me one of those," the old man said, pushing by Glen. He filled his cup halfway.

"Go easy on that, it packs a helluva punch."

"I know what I'm doing, don't boss me," the old man said petulantly.

"It's your life," Glen replied before draining his cup and walking out of the alley. Wandering the alleys, he found quiet places to stash all of the bottles. He wanted them to be out of the way, but in places where the bums would find them easily. He took the first drink and waited until someone came to check him out. He wasn't worried about leaving any witnesses. He was quite buzzed by the time the last set of bottles was placed. He sipped his drink and leaned against a concrete block wall. A pair of Mexicans, wearing white cowboy hats and worn cowboy boots, walked by kicking a plastic soda bottle.

"What are you doing, señor?"

"Having a drink. They're free gratis."

"Ha! Nothing is free in Norte America, amigo."

"Wiser words have never been spoken." Glen slurred as he said this and realized he was not safe in the driver's seat of his car. "Do either of you hombres drive?"

"No señor, we don't have no licenses."

"That wasn't my question, can you drive?"

"Si, we can drive. Stake bed truck, tractor, whatever you have, señor."

Glen waved at his Chevelle. "What about this? I'm too drunk to drive."

The men whistled. "Primo. Yes, we can drive it."

"Okay, twenty bucks to each of you if you'll drive me home."

"Of course, señor, tell us where to go, for twenty dollars, we'll drive you anywhere you want."

Glen felt queasy by the time they got the car to the parking garage. He paid them and they thanked him profusely and tried to get more work lined up.

"We do plumbing, construction, roofing, landscaping, anything, señor. My cousin, Ernesto, has a telephone, he can take a message for us. You call, señor, and we will come. Ten dollars an hour, no taxes. We're hard workers."

"I understand and if anything comes up, I will call. But now, I have to get upstairs before I heave on your boots."

"Okay, for you we will work for eight dollars an hour."

"Adios, señors," Glen said as he ran up the stairs.

He made it to the bathroom, but barely. He threw up a nasty mess of orange goo and undigested chunks of hamburger. His head was spinning and he swore he would never drink again. When Gerusha came home, he was still hugging the throne.

"You're disgusting," she said.

"I know," he replied, "now go away and let me die in peace."

CHAPTER SEVENTEEN

Glen

Glen slept through Gerusha's morning routine. He felt almost human in the morning, though battered, bruised and ravenously hungry. He foraged and found left-over Chinese Chop Suet congealing in a cardboard container. Once it came out of the microwave, it was edible enough and he gobbled down the whole package. Smoking a cigar, he watched traffic flow by on the street. The phone rang and he listened to the message as it was being recorded. The Mayor's assistant was trying to find him and schedule an appointment. He was not sure how they tracked him to Gerusha's place, but they had been calling all week. Eventually, Glen would have to go see Mayor Harry, but not today. He decided to visit the hospital.

He couldn't remember how he got home, all he recalled was an endless eternity staring into the toilet bowl. He wasn't drinking anymore and that was final, he decided again. He found a parking place on the street by Harborview and walked around to the employee smoking area to look for his friend Bill. As he sat there, he listened in on a conversation between nurses.

"Have you ever seen such a goddam mess? We have more stiffs than I've ever seen, the coroner is going nuts. What is going on out there?"

"They've gotten into industrial solvent or something. It's sad to see them drink themselves to death."

"Well, I can use the overtime, we're saving up to payoff a timeshare in Cabo, more dead bums means more cash to me."

"That's sick. Don't talk like that."

"Well, its true, I don't care about those stinky old losers. They deserve what they get."

"You're mad because your ex is living on the street and skipping out on his child support. How would you feel if you saw his body come through our doors?"

"I wouldn't care."

"You don't mean it, I'm becoming very angry with you."

Glen hid a small smile. He once knew a Brazilian girl who talked like that.

Gerusha Andersen

Walter poked his head into Gerusha's office. He admired the furnishings; she had potted plants and original watercolors hanging on the walls. Everything was color-coordinated and communicated a peaceful harmony. She stared intently at her computer screen while tapping at her keyboard.

"Hello, Gerusha," Walter said gently.

She jumped. "Shit, Walter, I didn't hear you open the door. I must have been zoning."

"Sorry. I should have knocked, but I'm the CEO so sometimes I don't. Did you see a requisition for DNA sequencing equipment come through?"

"Yes, I saw your name on it, so I pushed it. Let me check." She tapped on her keyboard. "The purchase order was placed yesterday and delivery will be in 60 days or sooner. That was a nice order for the Swiss company, they even agreed to net-60 day payment terms with no premium."

"Outstanding, thanks. I heard you saved us a hundred grand on proton splitters Bennie wanted."

"Yes, we caught the vendor near the end of their fiscal year and they were motivated to get the order on the books. They thought we'd found a second source, so I got them to squeeze their margin."

"Bennie was specific, the equipment could only come from one supplier."

"I know, but I allowed the vendor's imagination to wander. I didn't lie to them, but I did allow them to mislead themselves with subtle guidance."

"That's delicious, Gerusha. I'm proud of you. Nice work."

"Thank you, Walter. Can I ask, what exactly do we do around here?"

"Haven't you read the prospectus? It's online."

"Of course I've read the prospectus, the SEC filings, the business plan in all of its revisions and I keep up with the rumors on the chat boards. I've read everything I can find, but I am still not satisfied. What are we really doing?"

"We're selling a new lease on life, a second lifespan for very wealthy clients. An exotic rejuvenation treatment."

"I know all that. But how does it work?"

"Ah, Gerusha, you have peered deep into the heart of the matter. You're a clever girl. I will explain. We've created a cross-pollination between cellular biology and quantum physics. Bennie has a unique insight and made non-linear correlations. It's dazzling when you catch a glimpse of its implications."

"Does it work?"

"You know we've had very smart people put vast sums of money in. Obviously, they would not invest at that level unless our technology had value."

"Was that an answer?"

"The question is not so simple. Does it work? That is almost insulting in its audacity. Yes, it works. Are there quirks and side issues inherent in the process? Yes, of course, that's inevitable. Are there areas where additional work is required? Yes, there are and there always will be."

"Would you take the procedure yourself?"

"Yes, when the time is right, I will most certainly grasp at whatever approximation to immortality we can achieve. That is a basic human desire." He glanced at his watch. "I have enjoyed our little tête-à-tête immensely, but I simply must run."

"How is the baby doing?"

Walter's eyes narrowed. "Are you perhaps *too* clever?" He considered the matter while patting at his bushy white pompadour. "No, simply an innocent question from a considerate and perceptive young lady." He seemed to collect himself. "Was I speaking out loud just then?"

Gerusha nodded yes.

"I must stop doing that," he said. "To answer your question, mother and son are doing extremely well and are perfectly healthy. Mama has predictable mood swings and cravings. She worries about her figure and has redecorated the nursery twice, but those are minor irritations which are easily tolerated. All is well and I thank you for asking. Let's get together for lunch again and we'll talk things through more thoroughly, I would enjoy that very much."

With that, he pulled out his head and closed the door softly. Gerusha swiveled in her chair and stared through the window at the parking garage for a few minutes before remembering her work. The email would not answer itself, after all. If she didn't keep up, it would bury her.

Glen

Glen dug around the trash in the trunk of his Chevelle until he found the case of Roxinal. It came in small bottles, 50 ml, with a rubber seal through which a hypodermic needle could be slipped. He held one up to the sunlight, it was perfectly clear, like water. Sitting behind the wheel of his car, listening to Foghat on the tape deck, he scraped off the lot numbers so the bottles could not be traced. The Feds would have circumstantial evidence linking the drug to Immortality, but it would be hard to prove the link to the extent that would hold up in court. At least Glen hoped so, because there was a big difference between street bums poisoning themselves on grain alcohol and recreational drug users OD'ing on purified morphine. The cops would actually make an honest effort to solve the murder of white kids in the suburbs.

Glen's connection was a Honduran man who called himself Jorge. He was a short and unpleasant man with bad acne scars. It looked as if a dog had nearly chewed one of his arms off, his forearm displayed a knotted mass of purple scar tissue. He chewed bubble gum in a huge wad. They met in a gas station parking lot near the Harborview Hospital. Glen was selling him the drug, the whole lot, for a hundred dollars. It was worth a thousand times that price or more, depending on how much it was cut. Jorge was supposed to come alone, but Glen was unsurprised to see a group of young Asians with him.

"Hello, Jorge. You brought your friends."

"They wanted to meet you in person."

Jorge had recently lost a tooth and the whole left side of his face was bruised. Glen respected Jorge for trying to keep his word. After this brutal beating, his failure was understandable. As the group came closer, Glen revised his estimation of their nationality. They were Laotian or Vietnamese with hard and suspicious eyes that darted from side to side like trapped cats. They were high on something, probably crystal meth or PCP. All alarm signals in Glen's body were raised. He looked around for some sign of the Gray Brigade, but they would not get this far up James Street for another couple of weeks. Glen was on his own. Death was in the air. Glen thought back. *Which mistakes led him to this situation?* The path seemed twisted and arcane, he couldn't figure it out.

The leader was a tight-muscled little guy, his arms writhed with ropy veins and twitchy muscles. He wore a colorful Hawaiian shirt unbuttoned to the waist and a large gold chain. On the chain, a huge golden dragon was displayed, it seemed like a cliché to Glen, Asian dragon and all that, but he politely did not mention it.

"What's the problem? You're practically getting the dope for free."

Jorge shrugged. "They think you can get more."

"Shit," Glen complained. *Of course.*

The leader plucked one of the bottles out of Glen's grasp.

"Roxinal," he said in surprisingly squeaky voice. *Steroid abuse,* Glen thought. The side-effects rolled through his mind, unbidden. *Depression, heart attack, increased breast tissue caused by high estrogen levels in the blood. Mood swings. Sudden dangerous fits of 'roid' rage.*

"I don't know it," the leader said.

"Pure medical-grade Morphine," Glen said.

"Why are you selling it so cheap?"

Glen didn't have a good answer for this question, so he kept his mouth shut.

"We brought a junkie to test it."

They brought out Half-size Lucy, her skin was gray and she was shivering and sweating at the same time. She was hurting for a fix very badly.

"Let me talk to her," Glen asked.

The leader shrugged his shoulders and Glen walked over.

"Hey Lucy," he said.

"Hey, it's the wristband man," she said weakly. "What's up?"

"Listen to me Lucy, this stuff is pure and uncut. I don't know about your habit, go real easy on this, just a little skin pop."

"Don't tell me, I know what I'm doing. Give me the shit and I'll shoot it, I need it bad. These guys are giving me a free taste."

"Badly, you need it badly."

"That's what I said."

Glen handed her a bottle and watched as she pulled her works from her jacket pocket; her needle was wrapped in a dirty piece of towel. She wrapped surgical tubing around her arm and flicked at an abused vein with a fingernail until it popped up slightly. She drew almost a cc into the syringe.

"Too much, baby," Glen said.

"Never enough, baby," Lucy replied. She stabbed and eased in the fluid. She put the needle away and loosened the tubing.

"Oh, it's smooth, just like the first time. Beautiful. I love you, band-man," she said dreamily, wrapping her arms around Glen's neck and trying to give him a kiss on the lips. Her breath was putrid and Glen avoided her mouth. She kissed him on the neck instead. He eased her arms off. She took a step back against the back wall of the gas station, then her knees collapsed and she crumpled with her head at an uncomfortable angle. Glen thought he heard her whisper 'bliss' but he could not be sure. Maybe she said piss or kiss or something else.

"Seems to be good shit," the leader commented.

"The E-R is close, if we drop her off, they may be able to save her."

"She's a skanky old worn-out whore. Let her croak, who cares?"

Glen was strangely moved. Lucy was part of the dregs of humanity, but in her own way she was special and worthy of a better fate. He blinked away the thought. His own precious ass was in grave danger and he needed to focus.

I'd been drifting for a long time, since I decided my chance of escaping the treatment center in North Dakota was unlikely. Maybe a year in. I'd been sleepwalking. It's impossible to care about others when you don't care about yourself. The new feeling was interesting, like something had sprouted to life and I didn't realize it until this moment, this moment when death is so near.

I viewed this job as a license to kill. The Mayor would pull strings to make sure our contract would not become public. It was a level of protection I was counting on. I didn't think the contract terms would hold up, but the Mayor would have public opinion behind him with a lingering sympathy for the loss of his son. My thoughts are somewhat scattered, but the bottom line is I want to live for love and revenge. There is a huge imbalance that needs resolution. No universal equation can be allowed to bring disharmony to the cosmos. The events that led to my incarceration in North Dakota needed redress.

I also had a revelation about Gerusha. At first, I thought she'd be a good outlet for my pent-up passion, an interesting diversion, an attractive young vessel for my use and abuse. But, there was more to her than that and she deserved more from me. All these random thoughts led me to one conclusion. I was going to kill these creeps, quit my contract with the Mayor, quit screwing around and get serious about my life and my goals. Or die trying, I guess.

Glen lifted Lucy's chin, she was breathing, but barely. Maybe she'd built up enough tolerance that she would survive the dosage. He didn't see how that was possible, but there was still a chance. He tried to think of weapons he might have in his pockets, but he could only think of the coins and keys that he picked up in the condo that morning. Nothing useful.

He rose from Lucy's body slowly and smoothly. He visualized the liquid quickness of a snake. Not too fast, or the prey gets defensive. He held up the little bottle for inspection and the leader glanced at it with slight curiosity. What was Glen trying to communicate? He moved the bottle to eye level as if there was something the leader should see and then slammed it into his eye with the heel of his hand. It was a tight fit, but it squeezed into the eye socket. There was little blood, but the sight of the last quarter inch of the bottle protruding from the head was horrific. Shock and awe, baby. This gave a moment for Glen to slam the nose bones of the nearest banger into his brain with a sharp blow from the heel of his hand. The banger fell down like a bag of wet cement. Glen hoped that Jorge would join in and help, but the chances were equal that he would run. Glen turned to the pair farthest from Jorge and hoped for the best. They were starting to react and Glen could choose between being killed with a 9mm pistol or a switchblade that was already sweeping in his direction in a deadly parabola. He slipped sideways and pulled around the blade man's arm. He managed to get the blade man in front of the Beretta man before two shots were squeezed off. The blade man was thin and wiry, his heart and ribs only slowed the bullets and Glen felt them hit his back like hammer blows. A more meaty man would have absorbed the shots completely. Glen didn't think this was fair and intended to complain to management at his first opportunity. However, he had a shooter to dispense with first. The leader flailed like he was blind. Glen remembered that the left hemisphere of the brain dealt with visual information from the opposite eye, so he thought it might be possible, what with the trauma caused by the bottle and all. The real surprise was that Lucy was on her feet. The movement distracted the shooter while Jorge hit him on the head with a piece of masonry. Jorge's lopsided face exhibited a huge bloody grin. He'd lost another tooth, but he'd dealt with two of the thugs. The leader was crouched and ready to strike at anything that came near him, but they stayed out of his reach.

"We need to get out of here," Glen said. He tugged at Lucy's arm and she compliantly followed. They piled into the Chevelle and Glen eased down a residential street trying to draw as little attention as possible. The whole thing took thirty seconds and spectators were peeking around the corner of the gas station up to see what was going on. Glen hoped they would get away clean. His back was stiffening, he could tell something was not right. He dropped Jorge off on Madison up on Capital Hill. They clasped hands.

"You move like a ballet dancer, señor."

"Thanks, I think," Glen replied. "Take it easy out there, brother."

"And you, amigo."

Glen slipped back into traffic.

"How are you doing, Lucy?" he asked.

"Good," she said softly with her husky voice. "I feel good."

"I need your help."

They stopped at a Bartlett's Drugstore and Glen gave her money and explained what he wanted. She seemed to be functioning and repeated his instructions perfectly. He gave her a handful of bills, some with blood crusted on the edges, and sent her on her way. She was gone a long time, but finally appeared with a plastic bag filled with supplies. They stopped at an hourly-rate motel and Lucy handled renting the room. They got in and Glen, grimacing, pulled off his shirt.

"How bad is it?" he asked.

"You're a big baby. I can see the bullets, they're just under the skin. I can get them with my fingernails. Hold still."

"You bought tweezers, use them. Damn it, at least wash your hands first."

"Shut up and stop squirming."

She plucked out the bullets and dropped them one-by-one into the wastebasket. She wet hand towels and mopped his back. They were quickly stained deep red. She poured on peroxide, let it burble for a minute, then dried his back again and covered the wounds with gauze and medical tape.

"Okay, you're good to go. You'll have new scars you can make up fresh lies about."

"Thanks, Lucy." He rinsed his shirt in the sink and worked in bar soap, soon it was presentable. He put it on the shower rod to dry.

"You've earned yourself a free BJ, take down your pants."

"No Lucy. Let's talk for a moment. You're a good kid. Do you ever think about getting out of this life?"

"I think about it sometimes, but I was never any good at things. Everyday things like work and relationships."

"I can offer you a second chance."

"What do you mean?"

"Get out the phonebook. Pick a treatment place and I'll check you in, pay the bill and make sure you have money if you get through it. Enough money to go to vocational school or something."

"Why would you do this for me?"

"Because, deep inside, I'm a kind and generous man."

"No you're not. You're the biggest asshole I ever met. Running around town with your bicycle and your wristbands like you're some kind of whack case. Putting my friends on the bus and running them out of town. You're a crazy fucking bastard. Why would you help me? What's your angle?"

"I don't have an answer. I'm telling you, if you make a decision now while your mind is straight, I will give you a chance to get clean and try life again."

"If you're jiving me, I'll kill you."

"You'll have to get in line for that," Glen muttered. He tossed the phonebook to her. "Pick a place."

"It will hurt."

"Everything hurts, Lucy. The world is one pain-filled ball of shit spinning in empty space. So what? Make a decision. If you want to keep sucking dirty cocks in Pioneer Square back alleys, say the word and I'll drop you back down there."

Tears streamed down Lucy's face. "That was a mean thing to say."

"Choose!" Glen demanded. And she did.

Mayor Harry Silverberg

Bart Stanton, the Seattle Police Chief, sat in front of the Mayor. Not for the first time, he studied the Mayor carefully and wondered if the Mayor had become deranged. He seemed okay, but there were worrisome signs. What could be done when the highest-ranking city executive went insane? The Mayor was functioning on a day-to-day level. Bart hoped the problem would not fall on his lap.

"You asked for personal reports of anything to do with your man Glen Wilson. We had an incident up by the hospital. Two men are dead and another has brain damage. The prognosis is not good. A very messy situation. Your man Glen has a bright green Chevy and we have witnesses on the scene that describe a car like that. We're certain this is another of your man's adventures."

"If you call him 'my man' one more time, I'll —"

Bart held up his hand to stop the Mayor. "I'm sorry. I'll stop."

"Thank you."

"We have to put an end to this, it's intolerable."

"I agree. Bring him to me and I'll deal with the matter." *Yes, I'll deal with it. I'll break that wine bottle, bury the sharp ends in his face and grind them into his skull until that lousy fucker dies screaming in agony. I'll break his knees with my souvenir Mariners bat then shove it down his throat until the end is immersed in stomach acid.*

Bart did not like the emotions that flitted across the Mayor's face. They were scary even to man who had seen almost everything in his many years of experience with people. Perhaps *because* of this experience.

"If we find him, we'll bring him in. Will you authorize overtime for my people?"

The Mayor sighed. Overtime was expensive and the Police Guild always pushed hiring more officers, they flaunted overtime records in his face as justification. "Alright, I'll sign for overtime. Don't go nuts with it. He's one guy, you don't need to mobilize the whole city to bring him in."

"Thanks, boss. We'll be prudent about it, don't worry. The guys can use the hours. Except for the few exceptions, things have been pretty quiet out there."

Mayor Harry leaned forward. "Are you suggesting that 'my man' Wilson and his gang of grannies might be having an effect," he asked in a nasty tone.

"No," Bart backtracked, "I'm not suggesting anything of the sort."

"You're not finding shit while you're sitting here wasting my time. Get out, you're fraying my temper."

"Yes, sir," Bart replied.

CHAPTER EIGHTEEN

Glen and Gerusha

Glen bought frozen lasagna, garlic bread and salad in a bag. He lighted a candle and put it on a piece of foil in the center of the table. When Gerusha came home, she threw her handbag and laptop computer on a chair then collapsed on the couch.

"I am 100% frickin' exhausted," she said. "What smells good? I didn't get anything for lunch except chocolate covered macadamia nuts that someone brought back from Hawaii."

"I made you dinner," Glen said. "Come and get it."

He poured Italian wine into water glasses and, on the table, placed a steaming aluminum tin of lasagna with a big spoon stabbed in the middle. He grabbed handfuls of pre-mixed salad from a plastic bag and heaped it on their plates.

"It's hard to keep places on the earth clean, so it makes sense to centralize the hygienic areas. Frozen dinners probably save thousands of lives every year, deaths caused by contamination. Did you ever think of what a miracle frozen foods are?"

"No. Are you going shut up and let me enjoy my meal without thinking? I'm tired, I already told you."

With his lips pressed together in anger, Glen plopped a blob of lasagna on her plate. He tore a hunk from a hot loaf of garlic bread. Burning his fingers, he hurriedly tossed the bread over the table onto her plate.

"Shit Glen, you big baby, I'm sorry. This dinner looks great; I'm just hungry and grumpy. I appreciate the effort. Do you want to bombard me with philosophical witticisms? Go ahead, you've earned the right."

"I'm trying to enhance your dining experience with intelligent conversation. Pardon me for existing."

"Really, anything you want to talk about. I'll bet you can make a big deal out of anything." She looked around the room. "Like the microwave oven, I'll bet you think they are a technological wonder too, right?"

"Well," Glen said, loosening up a little. "Electric burners are dangerous. They take a long time to heat up and a long time to cool down. The old ones didn't turn themselves off. They probably caused thousands of deaths from fires and burns. Not to mention the hazards associated with open flames from earlier days. Microwave ovens won't work unless the door is closed and they turn themselves off. There are a few casualties from microwaving metal and from internal short circuits, but they are much safer than the old ways of cooking."

"Really, Glen," Gerusha said around a hot forkful of lasagna. "That's fascinating. I never thought things through like that. How about other technology, like TV remotes or cell phones or electric toothbrushes? I'll bet they save lives too."

"Now you're mocking me. Stop it."

"I know. Let's talk about wine in plastic bags. Less glass means fewer accidents. So, the inventor should get a Nobel Prize, right? A humanitarian award?"

"Do you ever shut up?"

"Okay, let's talk about something safe. One of the sales reps wants to meet you. He has a contract to provide us optical storage network equipment and software services."

"I don't think so. I'm not sure how involved I will get with Immortality, so I don't think there would be any point to it."

"He wants to meet the man memorialized by the statue in the reception area."

"I thought I told you to get rid of that. Throw it in the garbage."

"No. If its going anywhere, I'll bring it home. Maybe I'll put it over there in the corner."

"Oh, no," Glen groaned. "Do you enjoy torturing me?"

"Sure. If I scribble you onto the schedule at 10 o'clock on Thursday, will you come meet this guy?"

"Alright, I'll try, but only if you stop hassling me and eat your damn dinner."

"Deal. We should be able to find something harmless to talk about. I know, how was your day? What did you do?"

"I don't want to talk about it."

They ate in silence for a while, and then Glen commented: "You want to know about my day? I was shot in the back by an Asian street thug."

"You're such a bullshitter. South Americans chop off one of your fingers and you lose another to a psychopath in Florida. Honestly, do you expect me to believe all this malarkey? If you were shot in the back, you wouldn't be walking around, you'd be cooling at the morgue. It's the kind of thing I'd hear about on the news. Just because I'm a blonde woman, doesn't mean I'm going to believe any crap you come up with."

"Fine. I'm going to quit the job I'm doing for the Mayor."

"You're friends with Bennie and Walter and Emma and Angela, I know because I've seen this with my own eyes. But, at the same time, you're sleeping on a pull-out bed in my living room and wearing clothes that any self-respecting street bum would walk away from. I don't mean to be hard on you, but I'm having trouble figuring out where you fit. This Mayor stuff, I don't know. Alright, show me the bullet holes in your back."

"No."

"Why not? It would help me figure out how much I should believe you."

"I'm not going to make it that easy."

"Now I've made you mad. I'm sorry. I'll make it up to you. Look, we'll go shopping, you simply have to start wearing better clothing. I have money, it will be my treat."

"Oh, please, no shopping."

"It will be fun, I promise." She plucked at his shirt sleeve. "We simply have to do something about your attire."

The Gray Brigade

Old women pushed brooms and rousted sleeping men in an alley east of Pioneer Square. They filled garbage bags with trash and tied gray ribbons on everything they could reach.

"Ladies, leave us alone, we have humane rights."

"Wrong, deadwood, there isn't any constitutional right to panhandle or poop on the street. On the other hand, there is a constitutional right to bear arms. How do you like those apples?"

"Please, lady, don't point that thing at me. What is it anyway, a blunderbuss? I've heard about your guns."

"Would you like a demonstration?"

"No, we're moving."

As the pair of transients walked away, they turned and looked at the dust the ladies were kicking up with their brooms.

"What are we going to do?"

"Portland ain't so bad. We can hitchhike down there in a day or two."

"Alright. Seattle used to be such a great city, now look at it."

"Yeah."

Glen and Mayor Harry Silverberg

When Glen woke, Gerusha was gone. He peeled off bandages and carefully washed his back in the shower. The bullet wounds were painful, but Lucy was right, they were superficial. He may have cracked ribs, but nothing fractured. The shallow wounds didn't bleed much; he dribbled peroxide on them over his shoulder and was able, with contortion, to plaster fresh bandage patches onto them. He grabbed his bag and walked toward the city municipal building. It was windy and gray lumpy clouds moved quickly across the sky, but the rain held off.

He checked in at the security desk. The officer in charge looked at Glen suspiciously, not impressed with the dirty suit and his haphazard and wind-blown hairstyle.

"Wait a minute, I know you," the officer said. "Wilson. Everyone in town has been looking for you. You don't look like much, what's the big deal?"

"Beats me," Glen replied.

"Are you sure the Mayor will see you?"

"Sure, why not?"

"Okay, hang loose, we're looking for him."

Glen sat on a bench and read a pamphlet about 'Getting to Know your Building Inspector'. He found it riveting: *When the revolution comes, the building inspectors will be the first strung up by their heels from lampposts. Strong and safe lampposts courtesy of your friendly local building inspector.*

The officer approached. "It turns out the mayor has been looking for *you*. In fact, he wants me to make sure you don't run off, so don't try anything. I have to run your bag through the metal detector."

Glen couldn't think of anything in the bag that might cause a problem. The wristbands and cash should slide through okay. He shrugged. The officer escorted him up the elevator and soon Glen was back in the Mayor's office.

"Do you want me to stay, sir?" the officer asked. The Mayor shook his head no and waved him off. "I'll be right outside," the officer said, staring pointedly at Glen.

"Why don't you make yourself useful and see if you can round up some donuts. I haven't eaten breakfast yet," Glen said.

"Yes," the Mayor agreed. "See if you can find Danish pastries or something, thanks."

The officer's look was poisonous as he exited.

"I need to talk to you, Harry. But, since you were looking for me, maybe you should go first."

"Fine. I'll lay it out for you. I want you to stop whatever it is you're doing. I was out of my mind when I hired you and I want to negate our contract. So, cease and desist immediately."

Glen sat back in his chair. "This is your lucky day, because our contract has a termination clause and I'm prepared to execute it for you."

"Fine, that was easy. Now we're done, right?"

"Well, the termination clause requires you to pay an additional million dollars. The contract says cash, but I'm willing to accept a certified or county check if that's more convenient."

"That's not the way things work around here. I can't cut you a check for a million dollars."

"Sure you can, Harry," Glen soothingly. "You're a clever man, you can figure this out. Hide it in your limousine budget or something."

"This is bullshit. I don't believe you, let me see the contract."

Glen fished around in his bag and found it. "This is a photocopy, my lawyer has the original."

As the Mayor read the hand-written contract, a calm seemed to settle over him.

"Okay, Glen," he said slowly. "I'll do it. I'll have a check cut and I'll messenger it out to you by the end of the day. Where shall I send it?"

"Drop it off at Immortality, they'll hold it for me."

Glen didn't like the Mayor's demeanor. He wondered about the security of the Mayor's grip on reality. Murder was in the air, similar to what he sensed with the Asian gang.

"Great, Glen, it's done. Now what about the old women?"

"The Gray Brigade?"

"SPD counted over a hundred of them on the street and the numbers appear to be growing. When can I count on them being disbanded?"

"What makes you think I can stop them now?"

"You started this thing! You have to end it."

"Look at it this way, Harry. Suppose there is a huge boulder teetering at the edge of a cliff. It might be easy to start the boulder moving, perhaps a nudge would do it, but it is a different matter to stop it once its gathered momentum. Or, maybe a forest fire would be a better analogy. A tiny spark can start one, but they can…"

"I understand what you're saying, shit-ball. I don't care how, you have to stop this before it gets out of hand. We can't arrest all these old folks and more of them are going to be killed or hurt or will simply fall dead on the street from old age. With more publicity, there will be more of them. They have nothing to lose, so we have no power over them. Take responsibility, maybe they will listen to you. Look at these pictures, there are gray ribbons all over now: Denny Park, Capital Hill, and they are moving into the Central District. We can't allow individuals to understand the power they hold when they join forces. They pay us to do this work for them."

"Most people tolerate paying, but they get mad when the money is wasted. You have a huge budget, start spending the money on things that work and maybe the movement will fizzle out on its own."

"You're insane," the Mayor sputtered.

"No, I think *you're* insane," Glen replied.

The Mayor settled back in his chair. An unnatural calm washed over him. "Okay Glen. Let's forget about the messenger. I will bring the check myself. Someplace quiet and out of the way would be nice. How about in the parking lot over by the old theatres, 6th and Blanchard? Be there at 4:30 and I'll have your check for you. Sound good?"

"Sure." Glen held out his hand. "It's been a pleasure doing business with you, Harry. Take care."

"You too, Glen, see you at 4:30."

CHAPTER NINETEEN

Glen and Gerusha Go Shopping

Glen sipped a cup of drip coffee. It cost $1.80 and he muttered about the cost under his breath. The kiosk did not even offer free refills. Gerusha was a few minutes late, Glen hoped she'd forget so he could both avoid the shopping and have something to bitch at her about. But, she appeared at his elbow.

"Okay," she said, "I'm taking a little extra time for lunch, let's get to it."

She found the customer service desk and got an assistant to follow them and collect the purchases. This was a nice luxury, the personnel at this downtown store were already getting to know Gerusha. She recently spent a lot of her new paycheck there and was on a first name basis with the sales associates in several of the fashion wear sections.

They started with socks und underwear. Gerusha guessed his waist size and asked for six pairs of everything. The purchase of suspenders, belts, and an overcoat were quickly dispensed with. They arrived at the Men's wear section. After the measuring tape was wrapped around and placed on various uncomfortable parts of Glen's body, Gerusha quickly laid out gray, black and navy suits to try. She was surprised and pleased with Glen's compliance until he tried to pair up a yellow paisley tie with the gray suit.

"It will be safer for you to stick with solid colors when you're wearing a striped shirt," she suggested. However, the salesman sided with Glen and eventually Gerusha could see the effect. Glen looked regal in the suit and Gerusha made a realization.

"I don't know why I didn't see it. You haven't made a move on me yet because you're gay. You fooled me with the nasty clothes you wear."

"I'm not gay," Glen protested. "I don't mind wearing nice clothes, I just don't care either way."

"He's not gay," the clerk confirmed.

"Then I'm mystified," Gerusha said.

"I think your evil plan might actually work," the clerk whispered to Glen while Gerusha was huddled with her fashion advisor.

"Oh, it'll work," Glen confirmed.

At the same time, Gerusha whispered to a hovering clerk. "Take the old clothes out back and burn them before Mr. Dickhead catches on."

"I'll take care of it right away, ma-am."

The whole adventure took almost two hours, including a half hour in the shoe section. They finally found themselves at the cashier. Gerusha pulled her Amex Gold Card out. The total, with tax, was over $11,000 dollars.

"Hold on, I have it," Glen said. He rustled around in his bag and pulled out a bundle of hundred dollar bills which he handed over to the cashier. "Make sure that's ten grand and we'll go from there," he said. "I suppose you disposed of my old clothes already," he said.

"Yes, don't even bother complaining about it."

"Well, it was convenient having only one set of clothes, there were no tough decisions in the morning."

"Too bad. I'm pleased, I thought you'd be kicking and screaming the whole way. Now, if you'll get a haircut and a razor blade that actually shaves, you'll be presentable."

"I'll get a haircut."

"And take me to dinner, big spender?"

"Sure."

"Maybe you're not such a loser after all. How much more money do you have in that bag?"

"I have no idea."

"Okay, I have to fly. I have a meeting at three. I called it, so I'd better not be late."

Impulsively, she gave him a friendly kiss on the cheek and strode off quickly to hail a cab.

"If I pull my car out front, will you help me load up all this stuff?"

"Of course, sir," the clerk replied. "Don't forget your receipt."

"That's okay, I don't need it."

"But, you might need it if you want to bring anything back for exchange."

"Bring stuff back? I didn't know you could do that. In any case, why would I?"

"I don't know, sir, but some people do."

"Why would I go to the trouble of picking something out and buying it if I was going to bring it back? It doesn't make sense."

"It's a mystery to me too, sir."

Glen and Mayor Harry Silverberg

Glen parked his car in the appointed parking lot and looked around. Nestled in a busy location with traffic swirling on all sides, the parking lot itself was quiet and mostly deserted. A good place for trouble, that was obvious. Glen got out of his Chevelle and sat on the hood. The sun peeked through mostly overcast skies and it was chilly. A hint of winter was apparent in the gusty wind. The Mayor walked up the sidewalk looking furtively around the area. It was so obvious he was up to no good, Glen had to laugh.

"What are you grinning about, asshole?" the Mayor asked.

"You were marshmallow in Vietnam and you're marshmallow now," Glen replied.

"Save your wit for someone who gives a shit. Spending my money already? That's a nice suit, you look like a prince compared to this morning."

"There is no underestimating the transformative power of a good woman, is there?"

"Too bad it's wasted on you, Wilson. I've been waiting for this day for a long time."

The Mayor fumbled with something in his coat pocket. Glen hopped off the hood of his car and backhanded the Mayor across the face. Immediately, blood spurted from his nose as he stumbled and fell on his butt. Glen was on him in an instant. He pulled the revolver from the Mayor's pocket. It was wrapped up with white medical tape on the handle and the trigger. Glen also found a large hunting knife with a handle carved from a deer antler. "Is that all you brought?" He opened the Mayor's inside jacket pocket and pulled out an envelope. The check was inside, it was made out to Glen Wilson in the amount of $999,999.00.

"I think you broke my nose," the Mayor complained.

"I did not. What about my other dollar?"

"I went up to the limit for a check on that account with a single signature."

Glen reached around and pulled out the Mayor's wallet. When he opened it, he saw a picture of the Mayor's wife.

"You should expend more effort fixing your wife instead of messing with me. She's a lovely lady." He pulled a dollar bill out and then tossed the wallet onto the Mayor's lap. "Once the check clears, I'll send you the contract original and we'll be done."

The mayor pressed a handkerchief against his nose. "Will you at least try to stop the grannies?"

"No," Glen replied.

He drove to Gerusha's apartment and made several trips to get all his clothes in. There was only one closet, so Glen pushed her dresses aside to make room for his new suits. He liked the look of his clothes hanging next to hers. His cell phone erupted, this startled him. It took a minute to locate it in the pocket of his jacket tossed over the back of a kitchen chair.

"Wilson here," he said.

It was Gerusha. "Hi Glen. As an incentive, they offered me a cash bonus or stock options. What should I do?"

"Take the stock."

"Thanks."

"You're welcome. Was that it?"

"Yes. Did you have your meeting with the Mayor already?"

"Yes."

"Well, don't be reticent. How did it go?"

"It went fine."

"That's all you'll say?"

"I guess."

"Okay, are we still on for dinner?"

"Absolutely."

"Okay, gotta run, see you then."

"See you then," Glen echoed.

There was one more chore. Glen made several trips to his car and brought up cases of Roxinal. He put on a pair of Gerusha's rubber dishwashing gloves and, using a can opener, peeled the tops off each bottle and flushed the contents down the toilet. The empty bottles went into a plastic trash bag which Glen walked to a dumpster in an alley behind a Sushi restaurant. In it went with the fish heads and reeking guts.

I'll take Gerusha to a steak house tonight, Glen decided.

CHAPTER TWENTY

The Meeting

Gerusha met Paul in the lobby. He was accompanied by three other men, two were Japanese, and all wore conservative business suits with shiny shoes and expensive briefcases. Gerusha motioned for Paul to come over for a private conversation.

"Paul, what are you doing? I advised you to meet Glen by yourself first."

"I'm sorry Gerusha. The timing was perfect and I could not resist. I have executives visiting from Osaka and they very strongly want to meet Mr. Wilson. I'll make it up to you for this sin, I promise. This is a very senior team, they won't embarrass you in any way."

"It's not you I'm worried about. If this meeting goes bad, you remember what I said about meeting Glen alone first. You brought this on yourself."

"I have lots of experience with making things go smoothly, please don't worry about it."

"Very well, I won't." Paul was uncomfortable with the way she said this and for the first time wondered if he'd made an error.

He introduced her to the visitors and she led them into the elevator and to the top floor executive conference room. They were a few minutes early. Gerusha hoped against hope that Glen would appear on time. Or appear at all. Strangely, deep inside she was excited in not knowing how this would turn out. Secretly, she hoped Paul would get slammed hard and learn to listen to her. Regardless of the outcome, her conscience was clear, she didn't care if the visitors from Japan went away happy or not. What could they do? Fire her? Clearly, they were not impressed so far, they didn't offer business cards or hand shakes. *Did they think she was just a secretarial flunky?* The conference room table displayed a nice selection of pastries with orange juice and coffee that no one touched. They sat and waited quietly for Glen to appear. At precisely 10:00, he swept into the room. He wore his new business suit and the expensive shoes Gerusha bought him on their shopping spree. No socks. His tie was loose around his neck and his unkempt hair stood straight up in clumps. The whole effect worked, a stranger would not be able to tell if he was an eccentric rich power player executive or a street bum. The bruises on his face had faded and he had shaved poorly leaving stray gray hairs sprouting on his chin. When he walked in, he scanned the group and gave Gerusha an intense scowl. He immediately excused himself and left the room. Gerusha worried that he would not return, but he came back a minute later. He'd run his fingers through his hair and straightened his tie.

He shook hands and introduced himself to the group. He accepted business cards from the Japanese men graciously with both hands and made innocuous comments about each.

"Oishi-san? You are from the factory in Osaka? Very good sir. Nakahara-san, you are the executive director of worldwide marketing. I'm pleased to meet you sir." For the Caucasian visitors, he glanced at their cards and put them in his pocket. A young man, flamingly gay, breezed into the room and handed Glen a small silver case. Glen opened the case and took a quick glance at the business cards inside. He carefully proffered a card to each of the Japanese men and bowed politely.

"Mister Wilson, you are Chief Operating Officer?"

Glen nodded.

"An extreme pleasure to meet you sir," Mr. Oishi said in a thick accent. Glen gestured for everyone to be seated and offered to pour coffee for all. He poured a cup for himself and extracted a croissant from the pastry tray. Mr. Oishi plugged his tiny palmtop computer into the projector system. Soon, he was reading Power Point slides in a slow and monotonous voice. After about seven slides, the gay kid came back and handed Glen a small pile of papers. Glen interrupted the slide show.

"I appreciate the information offered, thank you so much. I apologize for being hasty and impolite, but I would like to see a presentation of your proprietary technology."

The Japanese conferred between themselves. Paul Butler and his boss looked at each other with confused concern.

"We are very sorry, but that would be quite impossible without signed agreements between our companies."

"I hope you will excuse my presumption, but I have downloaded Non-Disclosure Agreements from your company website." He motioned for Gerusha to give him her pen and he signed and dated each page, then filled in information on the last page and slid the documents across the table to Mr. Nakahara. Then he leaned back in his chair and watched, while chewing on his croissant.

He gestured to Gerusha with subtle motions which she interpreted to mean: "If you ever do this to me again, I'll cut out your heart with a dull knife and feed it to the wolverines at the Woodland Park Zoo. If you think I'm bluffing, then try me, sweet-meat."

The Japanese men talked between themselves for almost five minutes. At times the conversation was heated. Their exchange ended with Mr. Nakahara scolding Mr. Oishi very severely. Finally, however, Mr Nakahara signed the documents and slipped one set into his valise and pushed the other set back to Glen.

"This technology is not available in the United States and we will not provide technical details, just a high-level overview." Mr. Nakahara's English was much better than Mr. Oishi's, he spoke with a slight British accent which Glen had not noticed before.

"I understand completely," Glen replied politely.

The presentation was in Japanese, but as Mr. Oishi sequenced through the slides, Mr. Nakahara translated and commented on the information. The graphics were explanatory enough to get context on the products and technology. One slide in particular grabbed Glen's attention. He got up and poked his head out the door, but they could not hear what he said. Paul looked at Gerusha with questions in his eyes, but Gerusha shrugged to indicate that she had no idea what was going on.

"Shall we continue?" Mr. Nakahara asked as Glen returned to his seat.

"Please wait a moment," Glen replied.

Bennie rushed into the room. The first thing Gerusha noticed was he wore his T-shirt both backwards and inside-out. She cringed. Bennie waved at Glen then looked at the display being projected. He froze and stared for a long minute. Finally he rubbed his forehead. "Okay," he said to Glen before rushing back out of the room.

Glen leaned across the table toward Mr. Nakahara. "Bennie is impressed with your high energy containment system. I would like to propose a long-term cross-licensing agreement between our companies in the area of gravitron fusion technology. Bennie is preparing a tour of our laboratory and will give a lecture and presentation which we can connect to your scientists back in Osaka via our Internet conferencing system. Will you accept my suggestion to evaluate a codevelopment project, Mr. Nakahara?" Glen extended his hand across the table. Mr. Nakahara looked at Glen for a moment, then bowed his head and shook his hand. "Yes," he said.

Paul leaned toward Gerusha. "The Japanese never say yes or no to anything," he whispered.

"It is very important to me that Mr. Butler and Mr. Harris receive a small commission of zero point five percent on the total value of our transaction."

"I understand," Mr. Nakahara said.

"Our contract says we get two point five percent," Paul complained.

"Shut the fuck up," Harris hissed to Paul. "Please excuse our impolite outburst," he addressed to the table.

"While we're waiting for the tour, would you please continue with the presentation, Nakahara-san?"

"Yes, Mr. Wilson, I would be pleased to continue," Mr. Nakahara replied formally.

Glen leaned over and whispered into Gerusha's ear. "You're making me dinner tonight and if you serve anything frozen or pre-made, I will kill you slowly and with great pleasure."

She had a desperate moment, trying to figure out how she'd handle the afternoon appointments *and* cook dinner until she realized she could hire a chef to come in and help. *Outsource and delegate to the experts, that's the way to make things happen,* she realized.

"How about chicken?" she asked.

"I'd prefer something with beef," he replied.

The gay kid poked his head in the room. "We're ready to start the tour, Mr. Wilson," he said.

Paul huddled with Gerusha as the others filed out. "I think I have this guy nailed, I can give you a reading on him later if you'll meet me for lunch. I'll give you a complete personality profile based on my wide experience."

Gerusha smiled. "I don't think that will be necessary."

The Company Tour

Glen stood in a corner of the lab and watched Bennie and Mr. Nakahara talk. They were surrounded by the other members of the tour no matter how they tried to distance themselves by moving slowly away. Finally, Mr. Nakahara spoke quietly to his subordinate, Mr. Oishi, who bowed and walked off, tugging the arms of the rest of the team until Bennie and Mr. Nakahara were alone. Gerusha, belatedly reading the situation, helped with moving the team away. Glen smiled. Bennie scribbled on a white board and seemed to be arguing with Mr. Nakahara who only occasionally spoke. The issue seemed to be one term in an exponent buried in the middle of a long equation.

Paul Butler sidled over to stand leaning against the wall by Glen.

"I think Mr. Nakahara is testing Bennie," Glen said.

"I've met Mr. Nakahara several times over the years and he's hardly said anything until today. I'm not sure I understand what is going on."

"Don't bullshit me, Butler. Play dumb with someone else. You know perfectly well what is happening. In a minute or so, Mr. Nakahara is going to bow and allow Bennie to continue the tour."

They watched and this is precisely what happened with one minor exception. When Mr. Nakahara bowed, he touched Bennie briefly on the arm.

"I—," Paul started.

"I know, in all the years you've been representing Mr. Nakahara's company, you've never seen him touch anyone except to shake hands."

"Yes, that's what I was going to say. Can I ask you something?"

"Go ahead."

"Can you give me an idea what our zero point five percent might be worth over a couple of years? Just to give me a sense of it?"

"It will be worth jack shit if you piss me off." Glen sighed. "I suppose I can't blame you for asking. Let's say something along the order of seven figures, give or take."

"Holy shit. Thank you."

"You're welcome. Now let's talk about something else, the subject of money is tedious."

Gerusha cornered a lab tech and gathered the team, leaving Bennie and Mr. Nakahara completely alone. Bathed in pale blue light and wearing thick dark glasses, they peered into a thick port at a gravity fusion experiment

"That Gerusha is quite a girl, isn't she? She picks up things very quickly and is as cute as a bug."

"Quick enough, I guess."

"Can I ask what your intentions are regarding the young lady?"

Glen turned and focused his full attention on Paul who felt like a stripper on no-cover-charge night. "It is my intent to own her 100%, mind, body and soul."

"I read you. I was thinking of making a run at her myself, but I'll back off."

Glen laughed heartily. "She's free to choose who she wants, don't hesitate a whit on my account."

"Really?"

"No one embraces the concept of free will more than me. If you think you have a chance, you'd be nuts not to give it a shot, and may the better man win."

"You seem to embody a strange mix of personalities."

Glen shrugged. "It all seems organic and perfectly integrated to me. I'll do one more thing for you. I have a friend in India that needs a look at object-oriented hardware technology. Loan me your pen and a piece of paper and I'll give you his contact information."

Glen scribbled on the paper, and then examined the pen more closely. It was a heavy gold and walnut ballpoint, an antique.

He looked pointedly at Paul. "I think I'll keep the pen," he said.

"That pen was a gift from my —, oh fuck it, you can have it, prick."

Glen grinned. "Thanks, I appreciate it."

Gerusha walked over with the tour group. She huddled next to Glen and whispered to him.

"Mr. Oishi said something interesting, if you want to hear it."

"Sure," Glen responded.

"He said he'd heard there were intelligent Americans, but until he met Bennie today, he'd never met any."

"You're right, that is interesting. I'll tell you something. It's okay to generalize based on your own direct personal experience."

"You're giving me permission to be a bigot?"

"You can look at it that way."

"Gee, thanks, I think."

"Think nothing of it."

"I won't."

After the tour, they assembled back in the lobby saying goodbye. Paul cornered Gerusha by the Glen Wilson bust. He leaned against it with his elbow on top of the bronze head.

"I guess that worked out," Gerusha commented. "You took a big risk bringing them in here like that."

"If I didn't crave a little chaos, I'd be in the wrong business," Paul said, shrugging.

Glen chatted with the Japanese. He caught Paul's eye and motioned for him to get his arm off his statue. Paul quickly removed his arm, bowed slightly and mouthed the word 'sorry'.

Gerusha touched Paul's arm to make sure she had his undivided attention.

"Need I mention the consequences of blindsiding me again like this?"

"No, I understand completely," he said solemnly.

CHAPTER TWENTY-ONE

Immortality, LLC Executive Meeting

Glen took a butterhorn from a stack in the middle of the conference room table and tore it into pieces. One-by-one, he popped the pieces in his mouth. Bennie and Walter watched him eat.

"My Seattle job is done, so I want to get rolling with my next plan. It's back to Alaska for us. This is going to be good. Big fun, if we survive."

Walter glanced nervously at Bennie before addressing Glen. "We'd love to join up with you again, but we can't leave until our IPO is consummated. Even then, we'll need six months or a year depending on what our employment agreements say."

"That's no problem, I understand. There's no big rush."

"To tell the unvarnished truth, we're having problems. Bennie and I have talked about this and the IPO will go more quickly if you help us out of a rather big jam."

"What do you expect me to do?"

"The same as you always do. Spread chaos and mayhem. Sow the seeds of disruption. Force things to happen."

"Is that what I do? I wondered about that. I'm flattered you think I can help and I'd chop my fingers off for you if that would help. I'm not sure how I can be of service, but I'm willing to jump in and try. I'd like to pull the whole team together, let's see if we can get Murphy and Elke on the line."

Walter opened the conference room door and issued instructions to an unseen assistant. "This shouldn't take too long," he said as he came back to the table.

A young girl who looked to be about 12, came in and fiddled with the meeting room projector. "We got them on a net meeting," she whispered to Walter.

The display slowly faded into focus. Murphy and Elke were seen leaning against a wall. In the background, the sound of heavy equipment being rolled around could be heard.

"Hi guys," Murphy said. "Cripes Glen, you look a lot better than the last time we saw you. Raz wants to say hello."

A shaggy head appeared in the video frame. Raz was not wearing his stage makeup, so he looked like a skinny kid with long hair and piercing eyes. "Hello gentlemen. Hi Walter. Your gas dispensing system works great, I want to thank you for that."

"Think nothing of it, I'm pleased to help any way I can. Show business will always be in my blood."

"Sound check in twenty, no time to chat. Catch you guys later."

Raz waved and disappeared.

Elke appeared cool and composed as always, but Murphy's hair was askew and she looked haggard.

"We're calling to check your schedule. I don't know the details, but Bennie and Walter's company is having minor problems and we can use your help. I have a plan that takes us back to Alaska for an adventure but we need to get the Immortality IPO straightened out first. When can you wrap things up down there and come join us?"

"We can come up after the tour ends in a couple of months. Glen, we're glad you called because there are strange things going on. We'd like you to come and see for yourself. My gut tells me the situation is about to get out of hand. Please come, Glen."

Glen put down his coffee cup. "Ladies, if I come down there and lend a hand, you'll come up here and help Immortality? Then we can quit screwing around and dig into my Alaska deal?"

"That would work for us, we'd be happy," Elke said.

"Can you keep a lid on things until we wrap up the tour and get back up here?" Glen asked Walter and Bennie.

"Yes," Bennie said, "but no dawdling, please. Our multi-billion dollar deal will unravel if we don't get a grip."

"Fine, it's a deal. A year, right? Then we're all off to Alaska again."

"Yes, we agree," was repeated by all.

"Give me a couple of days, and I'll catch up with you."

"Thanks, Glen," the ladies said as the connection was closed.

The Gray Brigade

Mary Swanson stood before a large Seattle map which almost covered the whole wall of the game room. It displayed areas enclosed in arrays of gray stick pins. A few red pins were scattered in troubled areas, but the boundary defined by the pins was expanding nicely.

"Commander Mary, Colonel Eloise reporting as ordered, ma-am."

Mary turned and returned the snappy salute they had copied from an old war movie.

"At ease, Madam Colonel," Mary said briskly. She walked around her desk and unfolded and flattened the collar on Eloise's floral uniform dress. "What do you have to report?"

"All is well in the teal section and we're expanding that border by three blocks this week. Mr. Lehman expired while on duty and we're recommending he receive the Iron Cross medal to be presented to his family with his flag."

"I'm sure that request will be approved by the review board. He was a good man."

"Yes ma-am, he was. There is a delegation from Seattle Social Services, they want to discuss the terms of a cease fire."

"Don't they believe our pledge? We'll never rest until the streets are safe from Shoreline to Kent."

"They're desperate, ma-am."

"The executive command will meet them, but we will not back off, slow down, retreat or surrender."

"I will pass along the message." Eloise saluted and left the room. Mary turned back to the map allowing a satisfied smile to cross her lips. Every time the Seattle Police arrested a Gray Brigade member and the story hit the newspapers, five more signed onto the cause. Every time one died on the streets due to injury or old age, many more were sworn in. Money came in from across the country and she'd been featured on TV shows 20/20 and The O'Reilly Factor. Old folk's battalion groups were forming in Atlanta, New Orleans, Toronto and Detroit. The seniors were on the march and the whole world would soon feel their awesome power.

EPILOGUE

Glen and Gerusha

Glen sat up on the pull-out bed and rubbed his eyes. It was raining on this dismal Saturday morning and he did not want to get up.

"Hey Gerusha, make me coffee, will ya please, dammit!" he shouted.

Opening her bedroom door, her head was wrapped in a towel and she didn't seem to notice her bare nipples peeking from a partially buttoned nightgown.

"I'm not your fucking slave, dickwad, make it yourself," she called out, louder than necessary. "And boil me a couple of eggs while you're at it."

Glen cussed under his breath as he went into the kitchen. A minute later, Gerusha came out of the bedroom with her hair wrapped in the damp towel, but she'd thrown a robe over the nightgown.

"What happened to the scones I bought?"

"I took them to work. They were great, thanks. What are you complaining about? You can go grocery shopping. It's not like you have a job or anything."

"I could be your boss if I wanted a real job, then I could fire your flabby ass."

"I don't think Walter would let you. I signed a contract on Wednesday that saved us eight hundred thousand dollars and we get free research as part of the deal. I've been kicking ass and saving the company megabucks. Besides, my butt is not flabby. It's young and firm, not like your saggy old man's rear end."

"You don't know anything about my rear end."

"The hell I don't, the way you walk around here in your shorts with your ass cheeks and nuts hanging out all the time."

Glen poured himself a cup of coffee. Gerusha reached around and snagged it.

"That's it, the last straw that broke this camel's back."

"Does this mean you'll move out and get your own place?"

"What sense would that make? I'm off to Houston on Monday."

"It won't be the same around here without you using the last of my toilet paper and stinking up the place with your 'emissions'.

"Why don't you ever mention my good qualities?"

"Those are your good qualities."

"My check from the city cleared the bank."

"That's nice."

"I think we should celebrate."

"What do you have in mind?"

"I'm glad you asked, I've been thinking we should hop on a plane to Las Vegas and get married."

Gerusha choked on coffee. It spilled down the front of her robe.

"Ouch, hot, hot, hot," she said, gathering her composure. "What did you say?"

"You heard me, your grace."

"Say it again."

"We should get married."

She scanned him from tousled head to hairy and gnarled toes.

"Why not?" she said, considering the matter. "I don't have anything else planned for the day."

While throwing panties into a travel bag, the complete absurdity of the idea hit. Walking to the living room, she stood and looked into his face. He looked dapper; he'd shaved and wore one of the Nordstrom's suits.

"Wait a minute," she said. "I don't know anything about you. How many times have you been married?"

"Twice."

"How many kids?"

"None. Yet," he said while wiggling his eyebrows suggestively.

"How am I supposed to know whether you're some sort of evil genius or a disgusting and dirty old worthless geezer?"

Glen grinned and remained silent.

"You're not going to help, are you?"

Maddenly, Glen just grinned.

"Fine, I changed my mind, I will not marry you."

Glen shrugged. "Suit yourself. I already have the electronic tickets. As long as we hit Vegas and have lots of kinky sex, I don't care. Grab your bag, let's get the hell out of here."

"Okay, Glen," she said, sighing. "I'm coming."

The Gray Brigade

David Green, carrying a briefcase and umbrella, walked through Occidental Park on his way to work. The sun peeked through the clouds. He looked around. He hadn't noticed how clean the park had become.

Flowers were planted in a patch of dirt by the sidewalk and hundreds of gray ribbons, tied in the tree branches, fluttered in the air. A hundred feet away, a tramp was sitting on a bench, the only bum in sight. David decided to sit for a minute and collect his thoughts before going to his office. He closed his eyes and let the dappled sunlight caress his face.

"What's your name, young fella?"

David opened his eyes. Two old women stood directly in front of him. "David," he said.

"Got any kids, David?"

"Yes, two," he said.

The taller old woman pulled a clipboard out of a canvas bag.

"You see any needles or broken glass?"

Davis looked around. "No," he said. "I've never seen this park looking so good. Used to be I wouldn't even walk through here. Has the city cracked down?"

"Sort of. If we learned anything from the war in Iraq: it's not enough to clean out an area, you have to hold it or the enemy will come creeping back."

"What happened to the bums?"

"They're allowed to stay if they behave themselves. Most hate the new rules so they move on. I'm going to write you in for Saturday afternoon, three o'clock to five o'clock, okay?"

"What?"

"Bring your kids down and take a shift this weekend."

"A shift? To do what?"

"Nothing. Hang out. Play. Pick up trash if you see it, but you won't. There will be other kids, bring a checker game or something. Turn off the TV and come, there will be plenty to do. You'll have fun. We reclaimed this park, now we're going to keep it. You'll be here?" Her grandmotherly tone allowed no argument.

"Okay, I guess."

"Fine." The shorter lady pointed. "Mrs. Swanson, did you see that gentleman drop a bottle on the ground?"

"Yes, Mrs. Platt, I did," she said while adjusting the shoulder straps on her odd-looking canister gun. "Let's roll," she said firmly.

THE END

www.ingramcontent.com/pod-product-compliance
Lightning Source LLC
LaVergne TN
LVHW090940080826
845145LV00003B/827

* 9 7 8 0 9 7 5 4 3 1 4 3 6 *